IN
WINTER'S
GRIP

Brenda
Chapman

RendezVous
Crime

Cover design by Emma Dolan
Tree photo by Frank Bowick
Photo of woman by Emma Dolan

Le Conseil des Arts
du Canada | The Canada Council
for the Arts

We acknowledge the support of the Canada Council for the Arts for our publishing program. We acknowledge the financial support of the Government of Canada through the Canada Book Fund) for our publishing activities.

RendezVous Crime
an imprint of Napoleon & Company
Toronto, Ontario, Canada
www.napoleonandcompany.com

Printed in Canada

14 13 12 11 10   5 4 3 2 1

Library and Archives Canada Cataloguing in Publication

Chapman, Brenda, date-
        In winter's grip / Brenda Chapman.

ISBN 978-1-926607-05-4

        I. Title.

PS8605.H36I5 2010   C813'.6   C2010-904970-5

For Ted, Lisa and Julia
with love

One night came Winter noiselessly, and leaned
Against my window-pane.
In the deep stillness of his heart convened
The ghosts of all his slain.

-Charles G. D. Roberts, 1895

ONE

Tonight, I dreamed I was back in Duved Cove, dreamed I was sitting on the concrete steps in front of our house on Strathcona Road, the smell of pine and damp earth in my nostrils. The darkness thickened around me like a curtain falling. When I looked back at our house, the lights were out, and the emptiness I felt was mirrored in the drawn blinds and blackened windows. The air was still and silent like it gets when the day tucks itself in for the night. Loneliness rose in my throat and held me in its ache.

In my dream, I reach down to strike a match on the stone walk at my feet and watch its flame flicker, orange over indigo, travelling down the stalk before I wave the match like I'm shaking out a rag. I snap another red match head across the same stone, holding it in front of my eyes and blowing out the wavering flame just as I feel its heat on my fingers. I peer through the darkness, past the place where I know the pines and birch trees stand at the edge of our property, and I wait for Billy Okwari to come. Wait for Billy like we're sixteen again, knowing he'll find me in the shadows where I sit every night after supper. Fearful my dad will find me first.

I woke then, with tears on my lashes and a yearning for Billy Okwari that I could almost taste. Forty years old, and I still wanted him. I rolled onto my side toward the window and drew my knees up, curling into myself. I felt movement next to me. Sam reached over and settled his warm hand on my hip. He pulled me closer and mumbled, "You're dreaming again, Maj."

I nodded into my pillow, biting my bottom lip, and listened to Sam's breathing deepen into long, regular pulls. Already he'd slipped back into sleep. I envied him the simple ability to fall into it like a cat. I closed my eyes and thought again of my dream. It had been so real this time. Like the other times, I'd guiltily hold it to me for the rest of the day. I'd be careful to keep Sam from learning of the dream and the emotions rising in me like waves that he'd never been able to stir. I was thankful this dream had come tonight and not the nightmare that was its twin. A day of stirred feelings was preferable to one of trying to shake off fear.

I moved away from the heat of Sam's body and slipped from under the duvet. The morning's coolness caused me to shiver in my thin cotton nightgown. A car's engine grew louder as it passed by on the street and then silence. The ashy light through the window was enough illumination for me to make my way on bare feet to the stairs and down their length to the kitchen. Without turning on the light, I padded over to the window seat that looked out over the back garden and wrapped myself in the mohair throw lying at one end. I hoisted myself onto the corner of the seat and tucked my feet under the blanket, wrapping my arms around my legs and resting my cheek on one knee. My tangle of sleep-messed hair hung across my face like a veil. I pushed it aside and stared into the moonlit yard. Shapes of garden furniture and pots empty of flowers stood like sleeping fairies around the yard. Behind them, trees and shrubs held their dark limbs into the night sky.

Most times, when I dream of Billy, it comes out of nowhere. I won't have thought of him for ages then, without warning, a dream so vivid I can almost believe I'm a teenager again with nobody but Billy Okwari on my mind. Back in Duved Cove with my heart open and raw. Back when I believed in things,

2

back before my mother's death. Sometimes, it is too much. The restlessness will take me over for days afterwards until the dream's power recedes and I can return to my safe, middle-aged life with Sam. But this dream was different. This time, it hadn't come out of the depths of my subconscious. A phone call the day before from my younger brother in Duved Cove had shattered my forty-year-old peace.

I'd been at work when his call came, packing up my briefcase to go home. My last patient had mercifully cancelled, and I was thinking of the steak I would eat and the red wine I would drink in front of the six o'clock news. The phone had rung three times while I'd sorted papers and decided whether to ignore its unwelcome persistence. The work ethic had won out. I'd straightened as I picked up the receiver and lowered myself onto my chair behind the desk. "Yes? Dr. Cleary here."

"Maja? Maj, it's Jonas." My brother's voice, questioning and hesitant. I pictured him cupping the mouthpiece with his fingers, pacing the kitchen with his free hand wrapped in the coiled cord, twisting it into a tangle. His blue eyes would be focused on some distant point, and his blonde curls would be uncombed and lying every which way. It would have taken a lot for him to have made this call. My brother was riddled with self-doubt that kept him from spontaneous gestures.

"Of course it is," I'd teased. "But you've never called me here before." The implication hit me. I asked more sharply, "Is anything wrong? Are Gunnar and Claire okay?"

"It's Dad."

I closed my eyes. I'd known this call would come one day. I was not surprised at how empty Jonas's words left me. I asked automatically, "Is he ill?"

"Yes...well, sort of. He fell off the ladder cleaning ice from the roof. Luckily, he was on his way down when he fell. Doctor Galloway thinks he may have had a heart attack."

"That's too bad."

"Yeah, not the best. He's in the hospital but not because he wants to be. Galloway is keeping him there to run some tests."

Was I prepared for my father's death? Even if I never spoke to him again, it would be painful not to have the option. I didn't say anything, trying to settle all the feelings that rose to the surface with unexpected force.

"You still there, Maja?"

"Yes." A catch in my throat made the word come out raspy.

"Will you come? It's likely nothing serious—like, I doubt he's kicking off any time soon, but you never know." Jonas's voice trailed off.

"I'm not sure that I can. It means rearranging a lot of patients and," I took a breath, "it would just be hard."

"I know, but I thought you might want to come...after all this time. It would be good to see you, anyhow."

"I'll think about it, Jonas."

"Yeah."

"How are you and Claire and Gunnar?" I asked, anxious not to lose this tenuous line to my brother.

"Claire's teaching first grade this year. Gunnar's in sixth grade."

"That's right. Gunnar's twelve now, isn't he? Seems like he was just born." I was filling in space, all the time knowing I'd let these relationships slide. I should have known more about my brother's life than I did.

"And you and Sam?"

"We're fine. Fine. Sam is thinking of retiring next year."

"Talk about time flying," Jonas said. "It's hard to think of him giving up his work."

I picked up the stapler from my desk and squeezed until it hurt my hand. "I'll try to come, Jonas. That's all I can promise."

"Might be good for you to see him. Dad's got more interest in family these days. Hardly the father you remember." Jonas laughed harshly. I was startled by the bitterness.

"I can't imagine," I said, and I really couldn't. Memories of my father did not include meaningful family time. A flash of repressed childhood anger shot through me with unnerving strength. "I'm surprised he didn't get you to clean the ice off his roof. Seems to me Dad never liked to get his hands dirty."

"I'd offered to do it on Saturday, but he said it couldn't wait until the weekend."

"When I want something done, I want it done as soon as I ask," I growled, a weak imitation of my father's deep voice.

"It does no good, Maja. Don't even go there."

Suddenly, I was a child again with my brother trying to keep me from fighting our battles. Battles with my father that we'd never been able to win. I wouldn't let myself upset Jonas now. Besides, I'd given up the fighting spirit long ago. "How about I call you back tomorrow, Jonas?"

I could tell Jonas was relieved I wasn't going to pursue Dad's past trespasses, or maybe he was just relieved the call was coming to an end. "Okay. I'll be home late afternoon, or you can leave a message with Claire. Good talking to you, Maj."

"Yeah. Good talking to you, Jonas."

I stood gripping the receiver, staring at Sam's smiling face in the pewter frame on my desk. I picked it up. The picture had been taken on Sam's fiftieth birthday in our back garden next to the juniper tree. He'd posed under the rose arbour, a profusion of pink blooms hanging above his right shoulder. He'd just finished telling me that he had to go on a trip to China for two

5

weeks, and I'd been upset. We'd planned a long weekend at the seaside in Maine, and I'd been looking forward to getting away. Sam had picked a wise time to break the news; our friends would be arriving soon for his birthday dinner and it wouldn't do for me to stay angry. In the photograph, Sam's smiling at me like a guilty boy who's trying to win me over with shamefaced charm. He was like Dad in that way. Both could turn on the likability factor at whim, no matter the emotions whirling about them.

I sighed and set the photo back in its place. There'd been no recourse for me then, and there was no recourse for me now. I continued to come second place to Sam's import business. Like Jonas, I could not envision Sam retiring, even though he'd mentioned it twice in the last month. He might as well have said he'd be cutting off an arm.

I must have dozed, because when I opened my eyes, the room had lightened and there were violet shadows in the garden where there had been only darkness. I looked up and saw streaks of pinkish light lacing the grey sky. My neck felt tender, and I moved it slowly back and forth to work out the crick that had set in while I'd slept. With the mohair blanket held tightly over my shoulders, I went about making coffee. The morning ritual—drawing water from the tap, inserting a clean filter, grinding the beans and measuring out heaping teaspoons of coffee granules. Soon, the smell of strong Colombian brew filled the kitchen. I reached into the cupboard above the coffeepot and took my chipped, lemon-coloured mug and the oversized green mug that Sam favoured from the shelf. With two full cups, I ascended the stairs to our bedroom. Sam was just propping himself up against the headboard when I set the coffee cup next to him on the bedside table. He'd turned on the lamp, and the yellow light pooled around him.

"Did you have trouble sleeping?" he asked as he reached for the mug. He'd put on his glasses and peered at me from over the rims. His sharp blue eyes appeared to be sizing me up.

"I've had better nights." I climbed in next to him, careful not to spill coffee onto the duvet. We sipped our coffee in silence. I looked out the window.

"Snow's started. It should be a mucky morning getting to work."

Sam looked toward the window, where flakes were swirling against the pane as if they were inside a snow globe. "Isn't this your early morning?"

I nodded. "I'll have to finish my coffee and get moving. I have a couple of new assessments and then a facelift at two. I tried to talk her out of it, but she was determined."

"How old?"

"Thirty-five. She's a CBC reporter and thinks she has to look young to get the good stories. If I told you who I was talking about, you'd be shocked. She looks fine just as she is."

"Well, their vanity pays your salary. And pays it handsomely." Sam reached over and patted my knee through the blanket. He was only too aware of my internal struggle but always made light of it. He wasn't aware how my dissatisfaction with my work had intensified over the last year. Plastic surgeon to the rich was something I'd never wanted to become. I still wasn't sure how I'd allowed it to happen.

"What do you have on your plate today?" I asked.

"A full day of meetings. I may have to fly to New York tonight. I meant to tell you earlier, but it's a last-minute deal. I actually thought I was going to get out of it, but Lana tells me George is insisting."

"Why doesn't George go? You're partners, after all, but you seem to be collecting all the air miles." I tried to keep my voice even, but my words were accusation enough.

"George prefers to work behind the scenes. You know that." Sam said, annoyance making his mouth form a hard, tight line. "Why do we have to keep having this discussion?"

I didn't answer. It wasn't as if I had a chance of winning any argument with Sam. He never ended one unless he felt he'd won. Instead, I took a long drink of coffee and got back out of bed. "Time for a shower," I said, my voice lighter than I felt. I crossed the floor to our ensuite, conscious that I'd put on a few pounds, which Sam would be sure to notice if I undressed in front of him. I'd have to go to the gym to work it off. Unfortunately, it was true what they said about the forties signalling a slowdown in one's metabolism. I could be the poster child.

I adjusted the taps until the water was hot in my palm, straightened and stepped out of my nightgown. The first blast of water on my scalp and against my back sent a shiver up my spine. I began humming as I reached for the soap. I let myself luxuriate in the heat on my body and the soft lather on my skin. I tried to relax my mind as well but it wasn't long before I thought of my father.

I hadn't told Sam about the phone call from Jonas the afternoon before, probably because sometime between leaving for home and my first glass of wine, I'd decided not to make the trip to Minnesota. If I was completely honest with myself, I'd admit that I'd never stepped onto the side of going. I would call Jonas after lunch and leave a message with Claire. Dad was going to recover anyway, and I had so much work lined up that a trip now was out of the question. I'd seriously think about going to Duved Cove in the summer for a few days.

I let the idea roll around in my mind, pretending I was giving it proper consideration. It had been six years, the week of Gunnar's sixth birthday, since I'd last visited, so a few more months wouldn't make any difference. My father had come for dinner at Jonas's during those visits, but I'd not been interested in seeing him alone. I sighed. It was a good trait, being able to convince myself of something even when I knew deep down that I might never return to Duved Cove again. My hometown held too many memories that had never lost their power to cut like shards of glass into my skin.

Shower finished, I turned off the water and stepped onto the carpet. I grabbed a towel from the hook behind the door and bent over to rub the water from my hair. I straightened and wiped steam from the mirror. My face was blurry in the glass.

"You are a coward, Maja Cleary," I said to my reflection. "And there's just no way of getting around it."

TWO

I'll have the poached salmon and a glass of wine." Fiona snapped her menu closed and handed it to the college-aged girl taking our order. "The house white will do. Make sure it's good and chilled. No vegetables please, but could I have extra rice? Thanks. Also, bring two waters on your next visit." After she'd made her order, Fiona smiled widely and her stern face transformed into nothing short of beatific.

The girl smiled back then turned to stare at me. Her features settled back into polite disinterest. I glanced up at her over my menu.

"Never can decide," I mumbled and looked back down, my eyes skimming the choices once again. Von's menu offered several dishes that I liked. Fiona cleared her throat. I looked across at her. Her head was tilted to one side, and she was studying me with mock exasperation. She'd given up commenting on the tortured process I had for making meal decisions. I tucked my head back behind the menu and took a deep breath.

"All right. I'll have the grilled shrimp and a house salad," I said, all the time wondering if I should have ordered the steak sandwich. I'd certainly planned to when I'd opened my mouth.

"Anything to drink?" The girl shifted her weight from one leg to the other.

"The water will be fine," I said. I handed over the menu and tried to appear as officious as Fiona.

Fiona leaned forward as the girl retreated with our order. "You aren't joining me in a glass of vino? It'll take the edge off and make the afternoon go way smoother."

"I'm heading to the Riverside to do a facelift at two. The patients get a little nervous when the surgeon comes in smelling like they've belted back a few."

"I suppose. You really should find another line of work."

"You should talk," I said. "Child psychologist with the most troubled youth in Ottawa. Your job is much tougher than mine."

Fiona relaxed back into her chair, and it was my turn to study her face. Soft brown eyes, high cheekbones and oversized lips that gave her the pouty expression so in vogue with models. Her hair was gleaming auburn, cut in spiky chunks that would have looked boyish on most other women. Fiona had an Irish spirit that radiated from her eyes and creamy skin. The most attractive thing about her, though, was her indifference to her own beauty.

"I like my work," she said. "That makes what I do much easier than what you do."

"I don't hate my work." I met her eyes. "I'm just not convinced that what I'm doing now is one hundred percent worthwhile."

"Then quit and find somewhere else to use your talent. God knows there are people who really need a good plastic surgeon."

I looked past Fiona to our waitress, who was laughing at something the other waiter had whispered into her ear. Her cap of red hair crackled like fire in the overhead light. They looked so young and carefree that I felt a momentary sadness for a time long past in my own life. Had I ever been that happy?

"It's not that easy," I said at last, pulling myself back. "I signed a five-year lease on my office. Besides, if Sam is serious about retiring, we'll need my salary."

"Nonsense. Sam must have a pension, and you've got to have

enough socked away to keep you in fine style."

I didn't want to tell Fiona that I had no idea the state of our finances. It all went into a joint account that Sam looked after. If Fiona knew, she'd give me a royal raking over. She'd told me more than once that for a brilliant doctor, I was lax about the details of my life.

"I couldn't imagine not working," I muttered as the waitress placed water glasses in front of us.

After that, I steered the conversation away from me. I'd learned long ago that people like to talk about themselves and their own lives, and I could ask questions to nudge them there. Even Fiona, my best friend and a good psychologist, was susceptible. She went on at length about her latest patients—a child of ten who wet her bed every night and a seven-year-old boy who liked to light fires. We were sipping on steaming cups of coffee thick with cream when she finally stopped talking about her work and zoomed her attention back on me.

"Does Sam know how unhappy you are?"

"What?" She'd caught me by surprise. I should have remembered how astute Fiona was when it came to reading people. She was a psychologist, after all. "Whatever do you mean?" I tried a smile. "I'm not so sure happiness comes into it after you've been married ten years."

Fiona's eyes bored into mine, and I inwardly squirmed. I usually avoided any talk of my feelings. She continued, "I've known you five years now, Maja, and I've learned to read you, probably more than you'd like. It looks to me like you're having more and more trouble fitting into the world you've carved out for yourself."

"You've never said anything," I said, at a loss.

"I figured you'd tell me what you wanted me to know when

you were ready, and if you're never ready. . ." Fiona shrugged and smiled. "You're a very private person, Maja, and I respect that. You remind me a lot of my kid sister, Katrina."

"My life is fine. I am fine." The mantra I kept repeating, it seemed. "I'm not thrilled about my work, but neither are a lot of people." I suddenly realized that Fiona was my closest friend, and I barely shared anything that meant anything with her. Instead, I'd kept to safe topics like work and books and social functions. "I'm sorry, Fiona," I said. "I'm not great at this spilling my guts thing." I uttered a shaky laugh. "The irony is that I've picked you as a friend."

"I think one day, just like Sleeping Beauty, you're going to wake up and face life square on. At least, that's what I'm hoping for you." She hunched forward and spoke quietly, forcefully. "You've so much going on, my friend, and you have no idea."

"Will that be all?"

I looked up. Our waitress was standing between us, scribbling on the bill. She was staring over our heads through the plate glass window that captured the bustle of Bank Street.

"Yes, that's all for now," Fiona said as she reached out for the cheque and smiled at me. "It's time we put on our winter coats and got back into the fray."

When everything else in my life seemed out of my control, I could rely on my skill as a plastic surgeon to give me a feeling of competence and even peace. It was no surprise then, when the rhytidectomy went without complication. I'd opted for a local anesthetic, and our thirty-five year old reporter would be going home to spend the night sleeping it off at home with a tube for drainage behind her ear. I left her resting in the post-op room after leaving instructions with the nurses and went to the ward to check on another patient who'd had a tummy tuck the day before. She'd spend one more night in the hospital before release. I was pleased to see they'd removed her intravenous drip and that she was sitting up, sipping on some broth.

Seven o'clock found me backing my silver Ford Taurus out of the reserved doctors' parking to head to our New Edinborough home. I was tired but relatively happy with the day. A recent dusting of snow gave the city a softened, new-world patina which was caught in the beam of my headlights and the myriad lights of the city. The snow's whiteness lifted my spirits, and I was suddenly looking forward to a night in with Sam. I knew I'd been out of sorts and withdrawn lately, and we needed to connect. Hopefully, he'd have defrosted one of the many packets of frozen meals and started supper by the time I got home. We'd eat in front of the fireplace in the back room and listen to a classical recording from his extensive collection. He'd mentioned buying a rare Mozart recording that he wanted me to hear.

I took the long way, turning north along the canal past the University of Ottawa. I enjoyed this route, and it let me clear my head. By the Rideau Centre, I stopped at a red light and reached for my cellphone. I looked at the brown copper roof of the Château Laurier and its castle-like towers as I checked my messages. Two waiting. I played the first. Sam's resonant voice saying goodbye filled my ear, and I felt my spirits plunge. I'd forgotten he was heading to New York. He would be in the air now, likely sipping on a Scotch and soda and reading the paper. That meant I'd be having supper alone again.

The light changed, and I dropped the cellphone into my open purse. The second message would wait. I crossed Rideau Street and travelled north on Sussex, past the bustle of the Byward Market and the spired glass magnificence of the art gallery. I turned right and entered my neighborhood, passing the treed grounds of the Governor General's residence, the extensive property hemmed in by a black iron fence. One more right turn onto our street and the welcome sight of our driveway. I parked and stepped out of the car. The tire marks from Sam's Land Rover were filled with snow. He'd been gone a long time. I lifted my head and looked at our two-storey red brick house, set back from the street and nestled in behind conical cedar bushes and lilac trees, now encased in clumps of snow. Its narrow frontage kept it unassuming, hiding its spacious rooms, rich oak floors and high ceilings. I shivered in my wool coat and hurried up the stone walkway, careful not to slip on patches of ice hidden by the thin snow cover. The porch light was on a timer, as was the lamp on the post closer to the driveway. They lit my way through the early darkness of the cold February evening.

The first thing I did was run a hot bath. I'd been chilled by the day and soaked for half an hour, letting the Jacuzzi jets pulsate away all the tension from my neck and shoulders. By the time I dressed in flannel pajamas and a housecoat, my stomach was rumbling, and I hurried downstairs to the kitchen.

I heated up a packet of leftover stew from the freezer and poured a glass of pinot noir the colour of crushed rubies. The house was cool, and I settled in front of the gas fireplace in the backroom to warm up. Instead of classical music, I put Jim Croce's "Time in a Bottle" on our antiquated turntable and relaxed into his voice. The wind had picked up, and I could hear it battering the house and rattling down the chimney. Gusts of snow blew past the windows and danced in the lights placed about the backyard. Halfway through my meal, I remembered the phone message that I hadn't listened to. I took a forkful of food and pushed myself to my feet from where I sat in front of the coffee table. I waited until I was sitting once again in front of my meal before retrieving the saved message. It was a moment before I could place my sister-in-law's voice. Hysteria had sharpened Claire's usually level voice, and I felt prickles of fear rippling along my skin.

"Maja? Maja," a deep breath, "this isn't good news. I don't know how to tell you... It's your father. He was found dead in his backyard a few hours ago. They think...they think he may have been murdered. They've taken Jonas in for questioning." Another deep breath mixed with a sob. "Maja...call me as soon as you can."

I had to listen to the message three times before the words finally sunk in. Dad was gone. Part of me rejoiced. *Take that, you old bugger. I knew you'd get what's coming to you one day, but it took a hell of a long time.* Another part of me wanted to cry. I lifted my eyes to my ghostly reflection in the patio door. Jonas needed me. The wall I'd so carefully erected around my past was about to come tumbling down. I raised my cellphone again with a shaking hand and dialed Jonas's home number. Claire picked up on the first ring.

"This is so terrible. I just saw your dad, and he was looking fine."

"He left the hospital on his own?"

"Yes. Apparently before lunch. Are you coming? Jonas needs you."

"I'm...of course."

"Thank God, Maja. I can't talk now. Someone's at the door.

"I'll call you when I get in."

"I'll tell Jonas."

The first Northwest Airlines flight I could make was six a.m.

with stops in Detroit and Minneapolis. If the weather cooperated, we'd be touching down in Duluth a few minutes after noon. I booked a window seat and went in search of my suitcase.

By one o'clock the following afternoon, I was wending my way in a rented Chevy Cavalier up Highway 61, heading north through Minnesota towards the Canadian border. The snow was deep and mounded along the sides of the road, covering the rock outcroppings and lying heavy on the branches of fir and spruce. At Two Harbors, I pulled off the highway for a rest stop at Betty's Pies and bought a large cup of bitter coffee in a Styrofoam cup, and on the spur of the moment, a strawberry rhubarb pie to bring to Jonas's. The coffee warmed my hand through my thin glove, and I took small sips as I walked through the snow to my car in the parking lot. While I'd been inside, a layer of snow had fallen, and I swiped at the back and side windows to clear enough away to see, snow crunching under my boots as I circled the car. Even as I settled myself in the front seat, thick flakes had recovered the cleaned surfaces. I turned the heater on high and flicked on the windshield wipers. They thump-thumped against the glass and left icy streaks in their wake. Driving would be slow going for the last leg of my journey.

I'd called Claire from the Duluth Airport. The phone had woken her from an exhausted sleep, but she reported that Jonas was on his way home from the police station. The police had questioned him off and on for most of the night but couldn't come up with enough evidence to charge him. Her voice had been worried but relieved at the same time. She said Jonas would be thrilled to see me.

I pulled back onto the highway, sorry to leave the friendly

17

comfort and yellow lights of the restaurant behind me. Even though the falling snow hindered my view, I knew that the drive through northern Minnesota was a thing of beauty. The two-lane road curved through thick coniferous forests, and I caught glimpses of rocky shore and grey-white stretches of Lake Superior that awakened my senses. Town names rolled off my tongue—Castle Danger, Beaver Bay, Taconite Harbor, Lutsen. Near the town of Lutsen, I pulled off the highway and drove down a newly plowed side road towards the lakeshore. A rock face caked in snow cut steeply into the Lake Superior basin. The grey clouds hung heavy in the sky while the snow drove down past the ice cakes that rimmed the shoreline, the lake heaving. I stayed inside the car with the heater up full and prepared myself for the final few miles that led to Duved Cove.

Who would want to murder my father? I was at a loss. Jonas was not a choice I considered seriously. He'd never stood up to my father, even in the days when he had ruled our lives with an anger unparalleled, even after my mother made her last stand. Did it matter to me who had murdered someone of my flesh? I focused my gaze upwards towards the leaden sky. *My father had been murdered.* My breath quickened. Maybe it did matter after all. I'd loved him once, I'd tried to love him...and that should be enough to make it matter. The snow picked up steam as the wind pummelled the car. I shivered inside my wool coat and placed one hand over the heater. The air blasting into the car was still cold. I reached down and put the car into drive. It was time to face my demons.

I waited for three cars to pass by on the highway before easing into traffic. Twenty minutes and I would be home. Less than half an hour to Duved Cove.

THREE

My brother Jonas and I were thought to resemble each other, often mistaken for twins when we were younger. My father Peter Larson had Scandinavian roots, like many of the local families who had made the trip from Sweden to settle in Minnesota. My mother Annika Sigredsson was first generation American. Her parents had emigrated to up-state Minnesota six months before she was born. Jonas and I had the same blue eyes and white-blonde hair of our ancestors, although where Jonas had curls, my hair hung in poker straightness. Like my father, Jonas had grown to six foot while on that score I resembled my mother, both of us topping out at five four. When I wrapped my arms around my brother for the first time in six years that January morning, the bond was as strong as if we'd never been apart. After giving me a kiss on my forehead, he stepped back and looked at me.

"You haven't changed much," he said. "You're wearing your hair shorter, but the rest of you is the same."

"Thanks," I said. "I think. I was hoping you'd find me more sophisticated or something." Secretly, I was pleased that Jonas saw me as I'd been. There were many times when I felt like that young me had disappeared. I looked him over too. He was two years younger than me, but his hair had darkened and was streaked with grey strands. Tiny lines now rimmed his eyes. He still looked lean and slightly curved inward at the shoulders. "You've grown a beard," I said. "It suits you."

Jonas ran his hand over his chin and cheeks and grinned. "Keeps me warm." He lifted my suitcase, turned and motioned towards the house. "Come inside out of the cold. I've put on a fresh pot of coffee."

I followed him around the back of the house and climbed the steps to his deck. It had been freshly shovelled, and weathered cedar planks showed through the snow. I took a moment to look over his property. It extended back to the woods with a steep drop down to Lake Superior. His nearest neighbours, the Lingstroms, were a good mile away, half the distance back towards town. The snow continued to fall silently around us. I could smell their wood stove—he was burning spruce if my nose remembered correctly. We stepped inside.

My brother was a carpenter, and he'd built this house using local pine and cedar. Inside, the kitchen and the walls were red cedar, and the cupboards were painted a soft white. Jonas had built a table and stained the wood a golden brown, tucking it into an alcove encircled by windows that looked out over the side yard and a stand of birch and spruce. A gold and brown-glassed Tiffany lamp hung over its centre. I watched him pour two cups of coffee, noticing that his hand trembled. He set the cups on the table and we sat kitty corner to each other at one end. As he handed me one, some of the coffee slopped onto the table. I pretended not to notice.

"Claire's gone into town to buy something for supper and then she'll pick up Gunnar from a friend's. They should be back in an hour."

"It'll be good to see them." We both drank from our cups. The coffee tasted of hazelnuts and sweet cream.

"So, what's the situation with Dad?" I asked. With Jonas, I didn't have to couch what I said. We didn't speak often, but we understood each other. "How did he die exactly?"

Jonas held his coffee cup with both hands and seemed to hunch into it. He looked into its depths as he spoke. "Dad decided he was well enough to leave the hospital and checked himself out. That was Friday, the morning after I called you. First I'd heard that he'd left was when I drove into town to visit him in the hospital around two o'clock. Becky Holmes was on the floor and she filled me in. I told her I'd drive to his place to check on him."

"Becky became a nurse?"

"Yeah. She married Kevin Wilders, but I still think of her as Becky Holmes."

"There was a time I thought you and Becky..."

"Well, high school romances don't always end happily."

"That's for sure." *You and me, Maja, we'll be together forever. Billy Okwari's black eyes intense and certain. His lips warm on mine, sealing the deal.* "Did you find Dad?" I asked, more harshly than I'd intended.

"I didn't get over to see him until about five o'clock. I got held up." Jonas's eyes met mine then slid away.

What aren't you telling me, Jonas, I thought, but I let it go. He'd tell me when he was ready.

"It had started snowing just after lunch. I thought I'd shovel off Dad's back steps before I went inside to see him. I tramped through the snow to his shed and took out the first shovel I grabbed for. The sun was setting but there was still enough light to make out shapes in the shed. The shovel wasn't hanging up as usual but leaning up against the wall. You know how meticulous Dad is about putting things back in their place, and I guess that was the first indication that something wasn't right. Didn't seem like much at the time, though. Anyhow, I started back towards

21

the steps. Dad has his outdoor lights on a timer, and it was bright enough. I was about to start shovelling when I looked over and saw him next to the woodpile."

"Dad?"

"Yeah, Dad. He was covered in snow, but I could make out his shape. The snow was dark around his head." Jonas hesitated. "I took off a glove and brushed the snow off him. I don't know why, since I knew he was dead. He was lying on his stomach, but his head was turned to the side like he was listening for something deep in the ground. It was a shock to see his eyes open, frozen in place. His mouth was gaping as if he'd been trying to yell. The back of his head was caved in like a melon. I...I grabbed the shovel and leaned it up against the steps. I just left. Man, there was blood...everywhere. It looked like somebody'd spilled a bowl of cranberry sauce in the snow."

"You didn't call the police?"

Jonas shook his head. "I couldn't seem to make myself think. I sat in the truck for I don't know—a minute and then drove to Hadrian's bar. That's where they found me. I sort of blanked, I think. All that blood. It got to me, you know?"

"Oh, Jonas. I'm so sorry."

Jonas lifted one shoulder in a shrug. He didn't raise his head. I put my hand around his wrist that rested on the table. "Did they tell you what happened?"

"Somebody thwacked him in the back of the head with the shovel."

"The shovel that you got from the shed."

Jonas nodded. His eyes met mine. "The same shovel."

"But surely to God they can't seriously suspect you."

"Maybe. Maybe not."

I let out a sharp laugh. "Why, you were the one who stuck by him. That has to count for something."

"I had as much reason to want him dead as anyone." Jonas moaned, then rolled his body sideways and stood. "I can't talk about this any more now. Claire and Gunnar are home." Jonas rubbed a hand through his hair as he walked towards the backdoor to meet them.

I realized then that I'd heard tires crunching on the snow in the driveway even while my brain was taking in what Jonas had said. I kept my eyes on Jonas, but my mind was scrambling to make sense of what he'd revealed. What had happened between Dad and Jonas that could have Jonas wanting him dead? We'd all have understood if I'd done the murderous deed, but that anger was a long time past. I stared at Jonas's back, at the way his shoulders hunched forward and his hand rubbed the nape of his neck. He was more than just worried. Something was on his conscience. My stomach clenched in a spasm of dread. I'd always wondered what would happen if Jonas was pushed too far. I wished for that moment that I had never left the safety of Sam and Ottawa.

I'd lived a coward's life, avoiding anything that resembled strong emotion. I'd done it deliberately, accepting the sacrifices it had caused. My whole adult life had been spent avoiding just what lay before me now...and I would give anything to go back into the safety of my cocoon, back to the time before Claire's phone message had burst the illusion.

Claire and Gunnar brought in a blast of cold air and a lot of activity that eased the tension that had built up in the kitchen between me and Jonas. Gunnar was a slender blond boy, as Jonas had been at the same age, a jumble of gangly legs and arms that marked the beginning of his transformation into a man. He had Claire's eyes, soft, dreamy orbs that seemed to look right through you into another world. He accepted my hug without hugging me back before stepping back beside his father.

Claire wrapped her arms around my back and squeezed. She smelled of vanilla and Ivory soap. "So glad you're here," she whispered into my ear. "Come with me into the living room. Jonas will put the groceries away and start supper. He loves to cook."

"I'll bring you some wine in a minute," Jonas said, already pulling food out of a bag on the counter. "Sure, you can have a cookie before dinner, but just one," I heard him say to Gunnar as we started down the hallway. "Aunt Maja has brought pie for dessert."

The living room was lined with pine and as cozy a room as I'd ever been in. Logs burned in the stone fireplace, radiating a circle of heat into which we lowered ourselves after a quick tour of the room. We sat facing each other at each end of a deep, velvet-covered couch. A hooked rug of brown, red and plum rested cheerfully under my feet. Claire tucked a long leg under herself and leaned back into the pillows. "This is my one indulgence," she said, rubbing her hand along the couch's plush surface.

"It's beautiful," I said. "The bottle green colour is exquisite."

"I know it's impractical, but sometimes you just have to go with something you like and to hell with the consequences." She laughed, and her grey eyes narrowed as she looked past me. I turned and saw Jonas standing by the bookcase holding two glasses of white wine. His eyes lowered quickly, but the set line of his mouth let me know that he was not happy. He'd have been running a hand through his blonde curls if not for the wine.

"Thanks, darling," Claire said, reaching toward Jonas. Her long elegant fingers closed around both glasses, and she passed one over to me. Gold bracelets clinked and slid down her arm.

She was wearing a tight black turtleneck that showed off her muscular arms and boyish chest. Claire had been a champion cross country skier in her early twenties and obviously still worked at staying in shape. She'd cut her black hair short and spiky, and I thought it suited the strong lines of her face.

"Supper in an hour," Jonas said before disappearing back into the kitchen.

"Thanks, hon." Claire took a mouthful of wine and looked at me over the rim of the glass. "Has he told you about finding your father?"

I nodded. It looked like I wasn't the only one who could cut to the chase. "It's absolutely ridiculous that anyone would think Jonas capable of murder. I don't care how many times he grabbed the shovel."

"I know. It's craziness." Claire's fingers slid up and down the stem of the wine glass. I noticed how pale her skin was now that the rosy glow on her cheeks from the frosty outdoors had disappeared. Her eyes were tired and haunted. "He won't talk to me about what happened." She bit her lip. "We've had a hard day. We're both tired, and we had words this morning. Please know it's nothing, Maja. I stand behind Jonas one hundred per cent."

"I know that, Claire," I said. "We'll get through this. Truth has a way of coming out."

I took a long drink of wine, looking away and pretending not to notice the tear that was sliding down Claire's cheek.

"We've...we've drifted apart," she said, and at first I thought she meant me and her. I opened my mouth to reassure her that time had not changed us, but she spoke again before I did. "He needs constant reassurance, and the down times...it's been hard. Jonas has so many secrets, and I'm not a saint. How could I be?" Her voice lowered and tailed away. She seemed to want me to understand something that I was beyond comprehending. It was a shock to know that she and Jonas were in difficulty—a shock, but perhaps, not unexpected. I stared into her grey eyes, wide with torment and another emotion that looked a lot like fear.

"Jonas loves you," I said by way of benediction. "Love will get you through the worst."

"Will it, Maja? Will it really?"

"Yes," I said, but I turned my eyes away from hers to settle on the flames dancing up from the crackling pine logs in the cast iron grate.

FOUR

The next morning I woke early. I tried falling back to sleep, but too many thoughts were clamouring for attention. After a restless hour, I rose and dressed in a pair of blue jeans and a red fleece pullover before making my way into the kitchen. Claire had set up the coffee maker the night before with instructions to turn it on if I got up first. After two cups and a bowl of cereal and blueberries, I was ready to face the day and went in search of my boots and coat.

The rest of the household was still asleep when I stepped outside into a bitterly cold day. Sometime during the night, a north wind had blown away the cloud cover, and a high pressure system had pushed its way in. Already the sky was turning from black to midnight blue and frosted orange as the sun slipped over the tree line. Every so often weak, silvery sunshine glistened through the trees, casting slender lines of brightness in the snow. I'd gratefully accepted Claire's offer of her parka the night before and nestled into its fur-lined warmth. The coat fit well even though I was not as tall or slender as her.

I was relieved when my car started after two tries. I let it idle while I cleaned off the roof and windshields with a snow scraper. As I worked, my breath came in moist, white puffs as though I were chain smoking. With the plummeting temperature, the car should have been plugged in overnight, but it hadn't come with a block heater. It seemed negligent in this country, but the man who'd given me the keys hadn't had many to choose from in his lot. This particular car had just been driven up from Florida by a businessman. If I hadn't been in such a hurry to see Jonas, I'd have taken a taxi to a rental place in town, but I was too anxious to spend the extra hour driving into Duluth. The rental guy had assured me that the car would start no problem, but his confidence wasn't much help with the frigid temperatures in northern Minnesota.

The drive to Dad's house took all of fifteen minutes. If the roads hadn't been slick with ice, I'd have made it in ten. The route took me to the outskirts of the village, the road hugging the shoreline and winding slowly north. My car's tires valiantly gripped the road as I crept at a turtle speed up a steep hill and deeper into the woods. Luckily, the plow had been around early and the road was passable. Only a few houses dotted this back road, small homes with smoke pouring out of the chimneys and wood stoves the main source of heat. If I opened the window and leaned out, the smell of wood smoke and pine would fill my nostrils like a love note from the past. There was a time when I knew every family along this road, and might still, if the town held true to form. Most of the older people in Duved Cove lived their entire lives in the same house and their children married locally and moved into homes nearby. My generation was the first to go farther afield, to university then to towns and cities with better jobs.

Duved Cove had been a fishing village in the 1800s and a logging centre in the early 1900s. The mill was still operating, but on a much smaller scale than in its heyday. My father hadn't liked working with his hands and had broken with tradition by becoming a cop, a profession Grandpa Larson had viewed with a jaundiced eye, but even he had to admit that Dad would have made a poor logger. As it turned out, Dad wasn't much of a cop either. The year after I'd left for Bemidji State University to work on a chemistry degree, my father was implicated in a coverup of some sort and quietly dismissed from his duties. If he hadn't had such a good reputation, and if all the higher ups in the chain of command hadn't liked him so much, they might have made a harsher example of him for the benefit of the younger officers on the force. As it was, rumours of the dismissal were punishment enough in such a tight-knit community. Dad never told us the full story, and we knew not to press him for details. His dismissal was quiet enough that he was able to get a job as a customs officer at the Pigeon River crossing about an hour's drive from our house. It was a job he'd held until Friday.

My father remained in the house where I'd grown up even after my mother died. He owned a good twenty acres of land that had never been developed—land handed down from my great-grandfather, along with our house on the north-east corner. The house I'd loved as a child, in the middle of nowhere, surrounded by woods and rock that led to the rocky shoreline of Superior. The house where my father had found my mother hanging from an attic rafter one cold October morning.

I slowed the car and fought to keep the memory from surfacing. My hands had been clutching the wheel, and I tried to flex my fingers. If I allowed myself to think about the horror of that day, I would never be able to make this journey—one I'd been unable to make when my father had been alive. I'd visited my brother twice, the last time when Gunnar was six, but I'd never made the trip to my parents' house, even though Jonas believed it would help me to heal.

"I have nothing to heal from," I'd said angrily, and Jonas had watched me with veiled eyes. I'd tried to appear unaffected. "I just have no reason to go back there. I'm over it."

The last mile was almost too painful to bear; the big rock where I used to meet my best friend Katherine Lingstrom so we could walk to school together; the crooked tree Jonas and I had climbed; the path into the woods that led down to a sand beach where Billy and I had lain in the shadow of the woods. I took each landmark in with starved eyes. This was the part of me I'd shut away since my mother's death.

I could see her in my mind's eye, walking down the road, a cattail in her hand, twirling back to smile at me and tell me to hurry up. If I pretended time had stood still, if I believed hard enough...her hair had been white blonde like mine and fell almost to her waist. She wore it braided, but the days she'd let it loose had seemed a gift. She had a smile and blue eyes that had warmed me always, even when she was trying to contain me. Back then, I'd been a carefree and careless child, rushing headlong into every situation. My disregard for rules had gotten me into trouble with my father over and over again. I'd rebelled against his harsh, unyielding nature that turned monstrous when he drank. My mother had been powerless to protect me, to protect herself from his anger. I'd loved my shy, tormented mother with my whole being, and when she'd killed herself, she'd killed any part of me that could forgive my father. And yet part of me needed to with childish desperation.

I was surprised to feel my cheeks wet with tears as I started up the long driveway to our house. I lifted my brimming eyes to my old bedroom window in the second storey on the right side of the house. The blind was halfway down, as if it couldn't make up its mind. The symbolism was not lost on me. I parked the car and stepped outside. I'd come home at last.

I circled around to the backyard. The sun had risen above

the treeline, and the snow had taken on a rosy hue to match the sunlight filtering through the trees. I purposefully averted my eyes from the woodpile and scanned the yard. Dad had kept it free of clutter. I could see poles in the ground where he'd planted tomatoes and beans in Mom's vegetable garden. A concrete birdbath rose above the snow pile with a mound of ice capping its basin. Directly in front of me were a stand of birch trees and two spruce with birdfeeders hanging from the lowest branches. As I watched, a squirrel parachuted onto one of the feeders and scattered the last of the seed into the snow. Like so many properties in Duved Cove, there was no fence to encircle the yard except around the vegetable garden to keep out deer. I looked down. The ground had been trampled by a tornado of boot prints. I could only imagine what must have taken place after they'd found my father's body.

I turned and walked slowly towards the deck. When I reached the bottom step, I hesitated with my glove on the railing. I forced myself to look. The snow was piled in uneven patches around the spot where my father had fallen. I could see red and pink through the layers, and it was an eerie feeling to know that this was his blood. The place he had met his Maker. I moved closer and squatted in the snow. They'd dug around the area, probably looking for clues. As a crime scene went, it would have been a hard one to keep. Even now, the wind was blowing swirls of snow in intermittent gusts. I moved back towards the stairs, careful not to leave more footprints than necessary. I grabbed the handrail and leaned on it heavily as I maneuvered the icy steps. Once I reached the landing, I fumbled in my pocket for my keys. The key to this house was still on my keychain. I didn't know why I'd kept it after so many years, but I had. I supposed it could be construed as more symbolism, if you were bent that way.

The yellow and black tape across our back door made me pause a second, but it would not stop me now that I'd come this far. I pulled the yellow tape aside and fit my key into the lock. It turned as if I'd used it every day for the past twenty years. The familiarity of the key's weight in the lock brought back memories hooked onto feelings long forgotten. Once inside, I slammed the door shut and leaned against it with my eyes closed tight. I sucked in air like a drowning swimmer and tried to still my frantic heart.

"Mama," I whispered. "Your Maja's come home."

My father's kitchen had changed little since the last time I'd been in it. The same green linoleum on the kitchen floor, lifting a bit around the edges; the original tired oak cupboards; the old Frigidaire in the corner. A new rectangular pine kitchen table and matching chairs looked out of place in the otherwise drab room. I circled the space, trailing my fingers along surfaces. The house was still on its programmed heating cycle, and I heard the furnace kick in. I'd hardly noticed how cool it was until that moment. I heard the clock ticking loudly on the wall over the stove, the same clock that my mother had picked out of the Sears catalogue thirty years before. The room smelled stale, the dankness heightened by a mixture of cooking grease, overripe bananas and rotting potatoes, and I suddenly couldn't wait to leave it. I went quickly down the darkened hallway into the living room. Here Dad had splurged on a new couch and leather recliners that encircled a big screen television. He'd acquired a state of the art sound system too that had place of honor on top of a shelving unit. The ornaments and pictures Mom had collected were gone, but lower down on the shelving unit, my father had placed a framed picture of himself and two buddies dressed in hunting gear and holding rifles. In the photo, Dad was grasping a handful of dead ducks by their feet and grinning into the camera.

I walked over and picked up the frame, staring into Dad's face and trying to see any part of him that I could latch onto. I had no idea why I thought the essence of him would be captured in a photo when I'd never been able to find it in real life. He looked fit and ruddy-faced, as if time had held off aging him. His blonde hair had turned a soft white, cut in a layered style, and his eyes were still a deep vivid blue. I put his picture back next to framed photos of Gunnar. In the first, he is a baby in Claire's arms, and in the second he is school age, grinning into the camera with his top front teeth missing.

New carpeting led to the stairs and up to hallway on the second floor—forest green with a pattern of tan swirls. It wasn't thick enough to hide the creaks as I slowly climbed. I hesitated on the landing and watched dust dance in the sunlight seeping in through the slats of the metal blind that covered the window above my head. The same brown paneling I remembered lined the walls. It looked streaky in places, faded like well-worn leather shoes. The door to my parents' room stood open, and I stepped inside. I don't know what I expected to find, but it wasn't this. The bed was gone, and in its place were a stationary bike, a rowing machine and an apparatus that had weights and pulleys for working out the upper body. Free weights lined the floor in front of bright blue mats like the ones we'd had in gym class. I jumped when I turned and saw myself reflected in a floor to ceiling mirror that lined one wall. My face was pale and my eyes tired. I looked like I needed a hot bath and a good, strong drink. Those would come later.

My father had taken Jonas's old bedroom as his own. The double bed and oak headboard were new, but he'd kept the chest of drawers and my mother's hope chest. I crossed the room and tried to open the chest, but it was locked. I didn't feel like searching for the key—not yet in any case. The walls were washed-out beige, and I could make out the outlines of Jonas's posters that Dad had removed without bothering to paint. The one on the far wall had been the famous poster of Farah Fawcett, the one with her sitting nearly sideways in a red bathing suit with her head thrown back and a smile the size of a quarter moon on her face. Jonas had had a crush on her that lasted the entire television run of *Charlie's Angels*. A thick duvet covered the bed while curtains in a matching caramel colour hung at the window. If Dad had kept my mother's ornaments and photos, they were tucked away out of sight, perhaps in the locked chest.

I walked past the bathroom and kept going to my own bedroom at the end of the hall. The door was shut. I took another deep breath and turned the knob. Once again, the room's contents surprised me. My father had removed my bed and all my childhood things. In their place were piles of boxes and pieces of old furniture stacked against the walls, much like you'd find in an attic. The only item left in the room that I recognized was the faded rosebud wallpaper. All other traces of my occupancy were long gone or packed away out of sight. I moved closer and pried open the cardboard flaps of a large box, curious about what it held. Dozens of paperbacks were neatly arranged in rows, their covers glossy and brand new. I opened the large box next to it and found a boxful of hardcover books; the third box held bibles, black covers with gilt lettering. Had my father become an avid reader? Had he turned to religion? I couldn't remember that he'd ever sat down to read anything more than the newspaper, let alone consider theology in any form. In addition to the bibles, there were mysteries, historical fiction and *New York Times* bestsellers, light escapist reading.

I straightened and walked over to the window to look at the streaked sky through the boughs of the old pine. I raised the blind and a swirl of light dust drifted around me like flour. Lowering my gaze, I looked across the yard at the trees at the end of our property. As a girl, I'd spent many hours daydreaming at my desk, which had been positioned in front of the window. For the first time since I'd entered the house, I felt like I'd found something of my own. I closed my eyes and imagined myself back in high school with nothing in front of me but a school assignment and possibilities.

If I hadn't been so still, I might have missed the heavy creak of the loose floorboard on the stairs. I held my breath. A second creak even closer, and I exhaled slowly. I whirled around. Whoever had entered the house had done so without my hearing them. The half-open bedroom door seemed like an impossible distance away, and I knew I couldn't get to it before the intruder reached the landing. I was cornered. My breathing was too loud in my ears, but I willed myself to stay calm. If the person creeping up the staircase meant me harm, I'd know soon enough.

FIVE

The first thing I noticed about Tobias Olsen as he kicked open the door and stepped inside the room where I was standing was the Glock pistol he held with both hands, pointed directly at my legs. The second was the police uniform under his open leather jacket. I slowly raised my hands and grinned, even though my bottom lip and chin felt like they were quivering uncontrollably.

"Hey, Tobias," I managed to enunciate, since it felt like all the saliva had disappeared from my mouth. "Been a long time."

Tobias lowered the gun and squinted at me through pale green eyes. He was over six feet and on the husky side, big enough to put the fear of God into me. "As I live and die, if it ain't Maja Larson." He lowered the gun and clicked on the safety before slipping it back into the holster on his right hip. "It's been over twenty years, but you haven't changed much."

"The last time I saw you was high school graduation. You've taken up with the law, I see."

"Sorry about your old man," Tobias said, the corners of his mouth drooping momentarily. "Still, you shouldn't have crossed the police tape, Maja. Figured you'd know better."

I shrugged. "Just felt like something I had to do."

Tobias ran a hand through his bristly greying hair as he looked around the room. His eyes rested on the two boxes I'd opened. "Find anything interesting?" he asked as he crossed the floor to look inside.

"Just some books. This used to be my bedroom." I didn't know why I felt I had to explain.

"I remember," Tobias said.

"That's funny." I tried to look into his eyes to see what he'd meant by that remark, but they stayed fixed on the boxes. "I don't remember you ever being in my bedroom."

"You had all the guys dreaming. You must have known that, Maja. Every red-blooded boy in high school with an iota of testosterone knew where you slept every night."

I felt myself blushing. I lowered my head and started for the door. "You're as full of shit now as you were when we were teenagers, Tobias Olsen," I said.

He laughed. "How about we go into town and I buy you breakfast as a peace offering?" I could hear him rise from where he'd squatted to open one of the box lids and follow behind me.

I reached the door and put my hand around the doorknob. I turned and pretended to be considering his offer. "Okay," I said after a few beats. It would be a good chance to find out what he knew about who'd murdered my dad. Besides, I'd become hungry all of a sudden, and the thought of scrambled eggs, bacon and another cup of coffee was more appealing than poking around in my father's cold, depressing house.

Tobias followed me through town to Frida's Coffeeshop, which was located on a flat piece of land at the base of a hill. If I'd kept going on the same road, at the top of the hill I could have turned left onto Highway 61 to head north to the border. Frida owned a motel and some cottages that were strung out like a necklace around the bay. It was a pretty spot to have breakfast.

We found a table near the window. I sat so I could see the

woods and snow stretching down the incline toward the frozen lake while Tobias angled himself so he had his back to the wall and a good view of the room.

After the coffee'd been poured and we'd placed our orders to a younger version of Frida, likely a granddaughter, Tobias leaned forward and studied me as if I had something written across my forehead. "I see you got married," he said finally. "Word was you became a doctor and moved to Toronto or somewhere up in the wilds of Canada."

"Ottawa, actually. I married a businessman named Sam Cleary. We met through a friend when I was visiting her in New York City. My name's Maja Cleary now."

"He's Canadian?"

"Yup."

"So you took his name and followed him to Ott-ee-wa. Never been there myself. Would you recommend it as a place to end up?"

"You'd probably miss the lake. We have rivers but nothing like Superior." I took a sip of coffee and set down my mug. "What about you? Did you ever leave Duved Cove?"

"I worked in Duluth for a few years, got married, had a kid, divorced and moved back here."

"Do I know who you married?"

"Lindsey Schnerring. You might remember her. She was a year behind us in school."

"Wasn't she a cheerleader?"

"Yeah, that'd be her." Tobias stopped talking and took a sip of coffee. He set the cup down. "I'm thinking about heading to Florida soon."

"A transfer?"

"Sure. I'm getting tired of these winters and the snow. I want to try out beaches and heat for a bit."

"Are there many from our high school still living around here?" I asked. I would never ask directly about the one person I craved to know about. When I'd turned my back on Duved Cove twenty years earlier, I'd never said Billy Okwari's name again, not even to Jonas.

"Quite a few left from our class. Your buddy, Katherine Lingstrom, she married a dentist and moved to Madison. Her mom still lives in that house on Strathcona near your dad's place. Do you keep in touch?"

I shook my head.

"Too bad. You two were joined at the hip all through school— and pretty nice hips at that. I guess time and distance can end any relationship."

"I'm glad she's doing so well." I ignored his comment.

"Of course, your brother is still here. He's got a few buddies in town from his original gang. Adrian and Fish. They're both working at the mill."

"Jonas mentioned Becky Holmes is working in the hospital."

"She's Becky Wilders now. There's probably lots of people still around who you'd recognize, although we've aged enough that we're all starting to look like our parents."

I tried to hide my disappointment. Billy Okwari had been in our class at school but had been quiet and had kept to himself— I'd say invisible to almost everyone else. It had taken me some time to realize he'd wanted it that way. No wonder Tobias didn't give me any news of Billy now.

Our breakfasts arrived, and we ate without talking. I wasn't as hungry as I'd thought. The eggs acquired a rubbery consistency as they cooled, and I knew they'd come out of a package. I put down my fork and looked at Tobias. "So what do you know about my father's death? Have you any idea who killed him...or why?"

Tobias chewed on a piece of toast and waved the crust at my plate. He talked with his mouth full. "Should have warned you against the scrambled. If you want real eggs, you have to have fried or poached." He looked around the room as if it held the answers. "Can't tell you much about who'd want to kill your father," he said before taking a swallow of coffee. "Your dad was well liked. He'd recently notified U.S. Customs that he'd be cutting back his hours to part-time, which doesn't mean much as far as I can see. He also told them he was planning a vacation and needed a few months off. Not sure that was a cause for alarm either, but it marks a change in his pattern."

"Nobody had threatened him?"

"Not that we're aware of. Look, your dad was known for being opinionated, and he was a take-charge, bullish kind of man. That was balanced by his natural charisma and all around good nature. Bottom line, people liked him."

"What about when he got let go from the police force?"

"Yeah, that was a long time ago, but apparently, people felt like your dad was set up. Nobody liked what happened to him, so he was pretty much handed the customs job."

"How was he set up?"

Tobias slopped up the last of the egg yolk with the remainder of the toast and pushed aside his empty plate. He looked at me. His green eyes were thoughtful. "You really don't know much about what happened?"

I shook my head. "My father never spoke about it to us." I didn't add that we'd been too scared to probe. The temper my father showed with us had not extended past the inside of our home. I wasn't surprised that everyone liked him. He'd been adept at hiding his rages behind a mask of good old boy charm. It seemed unlikely that Tobias knew I'd been estranged from my father. My father would never have let on. "After my mother died..."

Tobias shifted uneasily in his seat. "Yeah, sorry about that too. I never saw you around Duved Cove after the funeral. She died soon after your father's dismissal, now that I think about it." I could almost hear the gears in his head clicking.

"It wasn't our best spring," I said.

"No, I guess not."

I reached behind me for my purse slung over the back of my chair. "Jonas said you'd let us know when we can have my father's body. We're going to have a quiet burial."

Tobias waved aside my money. "This is on me. The autopsy is scheduled for later today in Duluth. I'm driving down there after I leave you. We'll send your father's body back tonight to the Fisk Funeral Home."

"Thanks."

"You staying up at Jonas's then?"

"Yes. We'll be waiting to hear from you if you find out anything."

"I'm pretty sure the autopsy's going to show he died from the shovel blow to the back of the head." Tobias paused and added more gently, "At least it was quick."

We left the warmth of the restaurant and headed to our cars. Tobias walked past his to mine and reached around me to swing my door open. As I lowered myself into the seat, he leaned over the top of the window and said, "Don't go back into your father's house until we've had a chance to go through it, Maja. Unfortunately, we don't have the police force of a larger town, and Chief Anders is using up some leave and David Keating's wife just had their fourth kid, so he's been a little preoccupied."

"Okay." I wasn't sure if I'd keep my promise, but it seemed

41

best to let him think I would. "Is that the same Anders who was chief twenty years ago?

"The very same, but not for much longer. He's easing into retirement. I'm organizing the goodbye party for March."

"Nice seeing you again, Tobias." I turned the key in the ignition.

"Likewise," he said and grinned at me like I was someone worth smiling over. "It's just too bad it was your father's death that brought you home." He sounded wistful, like he'd hoped I'd have made the trip for more nostalgic reasons.

"It's not the way I'd want it either," I said as I swung the door shut.

When I pulled onto the main road, I could still see Tobias in my rearview mirror, watching me from where he leaned against the hood of his squad car with his arms folded across his chest.

I found Jonas out back in his workshop. He was slicing up a board with a table saw and the loud grinding noise of the blade kept him from hearing my approach. Thick glasses protected his eyes from floating sawdust, and with his fly-away mass of blonde curls, he resembled a mad scientist hunched over some fiendish experiment. I waited for him to finish his handiwork so that I wouldn't startle him. I used the time to look around.

Jonas was as meticulous as anyone I knew. He craved order, everything in its place and predictable. His workspace was organized and clean to the point of obsession. Hand tools hung in rows on the wall, while nails and other items were in pull-out boxes, carefully labelled. Directly in front of me was a wooden tabletop attached to the wall with a stool tucked underneath. He'd installed three fluorescent lights that illuminated every corner of the cedar-panelled room. The air smelled of sawdust, varnish and linseed oil—all comforting and solid. When Jonas finally saw me, he removed the glasses and smiled. "You were up early."

"I went to Dad's and had a look around."

Jonas's eyebrows shot up, and I knew I'd surprised him. "Was it like you remembered?"

"Pretty much. He had some new furniture and stuff. Same view out my bedroom window though. Where are Claire and Gunnar? I looked inside before I came back here, and they're nowhere around."

"They've gone to the school. Claire is getting some big art project ready for the kids tomorrow. She's also trying to keep Gunnar from thinking about Dad's death. Sam called this morning, by the way." Jonas ran his hand back and forth along the wood, feeling for rough spots.

"I left Sam a message on the kitchen table that I was coming. He'd gone to New York on business, and I didn't want to bother him." My voice came out false in my own ears. In fact, I'd tried calling Sam in his hotel room the night before I'd left and again in the morning before leaving for the airport, but both times he hadn't answered. Perversely, I'd chosen not to leave a voice mail. It struck me that I hadn't thought of Sam since I'd stepped off the plane in Duluth.

"Have you eaten?" Jonas asked.

"Yes. Why don't you finish what you're working on and I'll go amuse myself."

"Okay. I'll be up to the house in a bit."

"Take your time," I said as I turned to leave.

Sam answered on the second ring. "I'm sorry I wasn't with you when you got the news," he said. "Is it very bad being there?"

"No. It's okay."

"Still, it's always a shock when a parent dies. It must have been sudden?"

I could have told him then that my father had been murdered, but for some reason, I didn't. "It was...unexpected. The funeral's in a few days so I'll stay till then. Can you call Judith to let her know to cancel my patients for the next week?"

"Okay. Will it take that long?"

"I think so. There's a bit to straighten out."

"Was it a heart attack or stroke?"

"No. They're still not certain. The autopsy will show the exact cause. How was your trip?"

Sam's voice lightened, "Great. I sealed the deal, and it means a big bonus. I was hoping to take you out to celebrate, but that will have to wait."

"Yes. But we can do that when I get home." I heard a voice in the background saying something to Sam. "Is someone with you?"

There was muffled speaking, then Sam removed his hand from over the receiver. "Lana stopped by with some papers I have to sign. George should be here any minute."

"Well, I won't keep you then," I said, suddenly not wanting to keep the connection any longer.

"I'll call tonight," Sam said. "Try not to let your dad's death get you down."

"No," I said. "That's the last place I want to go."

SIX

At around two thirty, Claire, Gunnar and I decided to drive up the mountain to go cross country skiing. Claire more than any of us was showing signs of stress, and she'd leapt on my suggestion of an outing. She was unable to convince Jonas to leave the sanctuary of his workshop, to which he'd retreated after Claire and Gunnar had returned home early afternoon, and by the rigid way she held her neck and shoulders, I knew she was angry. It wasn't until after we'd parked in the empty parking lot backing onto Christie trail, unloaded our equipment, fastened our skis and started down the path, that she started to relax.

Claire had been a champion skier in her late teens and early twenties, even trying out for the U.S. Olympic team. Although she hadn't made the cut, she'd been first on the waiting list—no small accomplishment. Marriage to Jonas, a child and the need to make money had ended her Olympic dream. I sometimes wondered if she regretted the decisions she'd made. I'd known Claire in high school but hadn't been in her circle. Her father was a lawyer who started up a practice in Duved Cove when Claire was in tenth grade. By then, she was away training most of the year and back in the summers. We'd both worked as life guards one summer at the community pool, and through me, she'd met Jonas. I was still baffled as to how they hooked up, because Jonas was as far from self-assured and competitive as a dove from a hawk. Claire must have seen him as a gold-medal

45

challenge, because she'd done all the pursuing.

"I'll meet you at the lookout," Claire called over her shoulder just before she picked up speed crossing the field and disappeared onto the trail into the woods. She was wearing navy spandex pants, a turquoise shell and a red toque and made a vibrant splash of colour against the white snowscape and the darkness of the trees ahead. Gunnar was well in front of me, dressed completely in black with a grey toque. His gangly limbs couldn't match his mother's smooth strides, but he managed to widen the distance between himself and me with every ski stroke.

I'd borrowed Claire's old set of skis and boots that pinched. It had been twenty years since I'd last skied, and I struggled to find my rhythm. After a bit of awkward trial and effort, my strokes felt natural enough that I could enjoy the swoosh swoosh of my skis in the ruts of the trail and the reach and push of each arm as I jabbed the ski poles into the snow.

I entered the dark silence of the waiting forest. Snow weighed heavily on the overhead boughs and swooped in graceful arcs against the tree trunks. I raised my eyes at intervals to look up through the gaps in the trees. Since we'd left the van, the sky had changed from a silky blue to grey as snow clouds moved in from the north. I felt protected in the woods. Noises were muffled, and row upon row of giant pines encased the trail like a cocoon. I began to enjoy the solitariness of my path and the cold wind on my forehead and cheeks. The physical exertion felt good, even when I had to struggle up hills. I gained confidence on the downhill sections, invigorated by rushes of adrenalin. Time passed without me noticing. I rounded a long looping curve and climbed another hill. At its crest, I met Claire and Gunnar leaning on their poles and looking out over the cliff and the sharp rise of the mountain across the gully. They both turned their faces towards me as I glided alongside.

Gunnar's eyes flashed dark and angry. "I'm going back, Mom," he said.

"I'd like you to wait until we all head back together," Claire said, her body angled towards him, her face looking down at his.

Gunnar pretended not to hear. He adeptly rotated his skis and levered himself forward. One thrust with his ski poles, and he shot down the hill and out of sight.

Claire straightened and shrugged. "He's not very sociable these days. I think it's a phase. We'll rest a few minutes and then I'll start after him. He's mad that he can't keep up with me."

I looked across the fence that was strung along the edge of the precipice towards the snowy peak on the other side of the valley. The clouds had thickened, and I felt stray wet snowflakes land on my face. "Looks like we'll be getting another storm," I said.

"It was an early winter and could be a late spring." Claire hesitated. "Maja, has Jonas said anything to you about...about your father?"

I shook my head. "Jonas has hardly said anything to me about Dad. Why, is there something I should know?"

Claire began tracing a pattern in the snow with her ski pole. "Jonas was very angry with your father lately, but you know Jonas. He's not good at expressing his feelings. He just withdraws."

"What caused him to get angry? Jonas doesn't usually get worked up, or at least not so you'd know."

It was Claire's turn to shake her head. "I'm sure it's nothing to worry about. Maja, how come Jonas never talks about your mom or why you stopped speaking to your dad? He's never said boo about anything, even after all our years together. It's like there's a wall of silence between us that keeps me shut out."

"The things that happened were a long time ago and were

hard to talk about back then. Jonas has his reasons for not wanting to bring them up again." As did I. "Jonas never liked reliving those days or speaking badly of our father." I didn't know whether or not to be surprised that Jonas hadn't talked about our parents to Claire. I guess it put his relationship with Claire in a new light. He hadn't trusted her enough to share what probably still haunted him.

"I know," Claire said. "He avoids emotional upsets like the plague."

I smiled gently. "It's a family trait."

The snow was picking up steam, and a gust of wind rolled across the hilltop. It was time to go back. I took in a deep breath. It was now or never. "Claire, whatever happened to Billy Okwari? I was just wondering, because we've talked about everybody else that I could think of except him." I kept my eyes carefully averted from hers.

Claire wiped a gloved hand across her forehead. "Billy Okwari? That scrawny Native kid in our class?"

"Yes."

"He married some girl from Lutsen and moved away. Odd you should ask about him, though, because I saw him in town the other day. At least, I think it was him. Somebody said he'd moved back to the area recently. Boy, you have a good memory. It's not like he was part of our gang or stood out in any way. He was one of those kids who never spoke up in class or got involved in anything. Why do you want to know?"

"No reason. I just remembered him from those days."

Claire had given me more information than I'd expected. *Back in the area again?* No wonder I hadn't been able to find his name in the phone directory the times I'd looked. My heart beat faster at the thought of seeing him. We were both married, so it would be all right to make contact again, or at least that's what I

48

told myself. The rapid beating of my heart should have warned me otherwise.

Jonas had supper waiting for us when we got home around five. He'd stuffed a lake trout with crab, breadcrumbs and lemon juice and served it with baked potatoes and garden salad. We sat around the kitchen table and dug into the food like we hadn't eaten for days. A combination of fresh air and exercise had whetted our appetites. I couldn't remember when food had last tasted so good.

Gunnar sat across from me, and I watched him without him noticing. He kept his head lowered, his thin shoulders hunched inwards and his blonde hair hiding his eyes. His fork moved steadily from plate to mouth, the only sign that he was conscious. Finally, he stood and grabbed his full milk glass and the empty plate in one quick motion, leaving the table without having uttered a word. The rest of us had barely spoken either, except to comment on the food and the trek we'd made through the woods. It was as if my father's murder had sapped our energies, and we didn't have the strength to rise above our lethargy.

Jonas lifted his head. He pointed his knife at Gunnar's empty seat. "What's with him?" he asked Claire.

"He's been in a foul temper. I'll talk to him later." Claire stood and gathered up her dishes and cutlery. She carried everything to the counter then moved across the kitchen to the stove, where she picked up the kettle. "A cup of tea, Maja?" she asked.

"That would be lovely." I lowered my fork, realizing that there was nothing left on my plate.

Jonas pushed back in his chair. "Would you like to go for a walk after supper? We could make it as far as Hadrian's for a nightcap, if you feel up to it."

It would be good to have a chance to talk with Jonas, because I knew the next day we'd be making funeral arrangements. Tobias had stopped by while we were skiing and told Jonas my father's body would be delivered to the funeral home in the morning. Not to mention as soon as I laid my head on the pillow, all the worries would keep me from sleep. Maybe, a shot of something strongly alcoholic would help relax me. "Yes, that would be good," I said. "I'll wash up after my tea, and we can head out."

Jonas lumbered to his feet. "Come get me in my shop. I'll be ready to go when you are."

The wind was still blowing in gusts, periodically whipping up billows of snow that wet our faces, making us lean into their strength. The snow had stopped falling, however, so Jonas and I were able to make good time between the blasts of wind. The temperature had dropped since the afternoon, but the bank of cloud cover kept the cold from being unbearable. I'd dressed in the borrowed jacket, hat and scarf that Claire had said were mine for the duration of my visit. Jonas had two flashlights that we used for the first part of our trek because streetlights didn't extend this far out of town. Their two shafts of light crisscrossed through the darkness in front of us and illuminated shadowy hollows in the snow drifts as we trudged through the unpacked snow. The walk to Hadrian's was about two miles and would take us half an hour. We didn't speak much, preferring to let the night's silence and the soughing of the wind in the trees envelop us. I heard a wolf's plaintive howl from somewhere deep in the woods and shivered inside my coat. I was thankful to have Jonas's solid presence striding alongside me.

When we finally entered Hadrian's, it took a moment to

adjust from the darkness of the outside to the noisy brightness of the pub. The heat of the room struck me in a wave after the coldness of the winter wind. I took a moment to look around as I shrugged out of my coat.

During my high school years, Hadrian Senior had owned the bar, a squat, bald Swede who'd emigrated from Sweden at the age of five. His son, also named Hadrian, had inherited the bar when his father had retired ten years earlier, or so Jonas told me as we stepped away from the entrance. In some perverse trick of genetics, Hadrian the son was close to six and a half feet tall with a full head of cocoa brown hair that fell in lank strands to his shoulders and a bristly moustache trimmed in an uneven line above his lip so that he looked like he was perpetually sneering. He half-turned and glanced up at us from where he sat at a bar stool, both burly arms resting on the counter as he watched the wrestling channel on TV. His sharp blue eyes darted between Jonas and me, and I could see recognition glinting from their depths as they finally rested on me. He stood and stepped behind the counter as we crossed the plank floor. Bob Seger was singing "You'll Accompany Me" from speakers over the bar. Two men sat at the opposite end, hunkered down over pints of beer, and they shifted enough so that I knew they were watching us.

"Jonas." Hadrian nodded at the same time as he placed a mug under the tap and pulled a long draft of beer. "Howdy, Maja. Sorry to hear about your father."

"Thanks, Hadrian," I said. "It looks like you're doing well." I looked around the room. He'd kept the same oak panelling from his father's day, but the dark stained chairs and tables looked newer. A modern gas fireplace cast a cheery glow on the far wall; otherwise, the pub had not bowed to anything remotely trendy. This was a drinking man's bar.

Hadrian tilted his head in acknowledgment. He focused his eyes on Jonas. "So Tobias went easy on you?"

"I didn't have much to tell."

"Nobody can believe that somebody killed your old man," Hadrian said. "I'm sure going to miss him coming around. What can I get you, Maja?"

"A Scotch on the rocks."

"Coming right up." Hadrian reached for the bottle of Johnny Walker Red. "Jonas tells me you're a doctor living up in Canada."

"Yes, I married a Canadian."

"Haven't seen you back here in a long time."

He'd stated the obvious, and I didn't reply. Jonas reached for his beer.

"Let's sit at a table," he said.

"Staying with Jonas, are you?" Hadrian asked as he slid the glass of Scotch to me.

"Yes, for a few more days anyhow."

As I picked up the glass and turned to follow Jonas, I took a better look at the two men sitting on the barstools. One met my eyes, and an electric shock travelled up my spine. For one moment, I thought I was looking into Billy Okwari's black eyes until I realized time could not have stood that still. This man was half my age. He nodded at me before lowering his eyes and draining the last of his beer.

Jonas had chosen a table as far away from the other patrons as possible, and I slid into the seat next to him, still shaken but also exhilarated by the encounter.

"You look flushed," Jonas said.

"I'm getting to the hot flash age." I hung my parka over the back of my chair and ran a hand through my hair. It sparked with static from wearing the wool hat. "It sounds like Dad never gave up the drink if he was a regular here."

"He moderated his drinking after Mom died."

"God knows he didn't when she was alive. You've never told Claire about life with him when we were kids?"

"No point to that."

"It would have helped her to understand. . ."

"Understand what? Why I'm an emotional cripple?" Jonas's voice rose. He glanced around to make sure nobody had heard, and his shoulders relaxed when he saw nobody looking our way.

I couldn't explain the urgency I felt to disturb the family waters we'd avoided. I feared for what I'd seen in Jonas and in his interactions with Claire. "If Claire had known about the things he did, the things he made us do, she would certainly have given you strength. It would have helped your relationship."

"She married me as I was. I didn't need to explain myself. I didn't want her pity. The choices she's made had nothing to do with how our father treated us."

"Tobias said that our father was a charming, well-liked man. His mask never slipped in public then?"

"Only with his nearest and dearest. He fooled Claire too. She should have known. If she'd really loved me, she would have known." Jonas's voice broke and he quickly lifted his beer mug to take a long drink.

I wanted Jonas to understand about our father. I pushed on. "I studied personality disorders as part of my studies in university. In fact, I read everything I could about them, trying to sort out why Dad was like he was. You know, so outwardly friendly but so deeply disturbed and controlling at home. The times he made us get down on our hands and knees to clean and reclean every square inch of that house, and still we couldn't please him. The punishments and the groundings over nothing. Belittling us and making us feel so small then turning around and acting like we were the most special children on earth. We were always off-balance. That wasn't a normal way to grow up, Jonas."

"Knowing it and getting over it are two different things. I thought by not talking about it to anyone, I'd be able to live with it," Jonas said. "Did you ever tell Sam?"

"A bit. Not all of it. I never told him how Dad would wake us up with the muzzle of his shotgun and line us all up in the bedroom against the wall with the gun trained on us, where we'd stand for hours until he fell asleep."

Jonas hung his head. "I don't want to talk about this, Maja."

"I know. Mom wouldn't talk about it either."

"He was seeing a woman in town these last few months."

"Oh? Is she married?"

Jonas nodded. "The only kind he got involved with."

"Figures. It fed something in his ego. A narcissist doesn't care about anyone else—we may as well be hollow shells for all they care about us. They also have fragile egos that need constant reinforcement. Having married women fall for him would have given him a feeling of power."

"You figure he was a narcissist?"

"Yes, a person who has no empathy for others and needs constant adulation. They go into rages when they don't get their own way. They're also incredibly charming and manipulative."

"Dad's photo could be next to the definition."

"They also can make their spouses feel like worthless shit. It explains a lot about our parents' relationship." I sipped my drink, trying to keep my hand steady. "Do you know the name of the latest woman he was seeing?"

"I'd rather not say."

"I think it's important that I know. I'm not going to go to the police." I didn't add "unless I found out it led to the murderer". I looked across at the bar. The young Native man who so resembled Billy was putting on his coat and throwing money onto the bar. He had shoulder-length hair as poker-straight as mine and high cheekbones in a thin face. When he stood, he was taller than I'd thought and beanpole skinny. He headed towards the back of the bar, where an oversized finger on the wall pointed toward the washrooms.

"Maybe we should head back," Jonas said. He reached around and grabbed his coat. "Finish your drink, Maj."

I studied him over the rim of the glass as I swallowed the last of the Scotch. It burned my throat going down, but not unpleasantly. Jonas seemed to fold in on himself, his shoulders inverted and his hands tucked under the coat on his lap. When I lowered my empty glass, he stood and looked down at me. The expression in his eyes was sad.

"Becky Holmes," he said. "If you really want to know, our father was sleeping with my old girlfriend Becky Holmes— known to everyone in town as Mrs. Becky Wilders."

SEVEN

Your father lived a good life," said Ralph Kreighbaum in a voice as solemn as...well...as a funeral director's. At ten a.m. the next morning, I was sitting in his office facing him across a deep mahogany desk that glistened like a flat piece of ice. Every time I lifted my eyes to look at Ralph's emaciated face, I was thrown by the gigantic portrait of his wife and two sons that hung across the better part of the wall behind him. His wife, Sharon, was as plump as Ralph was thin, and unfortunately both sons had inherited her genes. I allowed Ralph to drone on about coffins and services for nearly fifteen minutes before holding up a hand.

"I'm sorry," he said while frowning at my interruption. I knew he'd been building up to lay out the burial costs. His eyes narrowed but he kept his voice friendly. "Am I overwhelming you, Maja? I know this can all be very technical for someone in your state."

I let his comment pass, but it gave rise to the picture of a pregnant woman with the vapors. I kept my voice low. "No, it's not that, Ralph." Out of nowhere, I remembered sitting behind Ralph Kreighbaum in grade school and smelling Vicks Vapo Rub that his mother had rubbed into his chest every morning to ward off colds. Back then, Ralph had been a sickly kid who missed a lot of school. He didn't look much healthier now. His skin was the colour of beach sand, a disturbing contrast to his shoe polish black hair. Maybe Sharon had taken over the role of chest-rubber. The image was not pretty, and I pushed it away.

"Jonas and I don't want a big funeral. We're thinking no service at all, actually. My father was not a religious man, and he wouldn't have wanted any fuss." I almost choked on those words. Dad would have wanted everyone in town to come out and honour him. He would have opted for the bloody parade package if there'd been one. But I wasn't about to let him go out like a hero.

"Maja, everyone knew your father. He was such a well-liked, outgoing man. They'll want a chance to say a proper goodbye."

"We were thinking of just having the family attend his cremation."

"Perhaps a small service in our very own chapel, and then the family can have a private cremation. That might be a nice compromise."

Claire stirred in the seat next to me. Up until then, she'd been staring out the window, where the sun glared off the snow-laden bushes. Today, she wore a bulky cable knit sweater and straight black skirt to her knees. She crossed one black-stockinged leg over the other and cleared her throat. "Actually, Maja, your father stipulated in his will that he wanted a service when he died. He'd set aside some money."

I turned and stared at her. Her eyes were too bright, and it looked like she'd been crying. She hadn't taken the usual time to fix her hair, and it was uncharacteristically messy. I'd heard Claire and Jonas fighting upstairs after I'd gone to bed and knew she was mulling over whatever had gone on between them. "How do you know...?"

"About the will? Your father made me executor a few years ago. Jonas wasn't in any shape to think about something so complicated, and there was no one else to take it on."

"Is Jonas aware of this? He didn't want a service either when we talked it over yesterday."

"He may have forgotten that I was named executor. It's not something we talked about after your father asked me."

My god. My father was manipulating us from beyond the grave. For the first time, I wondered what else was in his will. "Are there any more surprises I should know about?"

Claire avoided looking at me as she spoke. "He pre-ordered a large headstone and has paid for a plot. He doesn't want to be cremated."

"Shit." I stood and looked down at Claire. "I think I have to go for a walk. Why don't you finish up the details? It's probably better that you do."

I grabbed my coat from behind me on the chair and strode to the door. We'd come in separate vehicles, since Claire had to go to work afterwards. Now I understood why she'd insisted on coming with me, even though it meant she had to call in a supply teacher for a few hours. She'd known all along how this was going to play out.

I drove through town, past the street of little shops with their washed-out clapboard siding and faded signs hanging over the sidewalk—Gerta's Novelties and Flowers, The Early Bird Restaurant, Meghan's Foodmart and the Minnesota State Liquor Store. This last building was the best maintained, a red brick exterior with a freshly painted sign. The town had spent money some years back beautifying the downtown to attract the Vermont-type tourist crowd. It looked like that era had ended with a whimper. A decline in fishing and lumber had all but killed the welcoming spirit in Duved Cove.

I pulled into the parking lot, feeling like a little alcohol might help to fuel me through the next few days. The store was empty except for the man who greeted me from behind the cash register. It took me a few minutes to make my purchases: a French merlot and two bottles of sauvignon blanc for Jonas and Claire and a twenty-sixer of Chivas Regal for myself.

I got back into the car after depositing my package on the floor behind the driver's seat, then continued through town to the beach road. Houses clustered along both sides of the road at the turnoff from the highway, but they dwindled to one or two where the road curved to the left and began its descent to the waterfront. Luckily, this road was maintained throughout the winter because of a few homes strung along the point that stretched into Duved Bay. I drove past the last house as far as the road was plowed then parked. The wind was bracing nearer to the lake, but I welcomed it after the stifling air in the funeral parlour. I pulled the parka's hood up over my head and set out on foot down the skidoo trail to the beach.

The world was a white wonderland, and the sun glancing off the snow would have been blinding if I hadn't been wearing my sunglasses. I walked in the ruts of the path through a copse of trees. Exiting the stand of pine was like walking through a gateway to another world. I stepped onto a flat stretch of shoreline at least a mile in length and half a football field wide. The snow-covered beach extended as far as I could see in either direction, reaching around points of land where huge rocks had been tossed carelessly into glacial heaps. Gigantic chunks of ice crowded each other for position close to shore, but further out, the water reflected the crystal blue of the sky. A white lighthouse with a red cap stood guard on the peak of the cliff. It was this landmark that encouraged me to keep going toward the lake.

Skidoos had flattened the snow that covered the sand base, making walking uneven but easier than going through deep, unpacked snow. I trudged along, happy to enjoy the fresh, cold breeze on my face, the beauty of the lakeshore and the glorious sense of isolation.

Perhaps I should have been more wary, since my father's killer was still running around free. Here I was, far from town with nobody knowing my whereabouts. My anger at my conniving father and his accomplice Claire kept me from being overly concerned. Besides, I didn't believe that I was a target of anybody's murderous rage—my father a target maybe, but not me.

I reached the base of the cliff that rose steeply to the lighthouse, slightly winded but invigorated. Up close, its paint looked more weather-weary. I stopped and breathed deeply, looking across the lake to the line where the sky met the water, soaking in this view that I had ached for long after I'd moved away. Even now, back in Ottawa, I longed for Lake Superior, just as I imagined Maritimers longed for the ocean after they moved inland. I scanned the horizon—two lines of blue meeting. A sweep of emptiness rose in my throat.

I miss my mother. I miss my mother. I fought down the grief that I would not, could not allow out. I was too old to miss my mother. The dampness in my eyes was from the wind. I took off my sunglasses and swiped angrily at my eyes before pushing the glasses back into place. *I have no parents now.* The thought came unbidden. Even though I'd barely spoken to my father for years, I still knew he was living his life in our house in Duved Cove. In some corner of my mind, I'd held to the belief that we could patch things up. It was a flame flickering faintly, if only on those long, lonely nights when I couldn't sleep. It was an emotion I'd kept stubbornly to myself, half the time not even letting it into my heart. His death would not let me pretend any more. There would be no reconciliation. There would be no happy ending for me.

I turned and started retracing my steps, head lowered. So here it was. Somebody had killed my father in cold blood. Thwacked him across the back of his head and left him in the snow to die like an animal. For a reason bigger than myself, I needed to know why. I had no faith in Tobias Olsen's ability to untangle the truth. My father had been a complex man who did not reveal his true self to the outside world. If Jonas had killed our dad, I would find out before Tobias and would make sure he never learned the truth. It would be my turn to help Jonas heal.

By the time I reached the car, I was feeling chilled, but the new resolve in my belly felt good. Dad had been sleeping with Becky Holmes. She was the person with whom to start my investigation.

I checked for Becky Wilders' address in the payphone booth at the gas station near the highway turnoff. The Wilders' name was listed twice, but only one Kevin at 27 Rose Lane. It meant backtracking through town, but even at that, it was only a ten-minute drive.

I pulled up outside the Wilders' bungalow. Hunter green siding with mocha-coloured trim looked to have been recently installed. A child's red plastic sled lay in the pathway next to a snow blower. A green van was backed into the driveway.

I stepped carefully around the snow blower and climbed the front steps. Before I had a chance to knock, the front door opened. A more faded version of the Becky I remembered stood with one hand on the door and another holding the hand of a little boy who looked to be about three. He had the same red hair and hazel eyes as Becky.

Becky was three years behind me in school. She and Jonas had been an item from the sixth to twelfth grades, and she'd been as close to a sister as I'd ever had. She hadn't been very happy when Claire had pursued Jonas and lured him away. I recalled Becky's drunken crying on my shoulder at various parties over that summer when she'd found out that Jonas had been with Claire. In hindsight, Jonas and Becky might have been happy together if they'd stuck it out. Becky had suited him in a way Claire never would.

"Maja," Becky said, "come in." She reached her free arm around my shoulders and gave me a hug as I stepped inside. I hugged her back. She'd lost weight since I'd last seen her, and I felt her bony shoulders through her sweatshirt. Her face was thin, with high cheekbones and light brown eyes that seemed not to have any lashes. A black elastic held back her shoulder-length red hair in a ponytail that started at the top of her head. When she smiled, she revealed the same gap between her two front teeth that I remembered.

"It's good to see you again, Becky," I said. "I'm lucky to catch you on your day off."

"Timmy and I were about to have a snack. Would you like a cup of coffee?" she asked as she took my coat.

"A cup of hot coffee sounds wonderful." I straightened my black turtleneck over my jeans before following her and Timmy into the kitchen. "Do you have just the one child?" I asked.

"I have two older daughters, Leah and Gabrielle. They're twins, aged fourteen and the apples of their father's eye. Their picture is on the fridge."

I dutifully went over and lifted a photo of two dark-haired

girls with hazel eyes and attractive smiles. They were identical and pretty. "Great-looking kids," I said.

"Thanks. Please have a seat. Just push aside Tim's colouring."

I sat at the kitchen table and began putting crayons into their box. Tim had been scribbling with a red crayon over the picture of a bunny. "Where is Kevin working?" I asked.

"The garage coming into town. He bought it about five years ago from Lance Gibbons. You remember Lance, don't you, Maja?"

"How could I not? He was always, trying to take us for rides in his truck. 'Need a lift home, me lovely'?" We both laughed.

"Lance's moved to Florida." Becky slid a cup of coffee across the table with a jug of milk. "Sugar's there if you'd like it." She returned to the counter to get her coffee and a bowl of Cheerios for Tim, who was sitting on the floor playing with his toy trucks. She placed the bowl next to him. "Here, darling boy," she said, then straightened and plunked herself in the chair across from me with a sigh. "Geez Maja, I haven't seen you since your mother's funeral. How've you been all these years?"

"Good. Living in Ottawa. I'm a plastic surgeon there. I married a Canadian, so we ended up north of the border."

"Jonas told me you were a doctor. You always were smart—too smart for this hick town."

I'd thought it would be easy to bring up the subject of my father, but it took me twenty minutes of reminiscing about our youth before I mentioned him. It was a little odd to skirt around the reason I was in Duved Cove, but Becky seemed determined not to bring up his death before I did.

"I understand my father was in the hospital the day he died," I said at last.

Becky coloured slightly and lowered her coffee cup onto the

table with both hands.   "Yes. I...that is, the doctor thought he was doing fine. The tests for a heart attack came back negative, by the way." She faltered. "He was in good health, which makes what happened so much more tragic."

"Did you speak with him while he was in the hospital?"

"Yes. I was the admitting nurse. He seemed not quite himself, you know, agitated and upset, even after we knew he wasn't seriously ill or hurt from his fall."

"Did he give any indication why?"

"No." Becky shook her head, and her ponytail tossed from side to side. "He was supposed to stay overnight but checked himself out. I thought afterwards that if he'd stayed, he wouldn't have disturbed the burglar, and he might still be alive."

I studied her face. "You think it was a burglar?"

"It had to have been. Everybody adored your father." She held my gaze, but her eyes seemed filled with secrets. I could tell that she was keeping something from me.

"Is there something you're not telling me, Becky?"

"About what?"

"Did Kevin know you were sleeping with my father?" I asked softly. "Because Jonas sure did."

The impact was immediate. Becky's eyes widened, and she covered her mouth with one shaking palm. Tears rolled down her cheeks. "Oh my god," she wailed. "Jonas knew about me and your dad?"

I nodded.

"Oh my god."

I gave her a minute to recover. Timmy glanced at his mom a few times and pushed himself to his feet. He walked over and rested his head on her knee, whimpering in soft gurgles. Becky covered his head with one hand and smoothed his hair. The motion seemed to soothe her. "Kevin had no idea. It...we only got together a few times. Maybe ten in all. I'm so sorry, Maja. I never meant for it to happen. I know what it must look like, but we just sort of fell into it. Your father was so there for me, you know, and I was lonely, I guess. Kevin is just so wrapped up in that damn garage and I'm stuck here all day with Timmy when I'm not working. Your dad said nobody would ever know. He...he talked about taking me away from all this because I deserved a better life. Sometimes, I thought it might be nice to let him take me away and live the high life, but I never said that I would go."

My father had never *been there* for anybody but himself. I'd bet money he'd purposely let word of this affair slip to Jonas. He wouldn't have been able to keep something this flattering to himself.

"What makes you think my father would give you a better life than Kevin?" I asked, curious to know what hold he'd held over her.

A sly look crossed her face but quickly disappeared. "Your dad was resourceful, let's just say that. He tried to convince me to leave Kevin, and I was flattered, I guess. I might have strung your father along more than I should have, but I never intended to actually go with him. His life was just way more exciting than mine, and I got caught up in it for a while."

"Are you sure Kevin didn't find out?" I asked.

Becky sat motionless, and her bottom lip began to tremble. "Anything's possible," she whispered. "Oh god, Maja. What have I done?"

You've made a big fat error in judgment, I thought, but I said nothing.

EIGHT

I left Becky's without any clear plan, but by the time I reached the highway, I'd decided that I needed to see Kevin before Becky made some tearful apology and I missed the element of surprise.

I found him behind the counter, rubbing his hands on an oily rag and talking to a customer. I waited a few steps back and watched Kevin's double chin wobble when he spoke and the way his hands never stopped moving. He'd been a plump kid who'd grown into a massive adult. Yet there was something endearing about his friendly face and the way his straight brown hair fell into his eyes, like a boy of twelve. When the older man with whom Kevin had been discussing transmissions finally left, Kevin turned to me. It took only a second for his face to register recognition, but he grinned and stepped from behind the counter to envelop me in a hug. He stepped back and said, "Maja Larson, well I'll be darned. I was beginning to think you'd never come back to Duved Cove. I'm sorry to hear about your dad, by the way. An awful thing." He didn't look me in the eye until he said, "Becky will be pleased to know you're in town anyway."

"I just had a visit with her," I said. "It's nice to know you're both doing so well."

Kevin's eyebrows rose, but his voice stayed even. "Yeah. The garage is starting to make money, and Beck is great with the kids. They keep us hopping, but we like it that way."

"You must put in long hours."

"It's been a hard go, for sure, but I see some light at the end of the tunnel. It's all worth it, though. I want the best for Beck and the kids. Say, you staying with Jonas?"

"Yes, but just for a few days more. I have to get back to my life in Ottawa."

"That's right. Becky said you married a rich Canadian and set up a medical practice in the Great White North. No kids?"

"No, no kids."

"Kept your life simple." He chuckled and looked past me out the plate glass window. "Seems like I have a customer." He picked up the rag from the counter. "Will you be stopping by the house again before you leave?"

"I hope to."

"Well, great." Kevin was already halfway to the door. He turned as he pushed it open. "Sorry about your dad, but it's been good to see you, Maja. Becky wants to go to his service, so we'll see you then. Do you know the time he'll be buried?"

I listened for something more in his voice. I didn't know him well enough to tell if he was hiding anything. "Claire is working out the details. Call the house tonight and she'll be able to tell you."

"We'll do that. Beck and I wouldn't miss saying goodbye."

I watched Kevin walk away from me before I too started for the door. Suddenly, I was hungry and tired of my amateur attempts at investigating old schoolmates. Unless someone confessed to the crime, I wasn't so sure I had the ability to trip them up. I wouldn't give in yet, but I needed to sit somewhere over a few cups of coffee to figure out the next steps.

Frida's was empty except for a girl of sixteen behind the cash who sat on a stool reading a novel. She raised her head and smiled at me as I entered and told me to sit anywhere. I headed towards the windows facing the lake and sat in the same chair that Tobias had sat in on our visit the day before. I liked the feel of the room—redwood panelling on the walls and a view of the rocky beach and lake. I ordered the breakfast special with fried eggs as the girl poured me a mug of coffee. I sipped the hot brew and listened to James Taylor sing "Fire and Rain" from a speaker above my head. It was mid-afternoon, and already the day's light was less intense than it had been when I'd walked on the beach. A bank of clouds seemed to be moving in from the west. It wouldn't be much longer before the sun would be giving way to an early nightfall.

I'd just begun carving into my eggs and bacon when the door opened and the bell jangled to announce another customer. I kept my eyes on my meal, not all that happy to have to share my space with other people. I looked up when Tobias slid into the seat across from me. He was dressed in a navy police uniform, visible under his open parka. He removed his aviator sunglasses, and his green eyes looked me over. He'd brought with him a waft of cold air and the pine smell of the outdoors.

"A little late for breakfast." He reached over, plucked a piece of bacon from my plate and put it into his mouth. "See you skipped the scrambled."

"Once bitten," I mumbled, a little put out at having to share my thinking time. I swallowed a bite of toast and said, "Make any progress on finding who killed my father?"

Tobias shook his head. He sat sideways in the chair and stretched out his legs. "I have some...well, disturbing news, though. I just came from Jonas's, and I told him that somebody got to your father's house before we did this morning and went through it pretty good. I'm not sure if they stole anything, but

68

the place is quite a mess." He watched me as he spoke. "Were you back there by any chance?"

"No." I tried to hold his gaze. I wouldn't mention that I'd planned another visit but had gotten sidetracked. "I wonder if this has anything to do with his murder or whether it's just local kids taking advantage of an empty house."

"Jonas is at your dad's now with David Keating, having a look around to see if anything is missing."

I started to stand up, but Tobias motioned me back into my seat. "Finish eating. It's not like you can do anything now."

"I've lost my appetite."

"Well, you finish the toast, and I'll eat the eggs." Tobias reached for my plate. "Did I tell you that you're looking mighty fine this afternoon?" he asked as he picked up my fork.

"Are you always this forward, Officer Olsen?" I asked.

"Only when it comes to you, Maja Larson." Tobias grinned. His eyes held mine for a moment longer than necessary before he lowered his head to begin eating my meal.

Tobias followed me in his police cruiser along the road that hugged the coastline towards my father's house. We passed the turnoff to Jonas's place and continued the steep climb up the hill. The light was starting to fade, and shafts of golden, watery sunlight broke through the trees. The tops of the spruce and pine formed a black, jagged line against the sky. The heavy cloud cover had progressed rapidly over the course of the afternoon, promising more snow. It would be a dark, difficult drive home on the winding country road.

I parked my car behind Jonas's truck, and Tobias pulled in behind me. A second police car was angled into the clearing to the left of our vehicles. Tobias and I made our way to the back door, where we found the yellow crime scene tape flapping in the wind.

"Do you really expect a piece of tape to keep people out?" I asked over my shoulder.

"Most people are law-abiding," Tobias said. "If we weren't so short-staffed, we'd have finished our work long before now, and the parade of visitors wouldn't have been such a problem."

I stepped inside and stopped, shocked at the violent mess. Dishes were smashed on the floor, and all of the cupboards had been turned inside out. Even the fridge contents spilled onto the floor, its door hanging open and the smell of rotting food making me gag. Tobias and I made our way carefully around shards of glass and walked down the hallway into the living room. The same vandalism had taken place here: Dad's books strewn about the room, cushions ripped open so the stuffing spilled forth like soap bubbles, curtains torn from the windows, furniture upended and the large-screen television smashed beyond repair. I stood speechless, trying to take it in. Tobias put a hand around my forearm.

I shook my head. "Why would somebody do this?"

We continued upstairs. David Keating met us at the head of the stairs. "Hi, Maja," he said. "Sorry about your dad and all this." David had been four years ahead of me in high school, putting him at forty-four or five. He was completely bald but had a thick, grey moustache that drooped around either side of his mouth. He'd kept a runner's physique, and I remembered that he'd won several cross-country running trophies in high school. It was odd the selective memories that were coming back to me. Ones I hadn't had in twenty years.

"Prepare yourself for more of the same up here," Tobias said.

"It's not pretty. Luckily, the basement is still intact. Maybe, the intruder was interrupted."

"Jonas doesn't think anything is missing but he says he has no way of knowing for sure," David said to me. He shook his head in disgust before he and Tobias disappeared into the workout room. I walked down the hall to my father's bedroom. My mother's hope chest had been wrenched open, deep scratches marring its surface and its contents in disarray on the floor. The sadness threatened to well up inside me again. My mother'd loved this chest. Jonas was crouched in front of it, sorting through photograph albums with ripped pages. He was inserting photographs that had been thrown on the floor. Ornaments and mementos lay smashed and scattered around him.

"Hey, Jonas," I said and crossed to kneel beside him. He handed me a photo of the two of us, aged four and two, holding hands and standing in front of our house. In the picture, I'm wearing a red sweater with black kittens stitched on the pockets. My hair is long and white-blonde. Jonas is just as blond and a chubby toddler. We both look serious, not smiling for the camera.

"At least these are salvageable," I said.

"I can't see anything missing, but who knows, really?" Jonas repeated what Tobias had already told me. "It's not like I knew everything Dad owned."

"He had some expensive electronics and gym equipment."

"Dad never seemed to lack money. He bought a new boat and van last year."

"Oh? I haven't seen them."

"The boat is stored at the marina in Lutsen, and Kevin Wilders has the van in his shop. Dad was having a new sound system put in. I just haven't gotten around to picking it up."

"I didn't think he made that much working at the border.

71

Where was he getting that kind of money?"

Jonas shrugged. "He used to go to the casino on his way home after the night shift. He told me he won a few jackpots."

"They must have been big ones." I felt a fluttering in my throat. The rampage in my father's house spoke of an anger that had not ended with his death. My father had been up to something, and it looked like whatever it was had taken on a destructive life of its own.

Jonas rubbed a hand vigorously through his hair until it looked like a windstorm had swept through. His hands were shaking when he pushed himself to his feet. I stood too and put an arm around his waist to give him a hug. "You okay?" I asked.

"I think I need to see the doctor soon."

"Is it coming on again?"

"Yeah. I haven't had the feeling for a long time, but this week is taking a toll."

"I can drive you tomorrow if you like."

"The service is in the morning. We might be too busy."

"We'll make time," I said firmly.

A noise at the door.

Jonas and I turned our heads in unison to find Tobias just inside the doorway, watching us. He was standing perfectly still with his arms crossed in front of his chest and an odd expression on his face like he'd finally figured something out. His eyes had gone a darker shade of green in the dim light, and for the first time, I thought about the real danger he presented to my family. I quickly stepped away from Jonas, as if our physical distance would keep Tobias from knowing we'd been sharing confidences. All the while, I wondered how much he'd overheard.

NINE

It was a disgruntled assortment of people who saw Dad off to the netherworld. I sat in the front pew beside Jonas and Claire, who weren't speaking to each other. Gunnar slouched next to them, equally sullen and withdrawn. Becky, with Kevin in tow, made an entrance just before the service. Becky was dressed in a sapphire-blue suit with shoulder pads that hung loosely on her slender frame. She'd applied mascara and eye shadow with a liberal hand, perhaps to hide the tears she'd shed. Compared to the rest of us, she was a peacock of colour. Kevin had resurrected a brown tweed jacket and dress pants that were two inches two short. His slicked-back brown hair revealed a broad forehead of pinkish skin. He looked tired and ill at ease.

The chapel was crowded with townsfolk. I recognized my mother's old friends, the Mattsens and the Karlssons, both couples now in their seventies. The mayor, Jon Cronhielm, and his wife sat in the front pew across from us, and behind them were Chief Anders and David Keating, both in dark blue suits. Chief Anders nodded in my direction when he saw me looking, and I lifted a hand in a quick wave then turned to face the front as the priest began the proceedings. Anders had aged a lot since I'd last seen him twenty years before. His hair had turned a yellowish white, and pouches of flesh lay in half-moons under his eyes, which had retained the sharpness I remembered. He looked to have all his wits about him on the eve of his retirement.

We'd convinced Claire to keep Dad's casket closed, and that was about the extent of Jonas's and my input. She'd selected an expensive-looking mahogany number in rich brown, which we followed in a bleak procession to our seats. I'd kept my eyes focused on the cascade of white roses laid across its centre. The flowers were one more example of Claire's attention to detail. I was surprised that she'd taken on this role that should have been mine—surprised, but thankful. Claire had chosen a simple black dress that showed off her muscular arms and swanlike neck. She'd pulled her hair back with a black headband, but a strand of pearls kept the outfit from being austere. After a morning-long battle of wills with his mother, Gunnar had angrily given in to her insistence that he wear his grey suit. He'd outgrown the jacket and pants, and I'd silently rooted for him to get his way, but Claire would not be deterred. His teen years promised to be a battleground.

I don't remember details of the service. Hymns were sung and psalms read. The mayor and Chief Anders each spoke of Dad's finer qualities, and I had to keep reminding myself who they were talking about. A man with red hair that lay in curls on his shoulders and the complexion of an under ripe peach read the Lord's Prayer. I'd never seen him before.

"Who's that?" I whispered to Claire as the man closed his book, bowed his head and started back up the aisle to his seat.

"Charlie Mallory," Claire whispered back. "Dad's partner at the border crossing."

I leaned forward to get a better look. He had to be in his early thirties and had the face of a boxer with a crooked nose and scarred cheek. Nobody would ever mistake him for handsome. He raised his head and scanned our pew. I looked down so he wouldn't see me staring. He was another link in Dad's recent life

74

that I would investigate once the funeral was over.

The priest raised his hands for the benediction. I bowed my head and closed my eyes. I did not believe in God's grace. Not any more. Not after my mother's suicide. If there was a god, he would have embraced my mother's weary, hurting soul, not denied her burial in consecrated ground as her church had done. My god would be merciful.

Jonas took my right arm. "All set?" he asked.

"As set as I'll ever be."

I opened my eyes and stood. I could make it down the aisle behind the coffin. I would find it in me to make small talk with these people who had come to honour my father. I would try to read guilt in the eyes of the person who had swung the shovel and who had returned to destroy our home.

This time, I looked deeply into each set of eyes as we made our slow journey toward fresh air and freedom, once again in solemn procession behind the priest. Most nodded, and I smiled at them. Their eyes and mouths were a combination of sadness for my father and gladness that I had returned—the prodigal daughter, back from the wilderness. Faint sunlight brightened the primary reds and blues of the stained glass windows, five on each side of the church. The air was heavy with women's perfumes and the cloying scent of lilies in vases at the extremities of the chapel. It felt like an eternity before I was almost at the end of the red-carpeted pathway. I could see the foyer where we would put on our coats and go outside into the silver-blue winter day to follow my father's body to the graveyard.

I was steps from the doorway when I saw him. It was that sudden and that unexpected—Billy Okwari sitting in the last pew, the only person sitting amongst a sea of standing legs, his liquid black eyes watching me—the same eyes that haunted my

75

dreams. His hair still black, but longer and tied back, dressed in a well-worn grey leather jacket. He was stockier than I remembered, but familiar still in the way his shoulders curved forward ever so slightly and the tapered line of his jaw. He'd been all of eighteen the last time we'd been together—a child now grown into middle age. Our eyes held. His gaze burned into me, like he was trying to read the person I'd become. An electric current travelled up my spine. I let out a gasp, and Jonas slipped an arm around my waist.

"We're nearly there," he said, unaware that my distress was not from the strain of our father's funeral.

I tried to push past his arm, but Jonas held me fast and suddenly, we were in the foyer and people were swarming about us, shaking our hands and murmuring words of sympathy. I finally broke away, frantically searching those remaining. There was no sign of Billy in the crowded room. I turned and stumbled back into the chapel. My eyes scanned the empty pews. Billy Okwari was gone. Grief overwhelmed me. I stood bereft next to the confessionals, trying to still my breathing into a regular pattern.

Claire came up behind me. "Is everything okay? You bolted away from us like you'd been spooked."

"No, it's nothing like that," I said and half-turned to face her, not wanting her to see what was surely written in my eyes. "But I have to go to the washroom before we leave."

"We'll see you in the car then." Claire pivoted on the soles of her black boots and called to Gunnar as I made a beeline for the ladies at the end of the hallway.

I only just made it into the first empty stall and locked the door as my tears began to flow.

I recovered enough to get through the next few hours. Dad

wouldn't be buried until the ground thawed in early spring, but we saw him safely to the crypt. Afterwards, we drove back to the house, where Claire had arranged for a caterer to deliver sandwiches and squares for those who stopped by. For some reason, she'd insisted on serving sweet, sparkling wine, something I hadn't drunk since ninth grade beach parties. Jonas and I took one look at the green bottles Claire had arranged in ice on the kitchen table, then at each other. I motioned with my head towards my room at the back of the house, and we left the kitchen separately as soon as there was a break in the conversation. Jonas met me in my bedroom a few minutes later with two wineglasses he'd smuggled out of the kitchen. He'd loosened his tie and his shirt was wrinkled under his open suit jacket. I opened the bottle of Scotch that I'd kept in a bag next to my bed and poured us each a healthy measure. I put the cap back on the bottle and tucked it between the bed and the night table.

"How're you holding up, Jonas? Can you wait until tomorrow to see the doctor? Claire's insistence on a wake is making it difficult to slip away."

"Sure. This medicine will keep me going." He lifted the glass to his lips and took a long swallow.

I raised mine towards him. "A toast to our father and all he accomplished."

"You mean he accomplished something besides looking out for number one?"

"It's a long shot, I know, but people in town seem to have adored him. That must count for something. You know, Jonas, sometimes I think I dreamed all the bad stuff. You know, like we just misunderstood him, and the times he was nice to us were the real Dad...that maybe, we're the ones with the problem." It was the first time I'd voiced the uncertainty that had grown stronger as I'd aged and distanced myself from that time. I'd judged my father through child's eyes. Could we have been wrong or have exaggerated his faults? I knew he'd been flawed, but perhaps we'd been too harsh, building up hurts beyond what they were.

Jonas blinked rapidly and lowered himself onto my bed. He ran a trembling hand through his hair in the nervous gesture I knew too well. I immediately regretted upsetting him.

"Let's not think of it now," I said quickly and sat down beside him, reaching up and resting my arm on his shoulders. "I love you, little brother," I said. "We'll get through this. I won't leave until things are sorted out." I could feel him shaking under my arm, and I hugged him tighter.

"I feel like I'm just hanging on, Maja. Sometimes, I wonder if it's worth it."

My mother's gentle voice came back to me in sudden clarity. *Is it worth it, Maja? Sometimes, I'm just so tired.* Her hands fluttering like white birds. Her blue eyes wet with tears that had slid like pearls down her cheeks. I had known she was ill, and I had left her.

"I'll see you through, Jonas. This time, I'm not going anywhere. You have to hang in for Claire and Gunnar...and me."

Jonas turned his face toward mine until we were almost touching. His eyes were bruised by dark circles. He was having difficulty focusing, the irises of his eyes vibrating like tuning forks. These signs that a depression was imminent cut into my heart.

"You are wrong, you know, Maj," he said. "None of it was a dream. The monster we saw was the real Dad. All the rest was just smoke and mirrors. The man everybody knew and loved was one big lie."

TEN

After the third trip to my room to refill my wineglass, I began to almost enjoy myself. The afternoon light had given way to the dusk of evening before I stopped greeting neighbours and reminiscing about my childhood. It was a reminder that not all memories were bad.

I found Sonja Mattsen sitting on the green couch in the living room and sat down beside her. She'd lived up the road and had been good friends with my mother. She was seventy now and had lived a harder life than most. Two of her children had died—Danny had drowned playing in the lake at age five and Tommy was killed in the Gulf War. I wondered where she'd found the strength to carry on.

She patted my arm as she spoke. "You were the prettiest child, Maja Larson, with your long white hair and blue eyes the colour of cornflowers. I worried that the boys wouldn't leave you alone, you were that pretty. But you never seemed to have any interest. You were a smart one, that's for sure, and not a speck of vanity."

I thought I'd outgrown blushing, but I could feel the heat rise up my cheeks. "I never thought of myself that way. When the boys came around, it was to tease me or to hang out with Jonas."

Sonja's eyes were kind. "Your dear mother was so proud of you. She'd be bursting her seams to know you were a doctor up in Canada." She leaned forward, opened her arms and drew me into a hug.

"Thanks, Sonja. It warms me to hear you say that."

Would my mother be proud of me? I imagined that if she hadn't died, she'd have visited me in Ottawa in my upper middle class home during the course of my marriage, if I'd cajoled her into the trip. I would have had to use my most persuasive arguments, because she'd hated travelling far from Duved Cove. She'd have politely toured my home and mouthed the appropriate words of approval. She'd even have gone so far as to tell me how lucky I was to have such a fine life, but inside I'd have known that she did not approve of my closetful of clothes and my expensive furnishings. What would have disappointed her most would have been that I was using my talent to make people look younger, but she would never have told me that. She'd just have come up with excuses for not returning to Ottawa, and I would have tried not to let on that I knew the real reason she would not visit again.

Sonja stood to leave. She hesitated before saying, "Do you know that Katherine Lingstrom has been staying with her mother since Christmas?"

I was surprised by her words. "I thought Katherine was married and living in Wisconsin?"

Sonja nodded. "She was, but something has gone very wrong with her marriage. She's had a breakdown of some sort and doesn't want to see anybody. Her mother was out getting groceries last week, and we had coffee. She's been very worried. I know that you and Katherine were best friends before you both moved away, so I thought you might want to know."

"Thanks for telling me, Sonja. I will try to pay her a visit." I ran a hand across my forehead. "I can't believe it. Katherine was always so happy when I knew her as a kid." We hadn't been as close in our teenage years, but we'd spent our grade school years inseparable.

"People can change a lot, Maja. Life isn't always as kind as we'd like. Sometimes it damages people beyond repair."

I spotted Becky and Kevin Wilders standing in the doorway. Becky seemed to light up the room in all of her peacock blue splendour. She'd reapplied her eye makeup and lipstick; the bright colours were garish against her pale skin. Kevin had his arm around her shoulder and seemed to be saying something unpleasant into her ear, judging by the unhappy expression on her face. Curious, I skirted around a group of people until I got to them.

"I'm glad you could make it," I said, reaching out to shake Kevin's hand. He hadn't been able to remove traces of grease and car oil from the creases in his skin. "I thought the service went well."

"It was lovely. Just lovely," Becky said, stepping from the circle of Kevin's arm.

Kevin nodded. "I don't like funerals as a rule, but this one was okay. Something to drink, Beck?" he asked, taking a step into the room. He looked at her over my head.

"We have wine in the kitchen," I said.

"Okay. A glass of red. Thanks, Kevin." Becky took my arm and pulled me into the corner after he'd ambled away. "Have you told anybody about what we discussed?" She hissed the words into my ear.

"No, and nobody's said anything to me either."

Her fingers on my arm relaxed. "I'm pretty sure he doesn't know about your dad and me. Without coming right out and asking him, I've been trying to find out, because if Jonas knew, anyone could have. Lucky for me, Kevin isn't all that bright when it comes to sex and relationships. He's always at work in that garage or thinking about being at work. Shit, I could so use a cigarette, but Kevin thinks I've quit."

81

Was she honest with her husband about anything? "Do you know anything about my father's partner at the border? Charlie something or other?"

Becky nodded. "Charlie Mallory. He lives in Grand Portage. I was introduced to him once when I met your dad after work. It was when they were getting off night shift. Did you know Charlie is legally deaf? He lost his hearing in his early twenties from having meningitis, of all things. He picked up lip reading really quickly, so he was able to get a government job. The government can't discriminate, you know. Employment equity and all that."

"Must be tough being a border guard and not being able to hear."

"I think Charlie does the office work. Besides, it's not that busy a crossing at night."

I saw Kevin standing on the other side of the room with two glasses of wine. He was looking around for us. "Why were you picking up my father after his shift?" I asked. "It's almost an hour from Duved Cove."

Becky's face flashed crimson. "We were going to a motel, actually," she said. "I'd tell Kevin I was going to the casino with some girlfriends from work and then. . ." She held up a hand and waved. "Oh, here's Kevin." The fingers of her other hand bit into my arm. "Don't forget your promise not to say anything. I'll owe you big time."

I didn't remember promising anything. I also wasn't convinced Kevin hadn't found out about her affair, because secrets that involved cheating were as hard to keep in a small town as marriage vows.

Chief Anders made his way through the remaining guests to give me his condolences. I'd wanted to talk to him and was glad for the opportunity. His rheumy grey eyes studied me, and he nodded. "I'm very sorry for your loss. Your dad and I remained friends even after he left the force." He drank deeply from his wine glass. Then he tilted the glass and looked inside, grimacing.

"Thanks. He seemed to have a lot of friends. Sorry about the wine. Claire isn't much of a drinker, and she picked something she must have remembered from high school days."

Chief Anders smiled. He was a trim man with wide shoulders. He'd been famous as a lightweight wrestler in his younger days. "Not that there was any underage drinking when you were a teenager," he said.

"No, no. That would have been against the law." I rolled my eyes and smiled.

"Well, your crowd never got into much trouble, so no charges pending." He paused and looked around. "You're right. Your father did know a lot of people."

"Well, one of those people killed him," I said. "Have you any leads yet?"

Chief Anders shook his head. A lock of white hair fell into his eyes, and he brushed it aside. "Investigations take time, and as you know, we've been short-staffed. I have my best man Tobias working on the case, with David Keating helping out when he's not on regular patrol. They both send their sympathies, by the way."

It didn't seem like enough people working a murder case, but I kept that thought to myself. "I've always wondered why my father left the force. What happened exactly?"

"Old history, Maja. It had to do with some complaints we had about evidence going missing. It was strictly mismanagement, but I had to allow an external investigator to come in and go through the books and whatnot. Your father was in the wrong place at the wrong time. He'd been tasked with looking after what we'd confiscated and couldn't explain where it went. There was nothing conclusive against him, but he agreed it would be better to leave rather than drag the force through something messy. Luckily, the position at the border came up around the same time, and he accepted."

"But if he was innocent, wouldn't he have stayed and tried to clear his name? It wasn't like my father to roll over."

"I suppose, in normal circumstances. Your mother was having a difficult time, as I recall, and your father wanted more regular hours. You'd left for school, and he wanted to be around the house more."

That could have held a kernel of truth. However, my father had never been all that concerned about my mother's health, except when it came to keeping up appearances in the community. He might have wanted to appear the self-sacrificing husband, especially if it got him out of a sticky situation.

"I hear you're retiring soon."

His face relaxed. "Ah yes. My wife and I will be moving somewhere warmer. I think we've done enough service in the north."

"When is your last day?"

"A month tomorrow." He smiled at me. "It was nice seeing you again, Maja. I just wish it had been under better circumstances. I'll see you before you leave, although I'm sure you'll be flying out soon."

"I've decided to stay a few more days."

"Oh?" His shaggy eyebrows rose. "Well, then I'm sure we'll be in contact. I've told Tobias to keep me informed about the case and to let me know if anything develops. We'll be reporting to your family as soon as we have anything to share."

"Thank you. We're anxious to find out what happened, as

you can imagine." I made myself hold his gaze. I would not give him any reason to suspect that I intended to find out what happened to my father before Tobias did. He wouldn't know that I'd resolved to stay until I was satisfied that Jonas would never be found guilty of the crime.

Gunnar happily packed an overnight bag after receiving an invitation from a friend for a sleepover. This was the most animated I'd seen him since I arrived, and the sight of his smile was nothing short of uplifting. As soon as he left, Claire disappeared upstairs on unsteady legs to fall into bed. She wasn't used to drinking but appeared to have developed a taste for cheap wine. Jonas met me at the bottom of the stairs and gave me a hug. I inhaled the Scotch on his breath as he said good night.

"Don't worry. I'll lock up," I said.

"See you tomorrow then." He started slowly up the stairs. "Thank Christ that's over."

I took off my shoes, which were pinching my feet, and circled the living room, blowing out candles and picking up empty glasses as I went. I checked that the front door was locked and turned off the lights with my elbow. I carried all I could hold into the kitchen and put the glasses into the dishwasher. The kitchen counters were littered with half-eaten food trays, more glasses and wine bottles. The mess could wait until morning. I lacked the wherewithal to clean it up since I'd also had my fair share to drink. I turned out the kitchen lights and retraced my path down the hallway to my bedroom at the back of the house.

I dropped my clothes onto the floor, stepping out of my skirt and pulling my black cashmere sweater over my head. I unrolled my pantyhose and tossed them in the direction of the chair. They spreadeagled on the floor like a pair of splayed legs. I plopped onto my back on the bed in my slip and stretched my hands over my head. I should have been tired, but instead I felt wide awake and restless. I'd had enough to drink to dull any pain I'd been feeling. I spotted my cellphone on the night stand and rolled on my side to reach for it. Sam should still be up, and I hadn't spoken to him for a few days. It would be good to hear his voice.

He answered on the second ring. "Maja? I wondered when I'd hear from you. I've tried calling, but your phone's been off."

"I'm sorry. I've just been preoccupied with everything going on, and I forgot to take it with me."

"So, have you had the funeral yet?"

"Today. It went well as funerals go. Lots of people to see Dad off. Claire and Jonas weren't speaking to each other, and Gunnar was as sullen as a pre-teen can be, but we soldiered on."

"So you'll be flying out tomorrow? I can pick you up if your plane arrives after six. I'm tied up in meetings until then."

"No. That is, I'm going to stay on a bit. Jonas seems to be heading into another depression, and I'd like to be here."

"I thought we agreed you'd be back right after the funeral." Sam's voice stayed warm, but a familiar edge had crept in.

"I know, but it's important that I be here for a bit."

"What about your patients? You're already backed up."

"They'll keep. I've phoned the office and cancelled for the following week. Doctor Rajah is picking up the urgent cases." Not that there were many. Good god—a few more wrinkles before I could get them under the knife. It wasn't exactly life or death. I felt myself getting discouraged. "How are you doing?" I asked to change the subject.

"Okay. We're close to sealing that deal I went to New York

for. It should be a nice commission. I thought I'd take you somewhere warm for a vacation next week. How does Bermuda sound? A little sun, sand and sleeping in?" His voice was light and cajoling.

"Hmmm. I really have to finish up here, Sam. Then there is the matter of patients I've been putting off."

"Yeah, well, I'll check into some hotel packages and see what we can swing. It would be good for you to have a holiday."

When Sam got an idea into his head, there was no shaking it. I'd given him something to obsess about. He'd plot out his campaign to get me to Bermuda and would begin with sneak attacks. I knew his methods. "Gotta go, hon," I said. "It's been a long day."

"Yes. I'll talk to you tomorrow."

We both hung up, and I closed my eyes. He was probably already searching the internet for travel sites. Why was the idea of going to Bermuda getting under my skin? Was it too much Scotch...or not enough? And why did I have the feeling that the trip south was more for his benefit than mine?

ELEVEN

I got up and brushed my teeth then changed into a white silk nightgown before pulling back the covers and climbing into bed. After I turned off the bedside lamp, I noticed the moonlight streaming in through the window and catching me square in the face. If I didn't get up to close the blind, I'd be wakened too early by the rising sun. I climbed reluctantly out of bed and crossed to the window. The hardwood floor was cool on my feet, and I shivered under my light nightgown. Just as I reached up for the blind cord, a pebble clattered against the glass, making me jump back in fright. A second one followed, and I felt a stirring in my chest. This was a signal from long ago that I had never expected to encounter again. I unlocked the window and lifted it open a few inches. A cold blast of air made the curtains billow on either side of me.

"Who's there?" I called quietly, even though I knew.

"It's me, Maja." Billy's voice came out of the darkness.

"I'll meet you at the back door," I said.

I almost had an out of body experience—seeming to float through the bedroom and down the hallway to the kitchen. Would Billy and I have the same connection as when we were teenagers, or would this be a dream I should never have kept? Would he find me old and be disappointed in the woman I had become? But I *was* old—forty and counting. There was no way I was the same girl he remembered...and he would not be the same boy either. I wanted to see him, but I was afraid.

Conflicting emotions rose in me as I made that quick journey to the back door. When I finally unlocked it and swung it open, I was a bundle of apprehension, convincing myself not to expect anything much.

Billy Okwari stood on the back deck, hunched into the upright collar of his leather jacket, his black hair loose to his shoulders. He was dressed in dark blue jeans and work boots the colour of butterscotch. I took in these details in the blink of an eye, but my gaze was drawn to his dark, oval-shaped eyes that were openly studying me.

"You said you'd be back one day, Maja Larson," he said. "I just didn't know how long it would take." He smiled the sideways grin that had won my heart all those years ago, and in one swift motion, I crossed the space between us and wrapped myself around him. We stood that way for several heartbeats before he moved us into the warmth of the kitchen. I took a step backwards, and he leaned in to kiss me on the lips. His were cool from the winter night and tasted of mint. As I drew away, I opened my eyes. Billy was looking at me. I saw compassion and something else I couldn't read in his expression.

"You're shivering," he said.

I looked down. My breasts were visible through my nylon nightgown, and I wrapped my arms around myself to cover them. Gooseflesh marked my skin. "I'm freezing, actually," I said. "Do you want to come to my room? I can put something warmer on."

"Okay."

We slipped silently back to my bedroom, and I picked up my robe from the chair. It was a pale apricot colour that matched my nightgown. I put it on and wrapped the sash around my waist. Billy stood next to the door, watching me.

"Climb into bed under the covers and I'll sit in the chair,"

Billy said. "That flimsy thing won't keep you warm."

I nodded and climbed back into bed, pulling the duvet around my shoulders. I propped myself upright against the walnut headboard and reached over to turn on the bedside lamp. "Jonas lets the wood stove die down at night and keeps the house just above freezing. Claire says it makes her sleep better."

Billy crossed the room and pulled the desk chair closer, turning it so that he sat facing me. He stretched his long legs straight out, resting his elbows on the arms of the chair. "I'm sorry about your father. I didn't like him, but his death was a bad way to go."

"No, it's not resting easy with me. The more I dig around, the more people seem to have had a reason to dislike him. He was all charm on the surface, but his self-absorption seems to have had other victims than just his wife and children." In all of my imagined conversations with Billy, my father had never been the subject. With the Scotch I'd consumed still coursing through my veins, the whole scene had taken on a fantasy feel. I raised a hand to my face. I knew I must be flushed.

Billy rested his head on the back of the chair but kept his eyes on me. "You stayed away after your mother's death."

"I came back a few times. By then, you'd gone."

"You never got in touch. I had to make a life or go crazy."

How much would I tell? I looked at Billy's still face, his features older but the same. He was still lean, and the angles of his face were sharp, with high cheekbones. He knew me like nobody else, even Sam. I could let down my guard and let him see me. I knew without question that this was true. Billy would never judge me or find me wanting. The eyes riveted on mine did not lie.

"I gave up," I said softly. "I couldn't fight any more."

Billy shifted in his seat and crossed one booted foot over the other. "You married, I hear."

"Yes, ten years ago, to Sam Cleary. He's a businessman, and we live in Ottawa. I became a doctor, a plastic surgeon."

Billy nodded. "I can picture you as a doctor. You never had any children?"

If I hadn't known him so well, I wouldn't have detected the underlying pain in his question.

"I didn't want any kids." *Not after the abortion.* The words lay unspoken between us. We would not go there. Billy's eyes spoke without words. We'd never needed words.

"You married too," I said.

"Yes. Nina and I live in a little house on the Bois Forte Reservation at Nett Lake with my brother Raymond and his son. We just moved back."

"Ah. Would your brother's son be about twenty?"

"Wayne mentioned that he saw you at Hadrian's the other night."

"He looks so like you, I almost fainted."

"Wayne acts a lot like me too. Poor kid." Billy smiled.

"Do you have any kids of your own?" I asked softly, not sure I wanted the answer.

"A daughter. Her name is Ella, and she's nine."

"You've made a good life," I said, but inside I was wistful. This was the life I would have had.

"I'm happy with my life. Nina is a fine person."

His words were the slap that I deserved. I pulled my knees to my chest and wrapped my arms around them, letting my cheek rest on their hard surface. "Where does she think you are now?"

"I don't want to talk about Nina." A shadow crossed his eyes, but he kept them on mine. "This is about you and me. I've always missed you, Maja. You must know that would never change."

"I know," I whispered, the nights of misery slipping into my voice. All those nights of dreams had led me here. Before I could think twice, Billy rose from the chair and crossed the short distance to the bed. He stretched out next to me, pulling me down so that my head was resting on his chest. I could hear the comforting beating of his heart against my ear. I sighed, and Billy's arm tightened around me.

"I feel like I'm dreaming you," he said. "I imagined so many times that we would be together one day, just to talk and see you again, and now that you're here," he paused, searching for the words, "it's just such an odd feeling. Like real and unreal at the same time."

I lifted my head and looked at him. I traced the line of his jaw with my fingertips. "We were so young. I sometimes thought maybe I'd dreamed what was between us—that you'd have forgotten all about me. It's not like I feel that I'm anything special. I figured you'd forget me as time went on, and you'd make another life."

I felt his hand in my hair. "I've never forgotten you, and it feels like my connection with you hasn't changed." He was quiet for a moment. Then he said, "But we're both married now with people depending on us. That's our reality."

Happiness and sadness flooded through me in quick succession. "You're like a secret I've always kept to me, even all these years. You know, I never talked to Sam about you. He has no idea."

"Nina wouldn't have been pleased to know about you either." His voice trailed off. "Are there any leads on who killed your father?"

"No. He was having an affair with Becky Holmes. That's been my main lead."

"You've been investigating?"

"Just asking questions mainly." I propped myself on one elbow. "Jonas is tied up in this somehow, and I need to make sure he's okay. I promised him I'd stay around for a bit."

The hard line of Billy's jaw relaxed. "Then I can see you more than this one time. I thought you'd be going tomorrow."

"What do you do for work?" I asked.

"Raymond has an outfitters operation off highway 53 at Vermilion Bay, and I'm giving him a hand. We cater to the Fortune Bay Casino clientele. Nina is working at Lutsen Resort during the week, so she and Ella stay there, and I pick them up for the weekends. It's just temporary. She's got a job at the casino in April."

"Are you taking people ice fishing?"

"Yeah. Then fishing trips all summer and deer and moose hunting in the fall."

"Why did you leave Duluth?"

"Got laid off."

He reached up a hand around my neck and pulled me lower. We kissed for a long time, and it was like we'd never been apart. With Billy, I always felt like our souls were intertwining when we kissed, and I was sorry when he pulled back.

"I have to go, Maja."

"I know."

"I'll see you again."

His words were a promise, and I nodded. Billy rolled off the bed and bent to straighten the covers around me.

"I'll see you again," he said once more, and his eyes were black pools. "Sleep well."

He bent to kiss me one final time, and I watched him cross the room and disappear out the door. If I hadn't strained to hear, I would have missed the click of the back door. Billy had always come and gone as silently as that—one of the reasons we'd escaped my father's radar for so long.

I closed my eyes and turned onto my side. Billy Okwari had never forgotten me. I held onto this thought as I fell into a deep, untroubled sleep. For the first time in a long time I didn't dream. *Billy Okwari still loved me.* The knowledge filled something in my soul and gave me back a part of myself that I thought I'd lost forever.

TWELVE

I opened my eyes and immediately shut them again. I groaned quietly. The sun might have been up, but the light was grey in my room, and the air on my face was cool. I snuggled deeper under the covers and tried to fall back to sleep. Once awakened, my mind was racing so much that I couldn't relax enough to let go. After twenty minutes, I gave up trying to slip back into dreamland and began a systematic replay of the conversations that I'd had the day before with everyone who'd stopped by our house. Nothing stood out in my mind as relevant to my father's murder. I wasn't sure if I had the skills to unearth his killer, but I *was* sure that I wasn't going to give up yet.

Swinging my legs over the side of bed, I stretched my arms toward the ceiling and shivered as the cold air struck my skin. I forced myself not to dive back under the covers. I had to get Jonas to the doctor and shouldn't put it off any longer than could be helped. I also had to plot out my plan of attack for uncovering what was going on in my father's life before he died. There was lots to do and I didn't know how many days I could spare with Sam angling for me to come home.

I stood and felt for my slippers where they'd been pushed under the bed. I bent to tuck my feet into them, and a rush of happiness made me pause when Billy's image flashed through my mind. I touched my lips and smiled. I knew I should feel guilt for having been with him the night before, but I couldn't raise any remorse even after I reminded myself that we were both married. Perhaps the guilt would come later. I wasn't sure what to expect, because for the ten years of my marriage, I had never even contemplated being unfaithful. And what Billy and I had done, what we had always had between us, didn't make me feel like I was being unfaithful to Sam. It was like I was in my real life again, like I was finally being true to myself. What was between me and Billy had nothing to do with my life in Ottawa.

I looked over at the chair where Billy had sat watching me. I could still picture him there, his black hair loose about his face and his soft eyes the colour of onyx. He'd loosened his jacket, and underneath I saw a denim shirt open at the neck to reveal a beaded choker in black, white and red with an eagle design at its centre. Perhaps if I could conjure him up in my mind at will, that would keep me going. I could keep putting one foot in front of the other and carry on with my life in Ottawa with Sam; I could push my emotions back into the place where they would not cause me any more pain.

Claire was in the kitchen sitting at the table with a cup of coffee in front of her and a cigarette in her hand. She blew two smoke rings across the table as I sat in the chair next to her with my cup of coffee. Dark smudges ringed her grey eyes and uncombed black hair stuck out like so many clumps of grass. She'd thrown on sweatpants and a fleece pullover and didn't look her normal, pulled-together self. She tossed a scowl in my direction.

"Taking another day off?" I asked, then blew on my coffee before taking a swallow of liquid caffeine. It coated my throat in hot bitterness.

"A wee headache today. I planned to take the day off anyhow."

Claire sucked another puff from her cigarette and inhaled deeply. The smoke streamed out of her nose like a dragon breathing fire. "Jonas isn't doing so well today. Says he's not getting up."

"Oh?" I was sure he hadn't had so much to drink the night before that he couldn't function. This was not a good sign. I couldn't hide my worry from her any longer. "I think he's headed for another depression."

Claire's eyes were marble hard. "That would be my guess too. In fact, I just got off the phone with the doctor, and I'm to take Jonas in as soon as I can get him moving. I thought I'd give him till lunch to sleep."

"That's good," I nodded, relieved that she'd already started arrangements. "He'll be needing an antidepressant to get him back on track."

Claire turned her face towards me. "You doctors all believe in the power of drugs, like they're the answer to our problems. Maybe, they'll get him functioning again, but I'm not so sure drugs are enough to make him normal."

"Jonas has clinical depression, Claire. It's a real physical condition that happens when chemical messages aren't delivered correctly between brain cells. Sometimes, he needs medication to be able to function. If he doesn't get it, well, he just gets worse." *Till he cashes out, like my mother.*

"Well, sometimes it just seems to come at convenient times." Her tone was sulky.

"Is there something you aren't telling me, Claire?"

Claire met my gaze. She dropped her eyes first, but not before I saw into a well of anger. Her long fingers ground the cigarette into the ashtray like a pestle. "Jonas always falls back into depression instead of facing his issues. I swear to God, it's getting to be a tiresome record that keeps playing over and over.

I don't know why I've put up with it all these years."

"He really is sick, Claire. He can't control his depression. Stress makes it worse. I know you've had to shoulder a lot, but Jonas counts on you." I'd unconsciously slipped into my doctor voice.

Claire stood and looked down at me. "And maybe I'm tired of being the strong one."

I watched her stride over to the sink and pour the coffee down the drain. "It's not sitting well in my stomach this morning," she said with her back to me. She set the cup on the counter, then put both hands on the sides of the sink. "I'm sorry, Maja. I don't mean to burden you with this. Your father's death has been such a shock and...well, I'm just starting to question things, you know, like how quickly life can end." She turned quickly towards me and leaned back on the counter, folding her arms across her chest. "You know, whether I'm doing what I should be with mine."

"It's normal to question. I do too."

"Oh really? You, a successful doctor with a loving husband who's also making a good living?"

"Even me," I said.

"Well, misery loves company. I know you're probably ready to fly home now the funeral's over. Don't worry about Jonas. I'll sort it out. This has been a particularly trying time, but we're a good team and will put this behind us. I'm going to change my clothes." She attempted a smile. "I have some errands in town to do before I coax Jonas to the doctor's."

I didn't set her straight about my intention to stay on. "Do you need help with anything? I don't mind coming with you."

"No, that's okay. I'm just dropping by the lawyer's. She called to say that your father made a change to his will so that needs a review."

"I'd like to come too."

"It's no bother, Maja. I can tell you the details when I get back."

"It would be good for me to come along," I insisted. "I'll go brush my teeth and will meet you in a few minutes." I ignored the obvious displeasure in her eyes. Suddenly, I was extremely interested to know what my father had left and to whom. Maybe, the information would shed light on who benefitted from his death. I'd read enough murder mysteries to know that one should follow the money trail when looking for motive.

We took Claire's van into town. I decided that after the visit to the lawyer, I'd walk back to Jonas's with a stop to see Katherine Lingstrom along the way. She may not have any information about my father's life, but her parents wouldn't have missed much of the small-town gossip. I knew Katherine's mother couldn't resist sharing what she knew. Sonja Mattsen's words replayed in my head from the night before and I worried for my childhood friend. Katherine and I may have let our friendship go by the wayside, but perhaps there was something I could do to help her now. At least I could be a good listener if she wanted to talk about her troubles.

Claire was nervous high energy during the short drive to Greene and Reynolds Law Firm, housed in a heritage grey clapboard house that had been converted into offices. She talked nonstop about Gunnar and his troubling new attitude towards school and life in general. I listened sympathetically but figured the kid was likely showing the first signs of puberty. It became more and more evident that Claire was going to have a hard time letting him grow up. All of my dealings with Gunnar so far pointed to a troubled boy who might be carrying the depressive gene of my mother and brother. For his sake, I hoped he was just experiencing a domineering mother and raging hormones. I didn't hold out much hope during this visit for understanding what made him tick.

We parked in the post office parking lot and crossed the street, avoiding patches of glistening ice that had been exposed by the snow plow. The Greene and Reynolds sign, oval with gold lettering on a black metal base, swung gently to and fro above the front entrance. An oil lamp sent a welcoming glow through lace curtains in the bay window. Greene and Reynolds had nurtured their folksy, down-home image with a burnish of prosperity—they'd been in business for at least three generations and managed to outlive all competition.

Georgia Beaufort, a South Carolina transplant in her early sixties with hair the colour of pumpkin and skin the colour of coal, hustled us into Patricia Reynold's office. She delivered cups of coffee as we waited for Patricia to arrive. This room was bright and high-ceilinged with curlicue crown molding and tall windows that looked out on a large expanse of snow-covered lawn and woods beyond. Patricia had an oak desk clear of work and framed prints of cottages on the walls. Georgia seated us in arm chairs upholstered in yellow and green flowered fabric that were positioned in a semicircle around a stone fireplace original to the building. A crackling fire completed the tranquil picture. Claire appeared to sink deeper into her chair as she sipped from her coffee cup and looked into the fire. It seemed best not to interrupt her reverie.

I remembered Patricia Reynolds as a scrawny ninth grade girl who had mousy brown hair and thick glasses. The boys had given her the nickname Flatsy Patsy and delighted in teasing her until she learned to make herself almost invisible. I heard the click of high heels on the hardwood floor and turned my head, preparing myself for an older version of the girl I remembered. My brain did a double take. The voluptuous platinum blonde who strode across the room towards us was as far from the flat-chested girl I remembered as Twiggy was from Jayne Mansfield. I stood, and as we shook hands, I studied Patricia's face. Whoever had done her plastic surgery had done good work. Her nose was narrow and delicately flared at the nostrils, with red lips larger than humanly possible. Even her eyes were wide, with the lids pulled tight, and the glasses had probably been exchanged for laser surgery. Capped by a mane of tousled blonde hair, she looked more like a Barbie doll than the flat-chested, gawky girl I remembered in high school. For thirty-five, she was remarkably constructed, right down to her breast implants that in my view were too large for her tiny frame. She kept her face expressionless, but I couldn't miss the triumph in her eyes as she extended a cool hand for me to shake.

"Maja, so nice to see you after all these years. I'm sorry for your loss. Your father was a wonderful man." She let her eyes slide surreptitiously up and down my body as she spoke. If she'd meant to make me feel self-conscious and unattractive, she had succeeded.

"You're looking lovely, Patricia," I said as she arranged herself in the chair across from us, crossing one stockinged leg over the other. My professional training had won out over my own insecurities. I was sure this expensively packaged Patsy still held scars from her years of childhood teasing. Nobody could care so much for their appearance unless they had a reason to be obsessed. I knew the signs from my patients, many of whom I sent to counselling before agreeing to operate on them. Some just found another surgeon, but that was outside my control.

"Thanks. You're looking well too." She tilted her head towards

Claire. "Sorry I couldn't make the funeral. I had a few urgencies to attend to."

"That's okay. You said there were changes to the will?" Claire wasn't messing around with any niceties. She'd set her half-filled coffee cup on the end table and was leaning forward with her hands on her knees.

Patricia cleared her throat. I almost missed the look of dislike she shot Claire, because she just as quickly lowered her eyes to study her hands folded in her lap. "Yes. Peter was in, oh, the day before he died and asked that his house and land be left to Maja. He actually signed the new will straight out of the hospital." Patricia raised her eyes, and she and Claire turned their heads as a unit to look at me.

"Me?" I asked, taking a second to register what she'd said. *My father had signed a new will the day he'd died.* "But that makes no sense. He always said he was leaving the house to Jonas."

"This is ridiculous," Claire snapped. "This isn't a minor change to the will like you led me to believe. The house and land are a major part of the inheritance."

"Peter said he would tell you when he was ready, and I had to respect that." I could have sworn Patricia was smiling as she stood to get the folder with my father's will. She sat back down and riffled through the pages. "Yes, he had eighty thousand in retirement savings that he's left to Gunnar in a trust for when he reaches twenty-one. Jonas gets the new boat and the van. The remaining money in his checking account goes to the hospital, about twenty thousand dollars."

Claire's face had turned the colour of skim milk. Her grey eyes flashed anger. "This has to be some kind of joke. Jonas looked after his father's house for all those years, and he deserves to inherit. Peter held it over his head like a damned carrot to keep him in line, and this is the thanks we get? A stinking boat and a van?"

Patricia shrugged. "Peter made it very clear that this is what he wanted. He signed the new will, so that's about as definite as it gets. He'd intended to tell you, but then he had the...accident."

"Was Jonas's name on the will to inherit the house before the change?" I asked.

"Yes, it was, but now you inherit the house and property."

"I don't understand. Why would my father change his will? It seems so contrary." Maybe I'd just hit upon the truth. My father was a contrary man who liked to play God. It would have given him great pleasure to turn the tables on Claire and Jonas. Manipulating people was second nature to him.

Claire stood and looked down at us. Her breathing was so quick and shallow that she appeared close to panting. She spoke with difficulty. "I've got to pick up Gunnar. I'll talk to you later, Patricia. I have to think this through."

I watched Claire stride to the door then I turned back to Patricia and shrugged. "I have to say I'm shocked by this, but the house can't be worth that much. It's out in the middle of nowhere and not in the best of shape. There is a lot of land, but it's just wilderness. I can't imagine why Claire is so upset except for the principle, I guess."

Patricia's eyebrows rose. "You mean you really don't know?"

"Know what?"

"That the land has been expropriated for the new four-lane highway that's being built next year between the border and Duluth. The government had another piece of land they could have chosen, but your father put forward a case for his property, and they went for it. The government offered your father a tidy sum, and he's signed the papers to sell."

"You're kidding."

"Do I look like a woman who kids? I'm surprised your family didn't tell you."

"Was it common knowledge around Duved Cove that my father was selling the land?"

"No. We agreed to keep it quiet while negotiations were going on. Some people might have put up a fight over the whole idea of an interstate just outside of town."

"People here don't like change."

"Especially that kind of change. Your father may not have been as well liked around here when the news broke, especially if they knew the lengths he went to so that his property would be picked. The other land was further out of town but swampy, and that was the clincher."

I didn't answer. I was too busy trying to sort out what this new information could mean. The list of people who would want to kill him had just grown exponentially. I couldn't deny that Jonas and Claire were numbers one and two. Kevin Wilders was a close third, followed by every person in Duved Cove who cared about preserving their way of life.

I agreed to sign the necessary paperwork that Patricia laid out for me on the desk and fled her office, shoving my arms into my parka as I pushed my way out the front door. As I stood on the landing zipping up my jacket, I spotted Tobias Olsen with his back to me at a parking meter, locking the door of his police car. I all but leapt down the steps and darted across the street without him seeing me. From my position half-hidden behind a white van, I watched Tobias bound up the steps to the lawyers' office that I had just left. He would soon know the contents of the will. It wasn't going to look good for Jonas or Claire since they'd believed my father was leaving my father's oh-so-valuable twenty acres to them. I had no doubt that the part of Patricia that still held the Flatsy Patsy scars would gladly share that information with Tobias without qualm.

I pulled up the hood of my parka and started walking quickly towards the highway. I needed to find out more about what was going on if I was going to sort this out. My worry for Jonas was deepening. It far outweighed the fact that overnight I'd become flush enough to change the direction of my future. My father had just left me enough money for a comfortable retirement, and for the life of me, I had no idea why.

THIRTEEN

Mrs. Lingstrom had aged considerably since I'd last seen her over twenty years before. She took a long time to answer my knock on her back door, but the smile of recognition on her face was enough to make me happy I'd made the visit.

"Maja Larson! My goodness. Oh. Oh. Oh." She pulled me into an embrace with surprising strength. "I'm so sorry about your father. So sorry."

She stepped back and drew me into the kitchen. A smell of cooked cabbage and tomato sauce hung in the air. I closed my eyes and I was twelve again, invited in for a cabbage roll supper.

"You will have some fresh coffee and cake, yah? Such a joy to see you after all these years. You are so pretty still." She sat me in a chair and bustled about chattering all the while. Her back was rounded and she was tinier than I remembered, but she was dressed the same—a flowered house dress over beige knee-high stockings and sturdy brown shoes. "Katherine will be so sorry to have missed you," she said at last as she set a brimming cream jug next to a sugar bowl on the table.

"I heard she was home..." I didn't want to believe that I wouldn't have a chance to see her. "Has she gone back to Madison?"

"No. No. She's on a vacation." Mrs. Lingstrom set a cup of coffee in front of me and a slice of homemade cinnamon bundt cake that she'd warmed in the microwave, but she would not meet my eyes. She settled herself in a seat across from me with a

106

cup of black coffee. She rested her elbows on the table, holding her cup with arthritic hands. The knuckles were swollen and the fingers claw-like.

"Umm. This is so good," I said, chewing slowly to savour every morsel. I felt like I'd gone back in time. In a moment, Katherine would come bounding into the kitchen, cheeks red and her blonde pigtails lopsided and half-undone. She'd been wholesomely solid with a square frame and sturdy limbs. Even when she'd grown to be a teenager, she'd radiated good health and a carelessness about her appearance. I felt a sadness for those days before my mother had died. For our lost friendship—it was like a death when you realized how someone you'd been so close to was out of your life.

Mrs. Lingstrom reached over and touched my hand. "Do you remember the time you and Katherine came home with that dirty old crow in a box? It was nearly dead, but you paraded it around like your new pet."

"My father wouldn't let me keep any animals. I was desperate." I smiled. "Katherine named it Blacky. Not all that original, but an accurate name, nonetheless."

"I thought for sure you were both going to pick up a disease. When it died and I threw it in the garbage, Katherine wouldn't speak to me for three days." Mrs. Lingstrom's eyes were wet behind her glasses. "I had to buy her a kitten in the end."

"Spooky."

"Yah, Spooky. Katherine treated that cat like a baby."

"Katherine and I used to put a dress on Spooks and push her around in the doll carriage. In hindsight, it's unusual what that cat let us do to her."

"Katherine so wanted a little sister or brother, and I couldn't have any more children. I wonder if that would have made a difference."

"A difference?"

"Oh, about the time Katherine turned fifteen, she became rebellious, and I couldn't understand what to do with her. The more her father and I tried to discipline her, the worse it got. I don't know. Maybe, we were too strict or maybe not strict enough. We've struggled with what we did wrong. If there'd been a brother or sister, maybe we'd have spoiled her less."

"You were wonderful parents. I couldn't have gotten through those years without your home to come to. This was my refuge."

Mrs. Lingstrom shrugged. "Katherine left home first chance she got. She married and moved to Wisconsin and hardly ever comes to visit. They have two daughters. Lila is twenty-three and Maddy is twelve. I never see them."

I did a quick calculation. Katherine must have married the year I'd gone away to college. I hadn't kept in touch those years, I was so tortured by my mother's death, I'd just shut everyone out. "It's so hard to believe she hasn't kept in better touch with you."

"Yah. She couldn't leave home fast enough."

"I heard at my father's wake that Katherine was having trouble in her marriage and that she came home."

Mrs. Lingstrom took a drink of coffee then stared into her cup. "She was here, but she's gone again."

"Do you know how I can get in touch with her? I'd like to see her, if possible. I've let our friendship go for way too long."

Mrs. Lingstrom stood and picked up my empty plate. "Katherine is on holiday," she said with finality. "I'll let her know you were asking for her next time I speak with her." She set my plate on the counter and came back to sit down. She didn't look as comfortable now, and I decided not to speak of Katherine again.

"My father," I said, "had you seen him recently? I'm trying to understand what might have been going on before he died."

Mrs. Lingstrom frowned. "It's odd, Maja, you know? I saw Peter the morning before he fell off the ladder. He'd come over in the morning to borrow some eggs for breakfast. It was odd, because he never came by. We did not speak much after your mother's death."

My mother and Mrs. Lingstrom had been friendly, but I knew my mother had kept silent about the worst of what went on at home. Perhaps Mrs. Lingstrom had known more than I'd thought. When my mother killed herself, my father acted like the victim. Jonas and I kept up the façade, but I'd hated him then. It had taken many years before I could think of him without the rage making me nauseous. I pulled myself back. "Did my father seem out of sorts or was anything on his mind?"

"He was preoccupied. I remember that. Said something about going on a holiday soon. He wanted me to know."

"Did he talk about anything else?"

"He seemed agitated, like he couldn't sit still. After I gave him the eggs, he hesitated in the doorway there as if he was going to say something. Then he seemed to change his mind and left. That's the last time I saw him."

I stood to leave. There was nothing more to learn here. "It has been good to see you again, Mrs. Lingstrom." I reached for her hand and closed mine over her twisted fingers. "Please say hello to your husband for me."

"Yah, I will, Maja dear," she said. "He's in Maple Lodge now. I visit him every Saturday. Sometimes he knows me and other times not. I'll be sure to tell him you were by, though, if he's having a good day."

I felt a sinkhole of depression open under me as I walked slowly down the Lingstrom driveway to the road. I stopped at the edge of their property and looked back. Even the house had a forlorn aura about it, as if it had given up fighting against time. The siding had mottled from blue to grey, and the roof shingles were black and curled in places. The windows, original to the house, were now surrounded by peeling frames and dark streaks where rain had stained the paint. The swing set Katherine and I had played on stood abandoned in the side yard, rusted to a burnt sienna colour and tilted in the snow, as if it were having trouble standing. We used to ride together on the black strap swing, her sitting and me standing with my runners squished tight against her thighs. I could envision Katherine below me, her head back and her pigtails snapping in the wind as we pumped our legs to go higher. Her arms and legs, like mine, would have been a rich brown from days playing in the summer sun.

Katherine's mother had liked to dress her in matching short sets, pastel pink or blue, and she wore them without fuss, although I knew she preferred my denim pedal pushers and plaid shirts. My favourite of Katherine's clothes had been her mint green outfit with a fisherman on the sleeveless top and the line of his fishing pole extending down her shorts to a fish on the pocket. A fringe of thread tassels rimmed the bottom of the shirt. Katherine had told me that the clothes were hand-me-downs from a rich cousin in California, and they'd assumed an exotic appeal beyond our tiny world in Duved Cove.

I'd forgotten that Katherine had become rebellious in her mid-teens. By then, I was thinking of nothing but Billy and devising ways to spend time with him without my father knowing. My second biggest preoccupation back then had been staying close to my mother to protect her from the days of sadness. Instinctively, Jonas and I had put ourselves between her and my father, and that had kept us close to home. Katherine and I had still hung

110

out some, but not nearly as much as in grade school. When I remembered Katherine, it was from the younger years, before we'd found boys and started to grow apart. She'd run through a few boyfriends after she'd turned thirteen—boy crazy, my mother had said. It looked like boy crazy got you married at seventeen and separated at forty. I wondered if Katherine regretted settling for sex in the back seat of a car instead of pursuing her dreams. If she could go back and change those years, would she do it differently? Would any of us? *I wish I didn't know now what I didn't know then.* Bob Seger had gotten it right.

I turned towards the road and began walking towards Jonas's. With any luck, he'd be back from the doctor's. I hoped he hadn't sunk into a depression that would keep him from telling me what he knew about the will.

As it turned out, the doctor decided to keep Jonas in the hospital overnight. He wanted to try a new medication and thought it best to observe Jonas's reaction to the drug for at least the first day. Claire arrived home with the news mid-afternoon. We took glasses of wine left over from the wake into the living room and sat facing each other at either end of the green velvet couch. The fireplace remained unlit and the anemic sunlight sifting in through the windows made the room feel dreary and close. I felt a headache coming on and would have liked to soak in the tub then have a nap. I looked at Claire as she took a long swallow of wine. She appeared less agitated than the last time I'd seen her at the lawyer's, one leg tucked under her as she leaned back into the pillows.

"It really hit Jonas hard this time," she said, lowering her glass. "I think the stress of finding your father was too much. Doctor

Galloway took one look at Jonas and admitted him on the spot. The hospital's the best place for him at the moment."

"I'll drop by to see him after supper."

"He'll probably be sleeping. When he gets like this, all he wants to do is sleep."

"Has Jonas had many bouts depression? He never let on to me." I didn't want to think about how little we'd been in touch over the years.

"Off and on. Maybe once or twice a year, but usually he can feel an episode coming on and starts on medication right away before it gets too bad. He never wanted you to know."

Jonas had never wanted to make trouble for anyone, especially me. I took a drink from my glass and swallowed hard to keep from spitting it out. Sam would have thrown the whole lot of it down the sink if he'd been here. Its sweetness made my tongue curl. I turned as Gunnar walked into the room. I couldn't tell from his expression whether he was affected by his father's visit to the hospital. Gunnar's scowl had been a fixture on his face since my arrival.

"What's for supper?" he asked Claire, his eyes large and defiant.

She pretended to sigh then chuckled lightly. "Is that all I am to you? A cook? Well, I thought for tonight we'd order pizza. How does that sound?"

"Okay, I guess. I have hockey practice at seven."

"I hadn't forgotten. Get a start on your homework until the pizza comes. I'll order in a few minutes."

Gunnar nodded once and clumped out of the room. Claire shook her head in mock disapproval. "You're so lucky you never had children. They can drive you nuts."

I had desperately wanted children, "had" being the operative word. Once I hit forty, I'd finally accepted that children were not to be part of my life story. It had taken me many years to reach that acceptance. "I'm already nuts," I responded and drank again from my glass. It was starting to go down more smoothly.

"I'm sorry about my reaction this morning to the will. It was just a shock, you know? I figured Jonas deserved better."

Jonas or Claire deserved better? "It's okay," I answered. "It was a shock for me too. At least my dad looked after Gunnar."

"At least that." Claire fiddled with the stem of her wine glass, then turned her full gaze on me. "What will you do with the money?" She smiled to soften the blunt edge of her question.

"I'm not sure. It really wasn't anything I'd planned on." I should have told her that I'd be sharing it with Jonas, but I was still annoyed with her for all the secrets she'd kept about my father's funeral and his will. I'd let her stew a bit more.

"Well then, I guess you'll have some decisions to make." Claire stood. "Time to order pizza, if I'm going to get Gunnar to his practice."

"Claire," I called just before she reached the doorway.

She turned. "Yes, Maja?" Her expression was guarded.

"Did you see Katherine Lingstrom when she was home?"

"A few times in their yard. She's put on so much weight I hardly recognized her. Why do you ask?"

"I went to see her today, but her mother said she'd gone on vacation."

"Well, I saw Katherine two days ago walking down the highway. I was honestly surprised she didn't come by yesterday to pay her respects."

"Yes, that is odd," I said. "It would have been nice to see her again."

"She's changed a lot," Claire said. "God knows why she let herself go like that."

After Claire left, I finished the last of my wine then stretched out on the couch and closed my eyes. I was suddenly overcome by exhaustion. The headache had spread from behind my eyes to the back of my head, and I needed a break from the tensions swirling around me.

FOURTEEN

I woke up. Someone was stealing into my bedroom. Someone I hadn't invited. I sat up and asked, "Who's there?" A shadow crept forward.

"It' s me." Jonas was beside my bed looking down at me. His ghostly face was half in darkness, but I could still see the worry there. His hair, white in the moonlight, was standing every which way, and he kept running his hand through the curls in a nervous repetitive motion I'd come to know too well. His eyes were those of a wild horse, the pupils dilated and crazed. He couldn't seem to focus on me.

"Why are you here?" I asked as I sat up. The clock shone three thirty on my bedside table.

"To warn you. Dad is home, and he's had too much to drink." Jonas's voice was a harsh whisper.

"Is Mom awake?"

"She will be if she isn't." Before I could respond, Jonas had turned and melted into the darkness. I grabbed the pink velvet housecoat of my childhood and slipped it over my shoulders, belting the sash tightly around my waist. Already I could hear my father's heavy footsteps climbing the stairs. Thump, thump, thump, like a rabid animal closing in.

"Where's my fuckin' family?" he bellowed, and the hair on my neck stood on end. I heard the cocking of his gun, and I knew this was going to be bad. I wanted to hide, but I couldn't leave my mother and Jonas to face this alone. I stood still, listening until his footsteps stopped outside my door.

"Don't you hide from me, you little bitch." Jonas hadn't shut my door completely, and my father's boot hit it with a crack. Even though I'd made myself stand tall, the sight of my father in the doorway scared me almost to wetting myself.

"I'm here, Daddy," I said. "We're all here." The desperate words were meant to head off his madness. They only threw gasoline on his rage.

"Get with your damn mother where I can see you." He reached for my arm and crushed his hand around my forearm, tossing me into the hallway. I sprawled on the floor and scrambled to my feet. My knees stung from carpet burns, but I hardly noticed the pain. I ran ahead of him to find my mother. I started searching the rooms, one by one. I was frantic to find her.

"Mama! Mama! Where are you?" I screamed, but she wouldn't answer. The rooms got darker as I ran from one to the other until I felt like I was blind. I reached out my hands to feel my way, screaming for my mother.

"Aggg... I sat up and clutched my chest. My eyes shot open, and I stared wildly around me, willing my heart to slow so that it wouldn't break the confines of my body. I madly searched the corners of the room, gulping in a great breath of air. I was in Jonas's house, safe on his couch. The dream was just a dream—the same one I'd had since childhood. It always ended with me searching for my mother. Sometimes I made it as far as the front of the house and outside into the yard before I woke. This time, the dream had been mercifully cut short. I glanced towards the mantle, where the clock ticked in a comforting steadiness. Seven ten. I'd fallen asleep, and Claire hadn't wakened me. She must have thought it would be a kindness to let me sleep. I pushed myself off the couch and listened for noises in the house. It seemed that I was alone.

I walked quietly into the kitchen and found her note on the table, propped against the salt and pepper shakers. Claire and Gunnar had gone to hockey practice and left pizza for me in the fridge. They'd be home after nine. I looked around me. The house seemed suddenly too empty and the walls were closing in. I had to get outside and drive somewhere with people talking and laughing—people who had no reason to be afraid. I ran back down the hallway to get my coat and boots. It was with the greatest feeling of relief that I stepped outside into the cold winter night.

I stopped by the hospital first and found Jonas sleeping in a private room, just as Claire had predicted. It was a deep, medicated sleep and I didn't stay long. Rather than go back to the empty house, I made my way to Hadrian's, where I knew I'd find company. A few heads turned when I walked in. I recognized Billy's nephew Wayne sitting alone at a table in the corner. He lifted his eyes when I passed, and I sensed him watching me as I crossed to the bar.

Hadrian the younger was in the act of pulling a draught of beer into a frosty stein. I settled myself onto a bar stool in front of him, where I could watch the television, which was tuned to a football game. Hadrian was wearing a blue and red plaid shirt à la Paul Bunyan, and his curly brown locks were tied back with a rubber band. He placed the beer on a tray with two other brimming steins and left to serve a table. When he came back, he wiped down the counter with a stained rag as he talked.

"Evening, Maja. Sorry I missed your father's funeral. It was stock-taking day."

"No problem. My father would rather have been with you in the pub, if he'd had any say."

117

"Ain't that the truth." Hadrian grinned, revealing an uneven row of teeth and two pointy incisors that could have doubled as paper punches. "What can I get ya?"

"I'll have a caesar—lots of spice and celery if you got any." I hadn't eaten the pizza Claire left in the fridge and was hungry. I watched Hadrian's oversized hands prepare the drink with surprising dexterity. He set it on a coaster then reached under the counter and set a bowl of peanuts in front of me.

"Thanks," I said. The tabasco burned the back of my throat, just as I liked it. I set my drink down and reached for a handful of nuts. "Say, Hadrian. Did my father come here often the last while?"

Hadrian leaned on the counter next to me. A mixture of Old Spice and sweat tickled my nose when he shifted positions. I put the back of my hand up to my face and tried not to sneeze. "Your father liked a drink as much as the next guy, but he'd really cut back the last few years. He still dropped in to chat and have a few beers, but not like the old days when my dad ran the bar." Hadrian chuckled and began to tell a story about my father's glory days but then remembered who he was talking to and clamped his mouth shut. I was just as glad not to have to hear about the nights of drinking it up with the boys that had led to him staggering into our house with pent-up rage pouring out like lava.

"Was he in the week before he died?"

"Not that I remember." Hadrian made a circular motion with his index finger to someone behind me and started pouring drinks, his attention now directed to the task at hand. I lifted my face to watch the football game. Blasts of cold air caught me on the back of my neck as the door opened and shut a few times. Hadrian's had a faithful following, and if you sat there long enough, you'd see almost everyone in town stop in for a drink. I looked sideways. Tobias was standing next to me with red cheeks and a big grin.

"This seat taken?" he asked.

"Help yourself," I said, not unhappy to see him. I was still shaken from the dream and didn't want to be alone with my thoughts.

He opened his parka and removed the black toque from his head. Straddling the bar stool, he ran a hand through his grey hair and ruffled it so that it wasn't lying flat. "Just off duty," he said, rubbing his hands together to warm them. "Hadrian, I'll have what's on tap."

Tobias leaned into me. "So, you're still here. How long you planning to stay?"

"Till you find who killed my father...or hell freezes over, which-ever comes first." I frowned at him over the rim of my glass.

"Ouch. Thanks, Hadrian." Tobias lifted his glass and drank. A line of foam rimmed his lips. He licked it off slowly. "The way I see it, whoever killed your father did it in a fit of anger. If it had been premeditated, they wouldn't have used his shovel, which was probably the closest weapon at hand."

"Maybe. I guess that makes sense." Something was bothering me. "I've spoken to some people. . ."

"Oh?"

"Just casually, you know, to try to find out about my father's last few days." I spoke quickly, not wanting Tobias to know I'd been striking out on my own. "A few of them said my father seemed scared, or worried at the very least. Somebody might have been threatening him."

Tobias stared off as if he was pondering what I'd said. "Touch-down," he said.

"What, you've figured something out?"

119

Tobias pointed up at the TV. "No, touchdown. Florida State just scored."

I punched him lightly on the biceps. "It's coming back to me. Concentration wasn't your strong suit in high school."

"Only if the subject interested me." Tobias turned and looked me in the eyes. "I used to like sitting behind you in class so I could watch the way you pushed back your blonde hair when you were thinking about something and the way you'd raise your hand when nobody else could come up with the right answer. You were something back then, Maja Larson. Something to behold." He took another sip.

"I'm not liking your use of the past tense."

Tobias set his glass on the bar and grinned. "I'll let you know if you've still got it after I've studied up for a bit. A true scholar does their research before jumping to a conclusion."

"You've never given up the art of bullshit, have you, Tobias Olsen?"

He laughed. "It's what sets me apart from all the others." He reached out, took a handful of peanuts and popped them into his mouth one by one as he talked. "Nobody seems to have anything but nice things to say about your father. He worked the night shift at the border so the guys with families could have a life, and he was sociable enough. He had buddies at Hadrian's where he spent an hour or two the evenings he wasn't working. He kept to himself a lot this past year, but that could be a result of working nights. There is something odd, though."

"Oh? What's that?"

"Your father had a lot of money for someone who worked at the border. For instance, leaving eighty thousand to his grandson. He also had a lot of expensive sports equipment and electronics in his house, not to mention a new boat and car."

"He was frugal," I said, but I also began to wonder where he'd gotten the money. I'd been so shocked by him leaving the property to me that I hadn't thought much about the rest. "Perhaps my father bought those things with the expectation of selling the house and land, or maybe he got a signing bonus?"

"I checked that out too. As you know by your trek to the lawyer, your father signed away his land quite recently; however, he hadn't collected any money from the sale as of yet. That makes the fact that he didn't owe any money to anybody even stranger. Not one red cent. Nada. He liked to pay up front in cash."

"Well, I don't know what to tell you." I took a swallow of my caesar, and my eyes teared up while I tried not to choke.

"Hadrian has a heavy hand with the tabasco. You should stick to beer. No surprises." Tobias chugged down the last of his for emphasis.

"I like surprises." I couldn't believe I was having this conversation with Tobias, who wasn't known for being much of a talker. He'd been one of those quiet boys in my class who was always hanging around with the guys, drinking beer on the weekends and skipping class. He'd never come across as all that bright, which seemed snobbish to say, but he'd never given me any reason to think otherwise. He'd also never given me the time of day.

"Your father left you the bulk of his estate. Plan on moving back to Duved Cove with Saul?"

"Sam, his name is Sam, and no, I won't be moving back."

"Did you know about the will?" Tobias focused his green eyes on mine, waiting for me to respond. The strength of his gaze was disconcerting.

"I was completely in the dark about my father's business affairs," I said. "We weren't all that close, as you may have gathered."

"That's why I find it odd, him leaving the house and land to

121

you. A more logical choice would have been your brother, so I can't figure out why your father changed the will so spur of the moment. Could it be he'd had a fight with Jonas and told him what he planned to do? We're talking a lot of money."

"Jonas didn't know." I swallowed the last of my drink and pushed myself off the stool. "My father was not someone you could pin down. He liked to keep people guessing as to what he would do next. It was like a game to him. Stick in a pin and see which way they squirm, especially if you happened to be related to him."

I turned to go, kicking myself for having said anything. I'd given Tobias an insight into our family that I wished I'd kept to myself because I'd just remembered something else about Tobias Olsen. In high school, he'd played hockey and football and was probably the most talented athlete Duved High had ever had the luck to have enrolled in all its years of operation. He'd come complete with a stubborn streak two miles wide that kept him from giving up once he got involved in a game, even if his team was long past winning. If he turned his attention to Jonas or Claire, I feared they wouldn't escape unscathed from his bloodhound tenacity. It was time I started thinking outside the box. I needed to search farther afield, to try to make sense of all the loose ends that were flapping around me, before Tobias got to the finish line ahead of me.

FIFTEEN

Billy didn't come to see me that night. The nightmare didn't darken my door either, and I awoke rested for the first time since my arrival in Duved Cove. With my battery recharged, I leapt out of bed just past six a.m. and dressed in jeans, a navy turtleneck and white pullover fleece. I gave my hair, flattened in sleep, a good brushing before pulling it back into a ponytail. My ministrations over, I stood momentarily transfixed in front of the mirror, trying to see into the eyes of this woman who was me. I stretched and swivelled my neck like a pendulum, slowly back and forth, searching for clues of the girl I'd been twenty years, thirty years before.

I was halfway through my life. The tired lines in my face had softened in sleep, but there was no escaping the changes time had wrought on the line of my jaw and the papery lines around my forty-year-old eyes. This was my face, but also the face of my mother and of my grandmother and great-grandmother before her. I should be proud of this face which was mine and not mine. People might find it odd for a plastic surgeon, but I had no desire to alter this process and make myself appear younger. What I did for other people did not interest me. The slow settling of my features into those of my mother's was a comfort I couldn't explain.

I left a note for Claire on the kitchen table saying that I'd be back early afternoon and grabbed an apple from the fridge and a granola bar from the cupboard before putting on my parka and boots. The door barely acknowledged my exit as it swung shut behind me on silent hinges. The darkness, punctuated by fingers of pinkish light above the tree line, enveloped me like a shroud as I walked toward my car. I pulled the hood of my parka over my head and nuzzled into its rim of fur as the wind cut across my face.

This time, the car engine wasn't so eager to turn over. I tried the key five times before the motor grudgingly whirred into life, and at that, it took some coaxing to keep it from sputtering out. I let it run a full five minutes before putting it into drive and turning on the headlights. The heater blasted cold air, and it probably wouldn't warm up inside at all before I reached my destination. I cursed the feeble heater as I eased the car down the tire ruts in the snow onto the main road and pointed it towards the main highway, the headlights piercing the darkness in two long streams. Once at the highway junction, I swung the car north toward the Canadian border.

The drive took less than an hour, but it was an hour of beauty as the sky brightened from black to pink and orange, finally settling on a pale blue. The coniferous trees along the side of the two-lane highway emerged from a wall of black to a feathery line of boughs heavy with snow. At staggered intervals, copses of birch and alder nestled in amongst the denser pines and fir. Highway 61 wound through the Sawtooth Range, traversing corridors that cut through towering cliffs of rock. Every so often, I'd round a corner and discover a clear view of the lakeshore, rocks covered by snow and chunks of ice in the coves. Hardly another soul was on the road except for transport drivers heading south to take their produce to market. Each waved at me as we passed. I could have driven forever, but it wasn't long before the houses of Grand Portage came into view, scooped into the silver-white winter landscape of Arrowhead country. I stayed on the highway until I pulled into the parking lot at the Canadian border.

When I stepped inside the U.S. Customs office, Charlie Mallory was standing behind the counter, chatting with a tall Native woman with long black hair. Both were dressed in navy uniforms with badges on their shoulders and guns at their hips. Next to her, Charlie looked short and stocky, his red curls tied back in a ponytail. His eyes took me in as he looked over her shoulder. Recognition gleamed, and he nodded. I waited by the door as he said goodbye to the woman and grabbed his black duffle coat from the coat rack. He ambled over to me, his eyes friendly. I was careful to enunciate now that I knew he was deaf.

"Hi, Charlie. I wonder if I could buy you breakfast?"

"Sure. I could do with some grub before I crash. Why don't we meet at the restaurant on the highway just the other side of Grande Portage?" His low, even voice was pleasing to the ear. It was surprising considering the pugilistic state of his face.

"Sounds good."

With a population of under a thousand, Grand Portage was situated between Lake Superior and Pigeon River. From 1730 to 1800 or so, Grand Portage had been a trading post where hundreds of traders and voyagers from all over the world met to barter goods and furs. An Ojibway community still called Pigeon River home, making up about half the town's population. As I waited for Charlie in the restaurant booth, I thought back to the days I'd camped in Grand Portage State Park, with its Grand Falls, and climbed trails up Eagle Mountain, the highest point in Minnesota. I would have liked to have camped under the stars with Billy, but we'd never managed to escape our lives for more than snatched hours. My father would have killed him and maybe me if he'd known I'd fallen for an Indian. My father

125

had been as racist as the day was long. I'd hidden my love for Billy because it would have shamed my father and unleashed his unpredictable temper. I'd had an abortion to save my family name and to keep the peace. In the end, it had not been enough. I had lost Billy and any chance to be whole. I might have borne it yet and managed to find happiness but for my mother's death. The noose that encircled her white neck had killed my dreams as surely as it had ended her short life. That was my reality, and as I sat waiting for Charlie Mallory, the enormity of what I had sacrificed welled up and threatened to destroy the safe haven I'd carved out with Sam. Fiona, with her psychologist's insight, had been right. I was not happy—had not been happy for some time. Coming back to Duved Cove had loosed all my ghosts and turned my world on end. It had made me face what I'd tucked away as carefully as the memories in my mother's trunk.

The bell on the door jangled and Charlie entered, stomping snow off his boots onto the rug before walking over to the table I'd chosen beside the gas fireplace. The room had narrow windows and was lined in dark cedar panelling. It would have been dingy except for the red and white checkered tablecloths and hurricane lamps hanging overhead. Charlie slid in across from me. The waitress appeared with a steaming pot of coffee, and we placed our orders. I had intended to request bacon and eggs but ended up ordering the waffles with sausage. It was an odd trait—my mouth speaking a different meal than the one I'd chosen in my head. I looked across at Charlie, who was watching me intently.

"I'm sorry about your father," he said after the waitress was out of hearing. "It must have come as a shock."

"Yes. I thought my father would live forever. Funny how we don't really believe our lives will ever change. We believe that

126

people will always be there and defy time. It's a lie we tell ourselves to keep the certainty of our own deaths at bay, I suppose. I wanted...I wanted to ask you about his last year or so. It might help make me understand why he died the way he did."

Charlie nodded but took time preparing his coffee—two heaping spoonfuls of sugar and three plastic containers of cream. He stirred the mixture for some time before looking up at me again. "Your father was a complex man. I'm sure I don't have to tell you that."

"You seem to have more insight into him than most people."

Charlie nodded and smiled. His crooked nose and scarred cheek suddenly didn't look so disfigured. "I've had to make better use of the senses I have. I've learned to be more observant than most. I also read lips, and people forget. They say things..."

I returned his smile. "Of course. People would be more discreet if they realized they were being overheard."

"In a sense, I *am* listening in," Charlie shrugged. "Your father was the one who suggested I work inside. They were thinking of moving me off the border, because my hearing loss was giving me difficulty doing my job. They began to think it was unsafe if I was checking cars and couldn't hear what was going on around me. I didn't want to be sent to an office building doing paperwork, so your dad said he'd work with me on the night shift when it was quieter. I thought at the time that he was good to help me out."

"You sound unsure."

"I don't mean to badmouth your father. I just came to know that sometimes he did things for reasons he didn't share. Usually, whatever he did benefited himself more than anybody else."

Charlie was nothing if not astute. He was also very good at reading expressions. "You and your father were not close, I gather," he said.

I picked up my coffee cup. My hand was shaking, and I set the cup carefully back onto the table. "We were not on good terms. I don't want to go into it, but please know that nothing you say could startle me. I know he was seeing a married woman."

Charlie's eyes were sympathetic. "Yeah, she met him a few times over the last month. There were a couple of women, actually. Your father seemed to like them younger. He had a lot of charm, obviously."

"What did they look like? The women, I mean?"

"The one who came most often, he called Becky. The other one used to pick him up. She never got out of her red van, but she had dark hair, I remember. The van was one of those older models—a Dodge, I think. I never knew her name."

"Did you tell the police?"

"No. I don't like gossip. It's not my place to talk about your father's love life."

"Could my father have been involved in something illegal?" I watched Charlie to see any sign of guilt. He'd be a logical partner if they were passing contraband through the border crossing. He met my gaze with a level stare.

"Do you have any particular reason to suspect that?"

"My father had a lot of money, a new vehicle and boat. Just seems odd."

"Your father gambled at the casino on the way home. He could have made his money there."

"Grand Portage Casino?"

"No, I think he went to Fortune Bay. Kind of a weird choice when you think about it, since it would have been out of his way. Grand Portage is right here, after all."

"A bit off the beaten track for sure."

Why was my father visiting Fortune Bay unless he had a

connection? Billy and his brother Raymond had their outfitters business stationed near there and took people staying at the resort on day trips, but that couldn't be the draw for my father. He'd never had any interest in fishing or hunting. I was at a loss.

Our breakfasts arrived, and we didn't speak again until Charlie had finished eating. I could tell he was getting tired, and I waved off a second cup of coffee.

"Thanks for taking this time," I said, reaching for the bill.

"No problem. Your dad was always easygoing with me, and I'd like to see them find who killed him. Despite anything I said, he didn't do anything that deserved being murdered."

I nodded. "Thanks."

I shrugged into my coat and followed Charlie outside, where we shook hands before getting into our vehicles. I sat in the parking lot with the engine running for several minutes after he'd disappeared toward town. I watched the wind whip snow around the building and debated whether I should let the investigation go or keep pursuing leads that seemed to be heading down paths I'd just as soon not go down. The bleakness of the morning settled over me.

The way I saw it, there were two possibilities, neither of them very appealing. Either my father was involved in something illegal that was making him a lot of money and at least one enemy, or his involvement with a married woman had angered somebody enough to kill him. I knew about his affair with Becky Holmes, which was bad enough, but the second woman was even more difficult to contemplate. It wasn't the fact that there was a second woman. It was the fact that the second woman and the vehicle Charlie Mallory had just described bore a striking similarity to Claire and her red Dodge Caravan.

SIXTEEN

The drive to Fortune Bay Casino on Highway 169 took an hour and a half. Blowing snow and white-out conditions made me drive more slowly than I would have liked, but the thought of the car hitting black ice and sliding off the highway demanded caution. I stopped for coffee at a roadside diner and to rest my weary eyes. It was tucked off the highway below a looming rock cut that was capped with a ragged line of fir trees. The owner, who was dressed in a blue checked shirt, baggy black cords and a Yankee ball cap, was close to eighty. He peered at me through inch-thick, oversized glasses.

"Roads ain't safe, young lady. You should hunker down till the worst of the blowing snow is over."

"I'm ready for a break," I admitted and obediently took a seat near the window. He shuffled over with a mug of black coffee, a fresh piece of apple pie and the *Duluth News Tribune* tucked under his arm.

"No sign of the storm letting up, but you never know around these parts," he said after setting the coffee and pie on the table and handing me the paper. His eyes were watery and tinged with pink. "I've seen storms blow in quick and leave just as quick. You going far?"

"Just to Fortune Bay. I'm almost there," I reached for the fork he'd set on a paper napkin in front of me. The pie tasted homemade, cinnamon and brown sugar flavouring the tart apples. I swallowed appreciatively. "Say, do you know of an outfitter named Raymond Okwari?"

"Ray's the best muskie fisherman around, bar none. Owns a little lodge not far from here that brings in the tourists. Course them natives have a jump on the rest of us when it comes to knowing their way around the wilderness." He smiled, showing his nicotine-stained teeth.

"Where's Ray's lodge?"

"Just off Trail Road. Hang the first right past the purple house about ten miles from here. Only purple house in the area, thank Christ." He pulled a cloth out of his pocket and wiped his hands. "Some damn people have no taste whatsoever."

I waved my fork in a circular motion at chest level. "Great pie."

"Can't take any credit. The wife baked it. She's normally working but had to go into town. Expect she's holed up at the granddaughter's till the storm lets up."

He turned to leave just as the front door opened. I looked over then ducked my head. Wayne Okwari, Billy's nephew, had stepped into the hallway, shaking snow out of his long black hair and stomping his work boots on the rug at the entranceway. He was wearing the same hunting jacket he'd had on when I'd seen him at Hadrian's. I hoped he hadn't recognized me.

"Hey, Verl. Quite a day." Wayne's voice was deeper than I'd expected.

"Say that again." Verl blocked Wayne's view of me as he headed toward the counter. I waited a few seconds then glanced over. Wayne had his back to me, leaning on his elbows next to the cash register. I was thankful he hadn't noticed me. Maybe it was folly to have made this trip. What did I think I could find out about my father's tie to Fortune Bay Casino? Likely nothing, and

I'd only succeed in embarrassing myself. I lifted a section of the newspaper and pretended to read.

"Heading to your dad's?" Verl asked. Mercifully, he didn't mention that I'd been asking directions to Ray's lodge.

"I'm coming from there. I'm on my way to Duved Cove. I just stopped to fill up my thermos with coffee. Then I'll be heading out again."

"Hell of a day to be travelling." I could hear liquid splashing into the thermos. "Read in the paper that Peter Larson was hit over the head and left for dead at his backyard in Duved Cove. That true?"

Wayne lowered his voice, and I didn't hear his answer.

Verl laughed. A pause and then, "What's your old man up to? He hasn't been in for a bit."

"Ice fishing with Chinese tourists mainly. Damn, those people like to fish. Don't even seem to mind the cold. They've been flocking in like Canada geese all month. My uncle Billy is working with us, and they've been going flat out. We're looking forward to spring thaw so we can have some time off."

I lowered the paper enough to see over the top. Wayne was in profile, screwing the lid onto his thermos. He looked less like Billy from this vantage point, with sharper features and thin lips—thin lips that matched his thin body. His hair was plastered back from his face in a matted toss of wet strands.

"Bet they're taking lots of pictures. Never seen one without a camera around their neck," said Verl.

"Good one." Wayne started towards the door. "Say hi to Marco for me. Tell him I'll stop by and see him on Sunday."

"Marco's sleeping. Just came back from taking a load of paper products to Dallas. He's taken another load out Monday."

"I'll be by to see him before then. Let him know."

"Sure thing."

I folded the paper and placed it on the paper placemat then waited a few minutes before going to the counter. Verl looked up at me from where he leaned reading the sports section of the paper. "Leaving already?"

"I don't have far to go. Say, was that Wayne Okwari?"

"You know Wayne? He's a friend of my grandson Marco. Marco has a rig and works out of Duluth. Never can keep up with all his comings and goings."

"I don't exactly know Wayne, but I know his uncle Billy."

"Oh yeah, you were asking earlier about Ray. He'd be Billy's brother and Wayne's dad. Well, Wayne works part-time in Duved Cove at a garage then helps out Ray when the spirit moves him. Never know when Wayne's going to turn up either. Kids these days just can't seem to sit still like in my day."

"It is a different generation."

Verl took my money and handed me back some change. "Looks to be letting up out there. Hope the roads ain't too icy for you, young lady."

"I'll drive slowly. Thanks for everything."

"I'm sure you're welcome. Come again if you're back this way."

"I will."

I came suddenly upon the purple house with canary yellow shutters and green roof several miles up the road. As I rounded a tight bend, the house appeared through the blowing snow like a two-storey rainbow in a universe of white and grey. I slowed but not fast enough to make the turn. The car ignored my change in direction. I knew enough to pump the brakes but could feel the tires resisting as the car slid wildly sideways into a tailspin on a piece of black ice. The steering wheel didn't respond to my frantic cranking, and the brakes may as well have been severed. I felt a throbbing pain where the door handle suddenly dug into my hip as I was flung against the door. A sudden spin and the tires ground against the snow bank lining the road. The solid mass of snow directed the car back onto the highway. I was thrust back then forward. My neck snapped and my head banged against the steering wheel, then thumped hard against the headrest. The seat belt tightened across my shoulder in a band down to my waist. It felt like all the air had left my lungs. Pain darted across my forehead and throbbed down my side. I closed my eyes and prayed.

Just as I was beginning to believe that the car would never stop its crazed slide across the road, the tires gripped onto something solid, and the wild ride ended. I opened my eyes and leaned forward to peer out the front windshield through the falling snow. Miraculously, the car seemed intact and was pointed in the right direction. I put one hand on my heart to still its beating and took in a deep breath. Nothing was broken. My breath came easily. It took me a few seconds to regroup before I gingerly began a slow descent down the hill, not daring to pull over in case the fickle car slid off the road. I spotted a sign with a toque of snow draped over its top that announced the outfitters lodge a few miles further on. I would keep going. I needed to see Billy.

The road swooped down a hill and would have dropped into the white belly of the lake but for the sharp right turn at the base of the incline. I was driving cautiously now, little more than a crawl, covering the last mile in record slow time. A sign that said "Ray's Outfitters" came into view through the swirling snow.

Just past it was a newly plowed parking lot, which I pulled into, sidling up next to three skidoos and a truck with a blade for plowing snow attached to its front. I looked past the truck to a log cabin painted a chocolate brown, visible through a stand of birch trees and falling snow. Smoke rose from its stone chimney and billowed sideways, caught by the wind that cut across the ice coating Lake Vermilion.

I left the semi-warmth of the car and made a dash for the front door of the cottage, feeling my right boot sink into a drift. The sudden shock of cold inside my boot made me cry out. I stopped and emptied the snow from my boot while the wind did its best to blow me sideways into another bank. Boot back on, I struggled up the wide steps to the front door. As I reached for the handle, the wind caught me in a backwards gust that set me off balance. I pulled the door open, and it wrenched from my grasp and banged against the wall. The wind was stronger here than on the highway. It was a relief when I finally made it inside the cabin.

The first thing I noticed was the heat radiating from a cast iron stove in the corner and the smell of wood smoke in my nostrils. A two-seater couch and a recliner took up one corner of the office, and immediately in front of me was a counter with colourful postcards facing out from a wire rack next to cartons of gum and chips, fishing lures and maps. Above the desk, a deer head and shiny fish kept guard over the room with dead, beady eyes. As I stood looking around me, Billy and Raymond entered through a door to the right of the counter. I wouldn't have recognized Raymond, but then, it had been a long time.

"Can I help you?" His black eyes were like raisins in a doughy face. He must have been carrying three hundred pounds on a six foot frame. Now that I was here, I couldn't find the words to say why I'd come. Billy stepped from behind his brother.

"Raymond, you get the gear ready, and I'll look after this customer."

"If you like," Raymond said and ambled to the door. He looked me over as if he was trying to puzzle out where he'd seen me before. I smiled and looked away.

Billy crossed the floor and stood in front of me. He lifted a hand and touched my face. His eyes were filled with concern. Even though his touch was gentle, I flinched as pain throbbed across my forehead.

"How did you hurt yourself? Come sit and I'll get some ice." He took my arm and led me to the couch. I lowered myself onto the cushion while Billy went behind the counter and began rummaging.

"I hit a patch of ice and hit my head. It hurts now that you've drawn my attention to it."

"Car okay?"

"Yup, I think so. Just my head got damaged."

Billy returned with a bag of ice that he pressed gently against my forehead. The throbbing above my eyes started to numb. I tried to concentrate on something else.

"You're going to have a goose egg if we don't catch the swelling." He sat next to me, waiting for me to tell him what had brought me so far from Duved Cove.

"I don't really know why I'm here. I went to meet Charlie, Dad's partner at Pigeon River, and he said that Dad came to Fortune Bay to gamble. It seemed logical to check it out. I stopped at the diner and found out your brother's is on the way, so here I am." I took a deep breath.

"So here you are." Billy reached over and covered the hand that was resting on my lap. His skin was warm on mine.

"There was something else." I turned so I could look into his eyes. It was now or never. "I wanted to tell you, Billy, that I'm sorry. After all these years, I'm sorry that I ran away from Duved Cove and my brother and father and most of all you. I know it doesn't mean much now, but I wanted you to know before I have to fly home." I looked down at our hands intertwined. "I'd made a promise to you, and I didn't keep it."

"You promised you wouldn't be gone long," Billy said so softly I could barely hear the words. They cut into my heart. I looked into his eyes again. They'd become unreadable, and I knew then how much I'd hurt him.

I sighed the words, "I'm sorry."

"What you lived through—the abortion and then your mother..." Billy shrugged. "I don't blame you, Maja. I never blamed you. Besides, we've both done okay. Others have filled the emptiness."

I nodded. "And that's really what it's been. Pain and emptiness."

"Your father's death has made you face it again."

"I've been running from all that I didn't want to think about, but I can't leave Jonas now. I think he's in trouble, Billy."

"Jonas couldn't have murdered your father."

"I'm not so sure. The way it happened could have been spontaneous. Maybe, my father taunted him with...crushing information, and Jonas had the shovel in his hands and just... snapped. It might have been like that."

Claire's haunted eyes. Gunnar's anger. Jonas's descent. They were keeping a secret that was destroying them.

"Where is Jonas now?"

"The hospital. He's sunk into a depression, and they're getting him stabilized with antidepressants. He's got a frail soul. My mother was the same."

"Your father isn't blameless." Billy's eyes were angry. He'd been my confidant all those years ago, but even Billy I hadn't told the worst. He knew and he didn't know. He stood and looked down at me. "I'll drive you to the casino. I know the person you'll want to talk to."

"I wasn't sure if anybody would tell me whether my father'd been winning or racking up debt. That's what I need to know." I handed Billy the ice pack and stood to face him. "We can take my car."

"We'll find out, don't worry. I'll just tell Raymond I'm leaving. We have a new group coming over from the casino in the morning for a three-day trip, but he can get that organized without me."

SEVENTEEN

Within snow-laden stands of mature birch, aspen and pine, Fortune Bay Resort and Casino nestled against the south shore of Lake Vermilion. A deep carpet of snow covered the eighteen-hole golf course that stretched away from the low, sprawling buildings. It was breath-catching, beautiful wilderness. I wished we had more time for a hike through the woods to the lake. It would have been all I could ask to spend the day with Billy away from everyone and everything. I could tell by the way he looked from me to the trees that he felt the same way.

"The Bois Forte Band runs the casino," Billy said as we pulled into a parking space. "Sah-Gah-Ea-Gum-Wah-Ma-Mah-Nee. The Chippewa call Vermilion the Lake of the Sunset Glow. Twelve hundred miles of shoreline and close to four hundred islands with fishing second to none. Walleye, pike, muskie, bass—food of the gods." He grinned at me.

"Would you ever leave Minnesota?" I asked suddenly, but I already knew the answer.

Billy turned his dark eyes to mine and slowly shook his head. "This is my home. I'm here till the end."

"I understand," I said, and I truly did. That didn't stop the pain from welling up inside me. I smiled and looked away from Billy's all-seeing eyes.

The casino turned out to be a cavernous games room with gold-patterned carpet, high ceilings in red and silver and more slot machines than rides at a carnival. The clanging, tinging and jangle of money and machines and the flashing lights were harsh and disorienting. Casually dressed people with determined faces sat in front of one-armed bandits while waitresses circulated with trays of drinks. After the quiet of Raymond's lodge, this bright, loud room was a shock to my system. I was glad Billy had offered to come with me. I tried to imagine my father in this room, sitting at one of the slot machines, pulling down the handle and waiting for the swoosh of money to clank into the metal tray. More likely, he would have joined a poker or blackjack game in the farthest section of the room, where hosts in black and white were dealing cards behind low tables covered in green felt.

Billy stood silently beside me surveying the room, eyes alert, stance relaxed. I'd always liked his stillness. In a crowded room or alone together on the beach, he had the ability to suspend motion—to disappear inside himself—a self-containment I'd never learned. After he'd drunk in the lay of the land to his satisfaction, he touched my arm and motioned for me to follow him.

We walked past the waterfall in the centre of the room to a long hallway. The noise was less deafening once we'd left the main room, but there was no escaping its relentless throb. Billy led me to a green door at the end of the corridor. He rapped loudly, and a deep voice called for us to enter. I stepped into the room behind Billy. An aboriginal man in a khaki security uniform sat behind a bank of television screens that showed various angles of the room we'd just left as well as the corridor we'd just walked down. He had a long black braid that hung down his back to his hips.

"Hey, Billy. How's it going, man?"

"Good, Chitto. You?"

"Can't complain." Chitto stood and stretched. He had a broad forehead, wide nostrils and round chin made more defined by his hair pulled tightly away from his face. He extended a hand in my direction. "Pleased to meet you."

"This is my friend, Maja. We went to school together in Duved Cove, quite a few moons ago."

Chitto's black eyes travelled between me and Billy. It felt like Chitto saw beneath the surface to what really lay between me and Billy. It was disconcerting. I felt a slow blush heat my cheeks. I couldn't remember having blushed so much since grade school. I shook his hand and met his eyes. "Good to meet you."

Chitto sat down and turned his attention back to the screens. "Quiet so far today. Probably the weather's keeping the regulars home. Have a seat. What brings you this way?"

Billy pulled out a chair for me but stood leaning on the desk facing Chitto. "Maja's father was killed a few days ago in Duved Cove, and we're just tying up some loose ends."

Chitto took his eyes off the screen and glanced towards me. "Sorry to hear that. Did I know your father?"

"You might have." Billy's eyes jumped from Chitto to me and then back again. "He used to come here quite a bit, we think. Peter Larson. Do you know anything about him?"

Chitto's shoulders tensed visibly. He lifted a finger toward a screen that showed the entrance where we'd stood surveying the room. Two middle-aged men in suits stood talking together. "You're looking at the new owners of the casino."

Billy turned and squinted at the screen. "Aren't those the Motego brothers?"

"The very same."

"What happened to Rainy Wynona?"

"Gone. Left without even a goodbye party."

"When did that happen?"

"Last week. Surprise to me. Surprise to everybody."

Billy watched the screen a bit longer but didn't say anything. Chitto turned and looked at me again. "Your father used to come here to play blackjack a few times a week. Hadn't seen him for a few weeks though."

"Did he win much?" I asked.

"He won his share but nothing out of the ordinary. I'd say he was in the black more often than the red. He always played at the same table. Travis was the regular dealer. He told me your father usually won enough to leave with a few bucks at the end of the night. I'd have remembered if Travis had said it was more than that."

"Why's that?"

"Someone beating the house, I'd have to keep an eye on them, you know, for signs of cheating. The dealers tip me off if something's out of the ordinary."

Billy stood and took a step towards me. "We'd better leave so you don't get into any trouble. I know they don't like customers coming back here."

"Wouldn't want to piss off the new bosses, that's for sure." Chitto laughed. "I hear they're not the forgiving kind."

We were almost at the door when I stopped and turned. "Chitto, when my father came to play blackjack, did he come by himself?"

"He came alone, but I seen him with another guy the odd time. I never thought about it much before, but it was enough times that I noticed. Sometimes they sat together and played blackjack. The other guy wasn't a regular, and I can't recall his name. Always wore a black Yankees ball cap. He hasn't been around much either, now that I think of it."

"Would you have them on tape?" Billy asked.

"Not likely. They weren't in together this month, and we

don't keep the tapes longer than that. We record over them."

"Well, thanks for the information," I said. Nothing that he'd told me explained my father's financial situation when he died. There were probably a lot of men in ball caps who played blackjack, so that didn't tell me much either.

"Trevor working tonight?" Billy asked.

"No, he's gone south for a few weeks. Expect him back a week Sunday."

"Thanks again, Chitto."

"No problemo."

Billy took my arm, and we left Chitto to his television screens. It felt odd walking back down the corridor knowing that Chitto was watching our every step. It made me want to get away from the casino as quickly as possible and back to the world of silence and woods and winter calm.

I left Billy at the top of the hill leading to the lake. The storm had stopped, and the snow lay white with bluish hollows in drifts along the roadside. The cloud cover gave up its hold on the sky, and the feeble sun was visible for the first time that day. Billy wanted to get some exercise before nightfall, and this would be his only chance. Once he returned to camp, he'd be busy packing up for the morning's journey.

He'd kissed my cheek then my mouth before he left me. His eyes had been as black as I'd ever seen them when he'd looked into mine before kissing me. We kissed long and hard, but it hadn't been enough. If we lived forever, it could never be enough. Billy's eyes spoke of longing and forgiveness and resolution. His hands touched my hair and held it tightly, palms resting against my neck, and it was the gentle weight of his hands that I felt most strongly as I watched him walking away from the car, his shoulders squared and his lean body braced against the wind blowing in from the lake.

I knew this was the end. Billy and I would not be joining our lives together, no matter how much we wanted to be together. Billy had Nina and Ella, and I had Sam and my life in Ottawa. Our futures were not ours to give to each other. I watched him walk through the snow, completely at home in the wide expanse of sky and lake and woods. He looked so at one with the wilderness that my throat ached. He didn't stop once to turn and wave, even though we both knew this was the last time we would meet this way.

When Billy was nearly out of sight, I reversed in a wide arc and aimed the car back towards the highway and Duved Cove. The drive to Jonas's passed quickly as I focused on the last moments with Billy. I relived them over and over in my mind before tucking the memory away for safekeeping. When I grew old and grey, at least I would have this day. I'd have the knowledge that time and distance had not destroyed my love for Billy Okwari nor his love for me.

I made it to Duved Cove Hospital as the sun was starting its descent behind the black line of fir trees. A horizontal swath of peach light intersected the grey sky and the darkness of the horizon. I looked eastward and saw the sliver of moon waiting for its turn to claim the night sky. The early sunset made me want to tuck myself into the house to watch a movie or read a book with a glass of wine in my hand and a fire in the hearth. This dream would have to keep. I stepped out of the car and huddled into my parka. Along with the disappearing cloud cover had come a sharp drop in temperature, hovering just this side of bearable. My teeth all but chattered as I jogged across the parking lot towards the lighted entranceway, my breath leading the way in moist puffs of frosty white.

The sterile green walls, blue vinyl seats and fluorescent lighting of the waiting room made me feel right at home. I'd spent the better part of my adult life in one hospital or another as a medical student, intern and plastic surgeon. Unbelievably, the waiting room was empty. I imagined the constant lines of people waiting in Ottawa emergency rooms and marvelled at the difference. There were perks to practising medicine in a small town.

Directly in front of me, Becky Wilders sat at the admitting desk, head bent over a book, red hair pulled back taut, her face glowing in the light of the desk lamp. She looked up and smiled as I approached. "If you've come to see Jonas, visiting hours are from seven to nine." Then she grinned wider, revealing a gap in her teeth, and waved a hand towards the corridor to my left. "I have to officially tell people that, but you can go in if you want. He's on the second floor, room 235."

"Thanks, Beck. Do you know how he's doing?"

"I went up on my break and checked his chart." A rosy colour spread up her cheeks. "I know I shouldn't have, but we go way back, and I can't help but worry how he's doing. He had a bad afternoon, so Doc adjusted his dosage and gave him a sedative— just enough to relax him." Her hand nervously flipped through the book's pages.

"I guess he'll be in for another night then. I was hoping...oh well." I took a step towards the elevator but hesitated. I moved back towards the desk and leaned in. "Becky, I've been wondering about something." I waited until her hand stilled and I had her full attention. I spoke softly. "When did you actually start this fling with my father?"

145

Becky slowly folded the paperback novel over her hand and resumed ruffling the pages. She wouldn't look at me. "Why do you ask?"

"I don't know, really. I'm just confused and trying to figure out what was going on with him. I'm trying to understand."

"You really want to know the first time we got together?"

"Yeah."

"Even if you aren't going to like the answer?"

"Try me."

"It's not that easy to say this. I think if it wasn't for his death... well, the first time was after Jonas and I broke up."

"But you broke up in twelfth grade." My voice had risen several pitches.

Becky nodded. Her eyes were defiant, but something else was there too. Guilt? Fear? "I was sad about him and drinking too much. I went over to your house to try to talk Jonas into giving up Claire and coming back to me. I would have done anything back then. Your father was home alone. He started comforting me, and well, one thing led to another." Becky shrugged and held my stare. "It was the only time until this year, I swear to God. I should never have told you. You can't imagine what it's been like keeping the secret all these years."

I didn't know what to say. Becky had just shaken me to my very core, and all I wanted was to get away from her. "You never thought of telling anybody?"

"Who would I tell? Jonas? My parents? *You?* I was ashamed. I felt like I'd betrayed Jonas and...your mother. I really felt bad about her."

I couldn't go there with her. I asked, "Why would you have taken up with my father again after all these years?"

Becky's eyes filled with tears. "I don't know," she wailed. "I was lonely. Your father was there. Maybe it's that simple."

"I won't judge you, Becky, but I can't condone what you've done." I heard my voice break, but I finished what I'd begun to say. "You were little more than a child the first time, and he took advantage of you, but not now. This time you knew what you were doing."

I turned and walked down the hallway to find Jonas, desperate to erase the image of my father fucking Becky in our house when she was only seventeen and my mother was still alive. Had my mother known? Had Jonas known? Was I the only one who'd never guessed?

I found Jonas sleeping on his side, one arm flung over his pale face and his hair a wild tangle on the pillow. I lowered myself onto the seat next to his bed and reached for his other hand, holding it in both my own. Jonas's eyelids flickered, but he didn't waken. I put my head down on the bed next to him and closed my eyes.

You were right, little brother. The monster we saw was the real Dad. All the rest was just smoke and mirrors.

EIGHTEEN

I was shaken. More shaken than I'd been since my mother's death, but this would not be the end of it. Not by a long shot. Now that Becky had told me her story, she would tell others. It's always that way once a secret is out. Guilt makes people seek absolution, and Becky had a lot to atone for when it came to my family. Maybe that's why, when I found Tobias Olsen languishing against the hood of my car in the hospital parking lot, I agreed to have supper with him. I needed to distance myself from the disturbing picture of my father with a teenaged Becky Holmes. It didn't hurt that Tobias greeted me with a wide grin.

"We'll take my car and pick up some Chinese. I have wine and beer in the fridge at home. It'll give me a chance to fill you in on what I've found out so far about the murder." His eyes hadn't left my face, and I finally raised mine. The intensity of his stare was disconcerting. A shadow crossed his eyes and was gone. It looked like sadness, but I was probably imagining the emotion. Tobias wasn't someone I associated with deep feelings.

I shrugged. "Okay. I guess I could eat."

"Atta girl." He pushed himself from the car and crossed the short distance to a car I hadn't seen before—a 1979 black Mustang restored to mint condition.

"You aren't in uniform," I said, looking from the car to his blue-jeaned legs next to the driver's door.

Tobias stopped and looked at me with his hand on the key

already inserted into the lock. "The odd time they let me have an evening off. This is one of those times as luck would have it."

"Nice car." I ran my fingers along the chrome as I walked around it to the passenger side.

"Yeah. She's my baby. I only take her out for special occasions."

I didn't say anything. This didn't sound like his usual banter. It was close enough to a compliment that I didn't know how to respond.

Tobias lived alone in a second floor apartment in the Bayview Apartments one block in from the downtown strip. It was a tan brick six-storey high rise—high for Duved Cove—built in the housing boom of the late seventies. Tobias's balcony overlooked the back field of Duved Cove Public School, now an alpine field of white, shimmering in the lights strung atop wooden poles around its perimeter.

After a quick tour of his apartment, three sparsely furnished rooms, we sat together on his leather couch, holding plates of chicken fried rice, Szechwan chicken and broccoli beef on our laps. It probably wasn't a meal that called for a 1995 Sauvignon Blanc with a hint of lemon and rose aftertaste, but I wasn't complaining as Tobias filled my glass for a second time.

"Thanks." I took a bite of chicken, swallowed and said, "So what new information have you got for me? Are you close to solving the case?"

Tobias drank from his wineglass before answering. He grimaced. "Usually, I drink beer. This is a bit fruity for my taste." He set his glass on the coffee table. "Not too close to solving the case, no. Interesting thing, though. When I went to the border this afternoon to talk to your dad's usual partner, Charles Mallory, seems you'd already done the breakfast shift." He spoke the words lightly but couldn't conceal his displeasure.

"Yes, I wanted to get to know him better, since he spent so much time with my father these last few years. As you know, my father and I lost touch for the most part, and I just wanted to talk to someone who...well, someone who knew him." The words sounded lame even to me, and I took another large forkful of rice and studied the big screen TV, the only other piece of furniture in the room. It might have served as a more plausible distraction if it had been turned on.

"Charlie told me you seemed most interested in where your father went after work. He also told me your father had girlfriends."

"My father was allowed. My mother's been gone a long time." I was reluctant to share information with Tobias. I was on my own journey of discovery, and I'd found out things I never wanted anyone to know. Let Tobias carry out his own investigation.

"Younger girlfriends. He said you weren't surprised."

"I was surprised they were younger, but not surprised he had some."

"Why's that?"

"My father was in good shape and liked women. Women liked him back." I shrugged. "I'd have been surprised if he didn't date."

"Do you know their names, by any chance?"

"Charles didn't name anyone?"

"No. He said he didn't know."

"If I told you a name, it would only be hearsay. I don't want to spread rumours that could hurt somebody's reputation."

"The name won't be going any further than me."

"I really can't say, Tobias. If you find out on your own, that's one thing. I won't be telling confidences."

He sighed. "You always were stubborn and protective, Maja Larson. I admired that in you when we were kids—how you looked after Jonas like a mother bear. Remember the time you knocked over Eric Vogel when he took Jonas's lunch pail? Man, you were some kind of fierce. I like protective women." He set his empty plate on the coffee table and picked up his wineglass. "Is that what you're doing here, Maja? Looking out for Jonas? Making sure I don't find out anything that points his way?"

"You're the detective. You tell me."

"I'll find out, you know. One way or the other. It might be easier if you just told me and hand over what you know like you have nothing to hide. Might go better in the end." He sank back into the couch and stretched his legs out in front of him. He eyed me over the rim of his glass as he drank.

"So basically, you're no closer to finding out who killed my father, is that it?"

"I wouldn't say that. I know your father was making money, probably illegally." Tobias held up one hand to stop me as I began to protest. "And he was likely dating a married woman. I'd say that's two lines of possibility right there. Would you happen to have found out anything you want to share with me about his finances?"

I thought it over. It wouldn't hurt to give Tobias something to keep him busy. Tossing him a bone might even generate a decent lead. "Dad liked to gamble at the Fortune Bay Casino on his way home from work."

"Bit out of the way?"

"I thought so too. The guy I talked to this afternoon said Dad never won that much..."

"Whoa right there! You went to the Casino this afternoon?"

I nodded. "Seems it's just been taken over by the Motego brothers. I gather it wasn't a happy takeover for Rainy Wynona. Do you know the Motego boys?"

"Let's say they're well known to law enforcement. Shit." Tobias slapped a hand on the couch. "This could be the connection we're after."

I could see the wheels in Tobias's head grinding into action. It would be good if his investigation went the casino route and left my friends and family to me.

"This has been fun, Tobias, but I'm kind of zonked and should be getting home. My cellphone is out of battery, and I forgot the charger at home in Ottawa, so I haven't been in touch with Claire all day. She's probably wondering where I've gotten to." I set my plate on top of his and stood too fast. The wine and sudden motion made me light-headed. I waited for the feeling to pass.

Tobias stood too. "I was planning to take you dancing after we ate. Figured you should see the nightlife before you return to the staid married life in Ottawa with Stu."

"Who told you married life had to be staid, and it's with Sam, not Stu."

Tobias laughed. "That's the other thing I always liked about you, Maja Larson. It never took much to get a rise. Not to mention the only place people dance in Duved Cove is out of excitement when they knock down all ten pins in the bowling alley."

"Another time then," I said.

"Another time."

If I hadn't known better, I would have sworn the look on Tobias's face was wistful. It was a disconcerting thought.

"Mom's upstairs lying down," Gunnar said, spooning another scoop of Kraft Dinner into his mouth and turning a page of the comic book he was reading. His eyes weren't on the page, though. They followed my progress across the kitchen to the sink, where

I filled a glass with cold tap water. By the time I walked over to the table and sat across from him, his head was back down and he was making a show of ignoring me. His blond hair had grown into his eyes, and he was using it as protection from my gaze. I looked at his thin shoulders and felt a sadness for all he was having to deal with at such a young age. A murdered grandfather and a father with depression. It was a lot for anyone to handle, let alone a twelve-year-old kid.

"I saw your dad today," I began. This opening made him lift his head, although he kept his eyes focused on the comic book. "He was sleeping. I'm hoping they let him come home tomorrow."

"Mom says he's better off in the hospital. He can't hurt himself there." Gunnar spoke without emotion. If it wasn't for the tremor in his jaw, I might have bought his tough-guy act.

"I don't believe your dad would ever intentionally hurt himself. He just gets very sad sometimes and needs some medicine to balance what is going on in his body. It's the same as someone who has the flu or a broken arm. They need time to get better."

"My friends say he's crazy."

Gunnar's words were shocking, but I understood. I'd felt the same shame for my mother. I'd tried to protect my mother from my friends' curious stares and questions, to keep my family's secrets hidden away from public scrutiny. Gunnar was doing the same thing for his father.

"Your dad is definitely not crazy. Your friends don't know anything."

"I know that. They're all stupid."

"So how's hockey going? What position do you play?"

"Right wing. It's okay."

"Do you score many goals?"

"I was till the coach stopped giving me a regular shift."

"How come he did that?"

Gunnar's face twisted with sudden anger. "He said I was fighting too much on the ice. He *said* I had to learn a lesson."

"And were you fighting a lot?"

Gunnar shrugged. "I guess. He didn't need to bench me though."

We sat quietly for a moment before I said, "Did you spend a lot of time with Grandpa? You must miss him."

Gunnar finally met my eyes. His were filled with secrets. He seemed to be thinking about what he was going to say to me. Then he looked past me toward the doorway. I turned. Claire was standing behind me, her arms folded across her chest, dressed in a silk housecoat the colour of butter, her feet bare.

"It's time for you to do your homework, Gunnar. You know better than to sit there reading a comic." Her voice was firm— harsher than it needed to be.

Gunnar glanced back at me then collected his bowl and fork. "Okay, Mom."

I watched him skirt the table as he headed for the door to the hallway. Claire crossed the room and sat in his empty seat. She promptly pulled out a package of cigarettes and book of matches from her pocket. She offered me one, but I declined.

"Did you have a good day?" she squinted at me through a haze of smoke. "I was starting to wonder if something had happened to you."

"Yes, thanks. I thought I'd do a bit of sightseeing before I head back home. It's such beautiful country, and I've missed it."

"I guess we take it for granted. Did you make it over to see Jonas?"

"Yes, but he was sleeping. Becky said he had a bad day."

Was it my imagination, or did Claire flinch at Becky's name? Perhaps I was looking for signs and reading too much into her expression.

"I expect he'll be back home within the next day or two," she said. "How much longer are you planning to stay? Oh, I should tell you that Sam called earlier. He says your cellphone isn't working."

"My cell's out of battery. I'll call him in a bit. I'm not sure how much longer I'll stay. I want to get over to the house tomorrow and start tidying it up. It's in quite a state after the break-in."

"Sam mentioned he'd bought airplane tickets for next week. He wanted me to tell you."

"So the trip is on," I mumbled to myself, and for the rest of our conversation, my mind was working on how to swallow my anger and stand up to my husband. I had no intention of going to a tropical island, not while Jonas was struggling and not before I knew that he and Claire were safe from Tobias Olsen's investigation.

The first time I called Sam, I got a busy signal. A half hour later, I managed to get through. I'd almost decided to give up and try again in the morning when he picked up on the third ring.

"Maja, I've been trying to reach you. Where have you been all day? Claire wasn't certain."

"Oh, just doing some sightseeing. Tomorrow I'm heading to my father's to start sorting through his things. Jonas is still in the hospital, so it's up to me."

"Claire said Jonas had a collapse. I'm sorry it's been so rough. I'd come in a minute if it wasn't so crazy at the office."

"It's been toughest on Jonas, Claire and Gunnar. Did Claire mention they believe my father was murdered?" I was sure she'd let it slip and thought it best to tell him so he wouldn't think I was hiding information.

"She told me. I hope you're not getting involved, Maja. I worry about you with a murderer running loose."

"They certainly aren't after me. I think whoever hit Dad with a shovel did it in a moment of anger. I'd only be concerned if I believed it was premeditated."

"I miss you, Maja. Did Claire tell you I bought the tickets? I thought we'd try Cuba this time. We fly out Sunday."

"Oh, Sam, I'm not sure I can make such an early date. I might still have another week here and then my practice... Can we postpone a few weeks?"

"I had to lock in the package. No way to change or we pay a hefty fee."

"We may need to pay the fee. I can't see making it for Sunday. I wish you'd cleared it with me before booking."

I could hear Sam's sharp intake of breath. "I'll be going, even if you decide not to. I'm sure I can unload your ticket on somebody. I'd rather you came, but if not...."

I was suddenly wearier than I'd been in a long time. My head felt stuffed with wool, and pain had started behind my left eye. Was this what it came down to then? A contest of wills? "Do what you have to do," I said softly.

Sam didn't respond, and the silence lengthened uncomfortably. In the past, his silent treatment would have worked. I was always the first to back down.

"I'll call you soon," I said at last.

"Fine," Sam said. A moment later, the dial tone buzzed in my ear.

I hung up slowly and stared at the phone for a long time, wondering what had just transpired beneath our civilized words. Was I being contrary on purpose? Should I phone back and apologize? Would agreeing to the trip keep my marriage on course? I reached for the receiver and dialed the Ottawa area code before hanging up a second time. I wasn't ready to make nice yet. I'd sleep on the idea of going to Cuba and see how I felt in the morning.

NINETEEN

In the capricious nature of late winter weather, with morning light, the temperature began to climb. By the time I greeted the day, the mercury had settled some five degrees above freezing, and the sun was beaming down from a cloudless blue sky. Claire and Gunnar were long gone when I finally made my way to the kitchen, drawn by the smell of strong coffee that Claire had made and left warming. I poured a cup and stood in front of the kitchen window. Dagger-like chunks of icicles that hung from the eaves had turned into dripping faucets. Sunlight reflected off the snow in a shimmering carpet.

I took my time getting ready—three cups of coffee thick with cream while I read the paper, a generous, hot shower followed by a lost hour of morning talk shows on the television. Finally, I was ready to go to my father's house to begin the task of sorting through the remains of his life. I poured one last cup of coffee as comfort for the road.

The walk to the car was made treacherous by a mixture of patchy ice and water that pooled in the laneway. The cold from the icy puddles seeped through my boots, but my feet stayed dry. I approached my rented car slowly but still slipped on the slick ice hidden beneath the water. It would have been a certain tumble into the brink except that I managed to grab onto the car's roof. Afterwards, I stood fishing for my car keys in my purse, lifting my face to feel the full warmth of the sun. Today, I didn't mind that the car heater wasn't working properly. I even opened the window a crack to let in the fresh winter air that now hinted of spring winds, muddy fields and new growth. The strong sunshine had turned the roads into slush the consistency of cooked oatmeal, but even that wasn't enough to dampen my spirits. This change in the weather had invigorated me more than anything else in recent days—enough that I could face a day of family memories.

The warm weather had drawn my neighbours out of their homes. I passed two joggers then three boys huddled together in yellow rain slickers and black rubber boots, building a water dam beside the creek that paralleled the highway. Closer to my father's, I spotted Mrs. Lingstrom walking from town with a cloth shopping bag of groceries, a loaf of French bread sticking out of the top. I slowed and pulled onto the shoulder. Mrs. Lingstrom glanced my way and smiled when she recognized me. I leaned over and swung the passenger door open. She climbed in slowly, her movements deliberate, like someone who's being careful not to reinjure a sore back. Still, she was moving more easily than the last time I'd had coffee in her kitchen, and the hands that set the shopping bag at her feet were not as deformed as I remembered. Arthritis could be crippling one day and better the next, I knew. Medication helped, but it wasn't perfect.

"I thought that was you, Maja. Normally I don't mind the walk when I'm having a good day, but this is a nice chance to see you again. How are you, my dear?"

"Good. I'm finally going to my father's to begin sorting through his things."

"Yah, I wondered who would be getting around to that. I thought it would be Claire."

"Claire's teaching today, and Jonas, well, Jonas is resting."

Mrs. Lingstrom nodded. She'd tied a triangular-shaped gold scarf with a rose pattern over her hair, knotting it at the nape of her neck. The splash of colour contrasted with the greyness in her face and her black wool coat. She seemed unwell, the whites of her eyes tinged with yellow and an angry rash visible on one hand.

"Have you heard from Katherine?" I asked, taking my eyes from the road to glance at her. It would be good if someone were home to help Mrs. Lingstrom.

"Yah. Yah. Katherine is on a trip. She'll be back in a few weeks." Mrs. Lingstrom waved a hand back and forth as if brushing away a cobweb. "I tell her I'm going to be fine. I've been living on my own a long time."

"I'm glad Katherine is enjoying a holiday, but I'm sorry I'll miss her. Can I take you anywhere later? Do you have errands or appointments in town?"

"I have all I need, but thank you for asking, Maja."

The driveway was potted with tire ruts and melting snow. The house didn't hold up well under the scrutiny of the glaring sun. It needed work, but the sale of my father's land would devalue her property even further. The thought of what lay ahead for her and others along our road made me sad.

"I would ask you for tea, but my kitchen is a mess. I haven't done the dishes." She turned her face to me, but her eyes were lowered as if she was too embarrassed to meet my eyes. I didn't want her to feel that way because of me.

"I would have to decline anyhow. My father's house will take the entire afternoon." I smiled. "I'll try to see you before I leave."

"I would like that."

I waited until Mrs. Lingstrom had entered her front door then slowly turned the car back around and started down the drive, the tires jolting up and down like a bronco ride in the uneven grooves of slushy snow. Before turning onto the main road, I let the car idle for a moment and looked back at the house one last time. My eyes were drawn to a movement, a curtain dropping into place at the upstairs bedroom window, a glimpse of a ghostly pale face and tangled hair. I must have been mistaken. Mrs. Lingstrom hadn't had time to put away her groceries and climb the stairs at the front of the house. She wouldn't have had any reason to stand in the shadows of Katherine's old bedroom window watching me, just as there had been no need for her to lie about Katherine being on holiday if she was really still in the house, staring down at me from her bedroom window like Mr. Rochester's crazed wife in *Jane Eyre*. I wouldn't give in to such a flight of fancy, but for the first time that morning, I shivered inside the warmth of Claire's borrowed parka.

"Where are you, Katherine Lingstrom?" I said into the rearview mirror as the Lingstrom house disappeared from view. "And if you're home, why won't you come out to play?"

I was about to turn into my father's driveway when I saw a police car round the corner coming slowly towards me. At first I thought Tobias was popping up with uncomfortable regularity but then saw that it wasn't him after all. David Keating was behind the wheel. With his aviator sunglasses and black fisherman cap, I almost didn't recognize him until I saw his droopy moustache. He waved and turned right into the driveway ahead of me. I followed and parked alongside his car. We got out at the same time and walked towards the backyard, trudging together through wet snow that hadn't been shovelled since the last snowfall. I'd have to clear the laneway or it would freeze as soon as the temperature returned to below freezing. David had his dark green parka open, and I could see a radio and gun holster hanging on his belt.

"I didn't get a chance to say congratulations on your fourth child," I said. "Boy or girl?"

"Our fourth boy, if you can believe it. Olive was desperate for a girl and cried for a week solid after the birth. The doctor said it was hormonal, but that didn't make it any easier. Now she wants to try for a fifth." David grinned wryly.

"Wow, five kids. Is that Olive Chan, the math whiz from two years behind me in high school?"

"The very same. We married when I was six years out of high school. Our oldest is turning seventeen next month. I tell Olive I'm too old to change diapers, but she's determined. Says she's young enough for one more kick at the can. She has effortless pregnancies and is never happier than when she's carrying a kid."

We stopped at the bottom of the deck. I looked across the yard to where my father had been struck down in the snow. Then I looked back at David. I couldn't see his eyes behind the reflected light of his green tinted sunglasses.

"How about I help you clean up for a bit?" he asked softly. "I know it's a real mess after the break in, and I have a few hours to kill. I'm actually just off shift."

"Shouldn't you be heading home to get some sleep?"

"My sleep is all screwed up. This is my last night shift, and I try to stay up late so I can get to bed closer to when I should."

"Well, okay then. I could use the help." I started wading through the wet snow up the stairs to the back door. "I haven't actually been back since the time I saw you here. It's taken me awhile to get up my courage to face this again."

"I understand. I'm glad I was going by when you made your

return trip. It's not great to tackle these things alone if you don't need to."

I thought I'd prepared myself for a second look at the destruction in the house, but I was mistaken. We stepped into the kitchen, where the stench of rotting food and the violent mess strewn about the room made the bile rise in my throat. My eyes watered and the room blurred. I blinked rapidly.

"This looks as good a place as any to start," I said.

"First job is to clean out the food," agreed David.

For the next three hours, we worked nonstop. First, we put the kitchen back in order then washed down the cupboards and floor. The sickening smell of garbage was replaced by that of Windex and pine cleaner. I sat back on my heels, where I'd been kneeling on the floor and surveyed the space. David put down the sponge he'd been using to scrub the sink and leaned against the counter.

"Well, this room is livable. Are you ready to let me buy you a late lunch?"

"I believe I owe *you* lunch for all your help." I got to my feet. "How about Frida's?"

"Let's take my car," David said while putting on his parka. "We should be late enough to escape the lunch crowd."

David and I took the window table—the one that was becoming my usual place to sit. I ordered a club sandwich with salad and a coffee. David went for the breakfast special: fried eggs, slabs of ham, hash browns and heavily buttered brown toast. We tucked in like two starving waifs, and it wasn't long before my plate was clean. Not far behind me, David soaked up the last of the egg yolk with a piece of toast and popped it into his mouth. He leaned back

163

and sighed contentedly, rubbing a hand across his shaved head.

"This is the time I really miss smoking. There was nothing more enjoyable than a hit of nicotine to finish off a meal."

"How long since you quit?"

"Two years, three months and four days." He laughed. "Not that I'm keeping track. You ever smoked, Maja?"

Had I ever smoked? I thought back to the summer Katherine and I pulled out half a pack of Players that we'd stashed in the hollow of a tree trunk at the back of her property. We'd managed to smoke three each before rain filled the opening and the cigarettes became too soggy to light. Katherine had taken up smoking in her teens, but I'd somehow refrained, even though I'd liked the taste and the feel of the cigarette between my fingers.

"Luckily, nothing more than the experimental puff. It's never good when a doctor smokes. Hard to give people medical advice when you're doing in your own lungs."

David reached for his coffee cup. "So, you hadn't spoken to your father in a while before he died?"

I shook my head. "We weren't close. I don't know if I regret that now or not." I was speaking more to myself than David, but his head tilted as he studied me.

"Your dad was a hard man to know. I had the feeling he wasn't all on the surface."

"You're the second person this week to say that." Charlie Mallory had made the same observation the day before. Maybe Dad hadn't hidden his true nature as well as we'd believed when we were younger. "Do you know why my father was dismissed from the police force?"

"What have you heard?"

"That evidence went missing that my father had been in charge of, and he chose the job at the border over an investigation."

164

"That sounds about right. It was all before my time, so I can't add much more." David took a drink of coffee, his eyes never leaving my face. He grinned and his voice became playful. "I gather your father never kept a journal...or a safety deposit box full of secret tapes or anything."

"Nothing I'm aware of. He wasn't a man to spend a lot of time reading or writing, as I recall. Introspection was definitely not on his to-do list." Then I remembered the boxes of books in my old bedroom and shifted in my seat. I'd have to look through them more closely when I was alone. Maybe their subject matter would give a clue to the man he'd been at the end.

"Do you know what evidence went missing?" I asked.

"You've circled back to that, have you? From what I was told, it was money, which is never a good thing."

"A lot of money?"

"Several thousand. Nothing that would make anyone wealthy."

"Where did the money come from?"

"A raid of some sort, apparently. Afterwards, some of the cash went missing, and it was never recovered."

"I can't think that my father would chance his career over a small amount of money."

"It was never proven that he took it. He accepted the border job instead of putting the force through an outside investigation, which would have been stressful for everyone. Chief Anders said your dad had been looking for a change anyway."

"Convenient that the border job opened up just then."

"Yeah. Sometimes life works out that way."

David's eyes shifted towards the door. My eyes followed the direction of his gaze in time to see Tobias crossing the short distance to our table. He stopped a few feet from me. He was dressed in uniform under his open jacket and stood looking down at us, his hat in one hand. His green eyes flashed like flecks of jade in the sunlight streaming in through the plate glass window. He stared at me for a moment before focusing on David. His expression was grim.

"I'm glad you haven't made it home yet. We have a missing person call."

David's face transformed from relaxed to on-duty. He stood quickly and shrugged into his parka. "Child?"

"No." Tobias glanced from me to David. "Kevin Wilders reported Becky missing about an hour ago. I've been searching all the places she might be but could use help."

A fluttering rose in my chest. "I thought a person had to be missing forty-eight hours before the police got involved."

Tobias looked at me again. "She didn't come home last night. Kevin's worried." He shrugged. "It could be nothing, but it's not like Becky."

"This is on me," I said to David as he reached for his wallet. "Let me know if I can help with the search if you don't find her right away."

"Thanks, Maja. Been good talking to you. I hope to see you again before you go."

Tobias nodded and smiled quickly at me before following David toward the entrance.

I wasn't ready to think the worst about Becky's disappearance and chose to believe she'd left town voluntarily, maybe to get her head on straight. Her disappearance and revealing her affair with my father couldn't be a coincidence. If they didn't find her by nightfall, I would definitely let Tobias know about her relationship with my father. Their affair would be a secret that I could no longer keep.

TWENTY

I decided to return to my father's house to continue working. It wasn't quite four o'clock, and the fatigue coursing through my body had been replaced by a nervous energy at the news of Becky's disappearance. I needed to keep busy. I needed to stop thinking about the bad things that could have happened to her. The hardware store was practically empty of customers, and it didn't take long to gather up cardboard boxes, garbage bags, newspapers and tape. I intended to pack up my father's smaller possessions and put them into storage before returning to Ottawa. I'd phone for storage space first thing in the morning.

This time, I bypassed the kitchen and living room and climbed the stairs to my father's bedroom. I wanted to sort through what remained of my mother's possessions first, to make sure they were safely handled and organized in boxes. I ignored the ruined mattress and slit pillows and kneeled beside the maple hope chest, careful not to crush any of the scattered photos and ornaments that had been tossed about like so much garbage. I began with the photos, carefully piling them into a smaller box that I found amongst the jumble. I'd have to place them back into the albums when I had more time.

The pictures were a trip into my past—Jonas and me at different heights and ages, holding hands, smiling into the camera; my father and mother in front of our house; Katherine and me on the swing; me walking down the road with Katherine and my mother. I held up the last photo and placed my fingertips on my mother's face, tracing its outline as if I were reading a story in Braille. I could find no sign in her eyes or the curve of her mouth of what she would do to herself. In the photo she is smiling patiently into the camera while Katherine and I stand a little apart. We are thirteen years old, and the budding breasts and soft curves of the women we are becoming are visible through our cotton blouses and shorts. Our legs are coltish and brown from long summer days in the sun.

The details of the day came rushing back to me. My father had a new Nikon camera and had followed us up the road, clicking pictures and fancying himself a photographer for *National Geographic.* No matter what he did, he always believed himself the best, or at the very least, the expert. We knew better than to question his omnipotence. I looked closer. My mother and I are playing along with his latest obsession, posing prettily with demure smiles. Katherine is staring at the ground, her arms wrapped around her middle as if she is cold. She doesn't look happy. She'd been quiet that afternoon, and it wasn't long afterward that we stopped hanging around together. With a flash of insight, I see that by the time this picture was taken, she'd already taken up with the wilder crowd and was on the verge of leaving me behind. The realization of what lay ahead for each of us as I stared into our long-ago faces was difficult to take. I dropped the photo into the pile and scooped up the rest of the photos without looking at them.

I spent another hour wrapping the ornaments that hadn't been smashed before placing them gently into a larger box, tossing broken glass and ruined mementos into a garbage bag as I went. Partway through, I turned on the overhead light as the shafts of sunshine shortened and the room darkened into semi-gloom. I drifted towards the window but left the blinds raised as I looked through the dark, plumy branches of a spruce tree. It would soon be night, and I didn't want to be alone in this house much longer. It was silly, but I'd experienced a feeling of uneasiness in the restaurant that hadn't left me. I was trying my best to keep fear and grief from overwhelming me. My mother's and father's spirits hovered beyond reach in this house, and sadness rose in my throat. I wanted to sit down and cry, but once the tears started flowing, I knew I wouldn't be able to stop.

I returned to my task with renewed concentration, determined to finish the work I'd laid out for myself. The more progress I made now, the quicker I could return to Sam and the security of our lives in Ottawa. Once I was sure Jonas was safe and back on track, I would leave and never come back.

When I had wrapped and stored as many of my mother's possessions as I could find, I stood and stretched. My legs had cramped, and I walked gingerly around the space to ease the aching in my joints. Near the bed, I stopped and put a hand to my wildly beating chest. I turned toward the door and froze in place. Something had struck the floor in the hallway at the bottom of the stairs and clattered across the floor. Seconds later, a floorboard creaked. *Somebody was in the house.* Had I locked the back door? Was somebody even now creeping up the stairs hoping to catch me by surprise?

I forced myself to leave the bedroom and walk the length of the hallway, eerily layered in darkness. I stood at the head of the steep stairs and peered down into the shadowy blackness. "Tobias, is that you?" I called, my voice echoing hollowly in the stairwell. "Claire? Is anybody there?"

I could sense another person in the house. It was as if the walls surrounding us held their collective breath, waiting for me to make a move. I took a tentative step forward then stopped. If someone was here to do me harm, I would face them square on. I would not go gently. I stepped more determinedly back onto the landing and felt along the wall until my hand touched the light switch. The stairwell leapt into brightness. Nobody was standing on the stairs or in the hallway. I raced back into the bedroom that my father had made into a workout room and searched for a weapon by the light from the hall. My hand closed on a five pound weight, which should give me a chance. My movements were reflected back at me in the semi-gloom by the mirror lining the wall.

Seconds later, I was back at the head of the stairwell. A scramble of footsteps and the backdoor banging sent me racing down the stairs two at a time. I was too late to catch them. I flicked on the outside lights, but whoever had been in the house had disappeared into the night. Mushy footsteps were visible on the deck, but half-filled with water. They offered no clue that I could see. I leaned against the doorjamb and considered my options. I could give chase, or I could lock up the house and tell Tobias what had happened. I preferred the second option. I'd used up all the bravery I had in my frantic rush to meet the intruder. I shut the door hard and locked it before going in search of my jacket and boots.

I drove faster than I should have down the country road to my brother's house. It was a relief to see Claire's van in the driveway. Lights were on in the kitchen and living room as well as the back porch. I parked behind Claire, took my glove off as I walked, and slid my hand along the hood of her van. Heat radiated from its engine. Claire must have gotten home not long ahead of me.

I found her reading a magazine at the kitchen table, a cup of coffee in front of her and a fresh cigarette burning in the ashtray at her elbow. Her head was tilted and resting on a hand cupped under her chin. She looked up as I entered. Sometimes I forgot how beautiful she was. When the tension left her body and her features were relaxed, she was very striking.

Black hair tucked behind her ears emphasized high cheekbones and wide doe-shaped eyes, steel grey in the bright kitchen light. "There you are, Maja. I was about to send out the troops."

"I was at Dad's most of the day."

"Ahh. Well, I had a pleasant surprise today. I came home and found Jonas sleeping on the couch."

"He's home?"

"He is. He was discharged in the morning but didn't tell me. Says it felt good to walk outside again, and he didn't want to bother me at work."

I dropped into the chair across from her. "That's good news anyhow. Where's Jonas now?"

"Sleeping upstairs. I nipped out to get some cigs, and he was heading up to bed. Said he was still exhausted but feeling more like himself. Gunnar is spending the night at his friend's."

I watched her eyes. "Have you heard that Becky Wilders is missing?"

Claire's gaze didn't waver. "No, I didn't know. Has she skipped town?"

"What makes you think that?"

Claire picked up her cigarette and inhaled deeply. She blew the smoke out in a stream. "It didn't look to me like she and Kevin were getting along all that well. He's at the garage all the time, and she's stuck at home with his brats."

"It doesn't sound like you're very fond of Becky...or her kids."

"Why would I be?" Claire's jaw jutted out stubbornly. "It was awfully uncomfortable with her around when Jonas and I were first married, and it's never been great between us. She told people she was waiting for Jonas to see the light and go back to her. I hate it when women can't let go, especially when they're not wanted. Jonas needed her clinging onto him like a hole in the head."

The cold animosity in Claire's voice was reflected in the hardness of her eyes, and I couldn't match her stare for long. "Did you know Becky was seeing Dad this past year?" I asked.

Claire snorted. "The whole town knew. I'm surprised Kevin didn't do something about it." Her eyes turned cunning. "Or maybe he has."

A noise in the hallway made us both turn our heads toward the door. Jonas was standing in the entranceway with his hands at his side, watching us. He wore jeans and a cable knit sweater, and he hadn't shaved in several days, but his eyes were clear and his hands were still. I stood to hug him, my discussion with Claire momentarily forgotten. Jonas hugged me back, but just barely.

"I see my wife's been keeping you amused. She's good at keeping people entertained." Jonas's voice was bitter.

A look that was so angry passed between them that I felt a rush of heat to my cheeks. Suddenly, more than anything, I wanted to walk out into the night and never come back. I'd leave Jonas to his fate and Claire to her misery.

Jonas sensed my change in mood. He'd always been sensitive to me, even when his despair was at its worst. His eyes softened. "Want to walk with me to Hadrian's?" he breathed into my ear.

I hesitated, then nodded. "If you're up to it."

"I am." He looked back at Claire. "Maja and I are going out. Don't wait up."

Claire didn't bother to respond. She'd already lowered her head to read the magazine, her hand reaching for her cigarette, her beauty momentarily extinguished by the ugly scowl marring her features.

In the end, we drove to Hadrian's in my car. The melting snow had created huge puddles that made walking unpleasant, especially in the dark. Jonas looked worn out from his stay in the hospital and agreed without arguing to my offer to drive. We chose a table in the corner near the fireplace. Somebody I didn't know was celebrating a fortieth birthday on the other side of the room with a boisterous crowd of friends. The noise was a welcome kind of energy. It had been a while since I'd heard laughter and people having a good time. It took my mind off the fear I'd experienced in my father's house. This was an ordinary night with ordinary people who weren't worried about a killer breaking into their home. Hadrian brought us a couple of beers but didn't linger. He was alone and the place was hopping.

I angled my chair so that I could study my brother. His hair had the brittle look of someone who's been ill, and his skin was just this side of waxen, but the anxiety was gone from his eyes. By the looseness of his shirt, he'd dropped several pounds, weight he could ill-afford to lose. He met my stare.

"Just a mini-meltdown, but sorry you had to see it." His crooked grin was tired.

"Don't concern yourself. I'm glad you're feeling better." I put my hand on his wrist for a moment before pulling it back to lift my beer.

"I'll be sleeping more than usual, but the hole is getting some sunlight. Galloway is getting good at pumping me with the right dose of medication now. It doesn't take as long as it used to before the fog lifts. There are shades of grey now and not just bottomless black."

"Gradients of light are always there in the black, even when you think nothing will be right again," I said.

Somebody let out a whoop at the party table. Mick Jagger began singing "Brown Sugar" in the overhead speakers. Jonas and I watched the drunken revelry for a bit, each lost in our own thoughts. Hadrian crossed the floor to another table with a full tray of drinks held high above his head.

"Did you know Dad was visiting the Fortune Bay Casino on a regular basis?" I asked.

'Doesn't surprise me. Is that where he got the money for the boat and truck?"

"No. Does make you wonder what he was up to, though."

Jonas started peeling the label off his bottle. "I found her, you know," he said. "That day. I wish I'd never gone. It always slides back to that moment whenever I have these...episodes." His fingers began picking more frenetically at the paper. His eyes were wide and unblinking.

"Found who?" I wasn't following his train of thought. Maybe the medication was affecting his short-term memory.

He set the bottle on the table but kept both hands wrapped around its base, like he was holding onto a lifeline. "Mom. Mother. That day. It was me who found her." Jonas turned his tortured blue eyes to mine, and I knew it was the first time he'd spoken of it.

"I thought it was Dad who found her." My voice was rising, and I made myself stay calm. "Why did you never tell me?"

Jonas shrugged. "What good could it do? It wouldn't have brought her back."

My mind scrambled back in time. I'd been as much a basket case as Jonas. I'd avoided Duved Cove after the funeral. Guilt filled me. Jonas kept talking.

"I still wake up sometimes, seeing her swinging there from the rafter—I cut her down and tried...tried to breathe life into her. Her feet and hands were blue. Her tongue was sticking out sideways, and her face..." Jonas's voice trailed off. He dropped his head and clasped both hands in front of him as if he were praying. "She would have hated anybody to see her that way. I knew she was gone, but I tried. I got her down and did mouth to mouth and pumped her chest. I kept thinking it couldn't be true, that I was going to wake up from the nightmare. I couldn't believe she'd leave us that way. I didn't know how I was going to tell you."

I slid off my chair and knelt beside him. I wrapped my arms around his waist and held him tight, my head against his stomach. One of his hands came down to rest on my head, and he smoothed back my hair over and over again. When I finally sat back in my chair, my cheeks were salty with tears that I brushed away with the back of my hand. I looked past Jonas towards the bar and saw Hadrian quickly avert his eyes from mine. I couldn't worry about what he had seen. Let him think what he would.

"I always believed it was Dad who'd found her," I said softly. "How cruel that it was you."

Jonas squared his chair so that he was facing me. Our knees were touching. "Something happened that pushed her over the edge. Dad was gone for a reason, and I don't know what it was. I couldn't reach you until the next morning, and he showed up home just before you made it from Bemidji."

I shook my head. "This is not how I remember it. You're rewriting history, and I can't take it in." Questions needed answering. "How did Dad seem when he got home?"

"Tired. Hung over...relieved when he found out."

"No," I wailed.

"I thought I was mistaken, that he couldn't be happy that she was dead. I've spent a lifetime trying to believe I misread his look."

"Did he ever say where he'd been? What their last conversation was about?"

Jonas shook his head. "He never spoke of it. The times I asked, he changed the subject."

We looked at each other then, mutual horror rising in our psyches like a Fundy tide. I had blamed my father for my mother's death, but never like this, never contemplating that he'd been happy to have her commit suicide.

"My god, Jonas. *What happened?* What was so much worse between them that she killed herself?"

Jonas whispered, "And why was he so glad she did?"

TWENTY-ONE

I drove Jonas home and went in search of Tobias. It was time to tell him about Becky's affair with my father and his possible affair with Claire. I was too tired to tackle Claire on my own. I knew that my close relationship with Jonas would prevent her from ever confiding in me. By telling Tobias, I knew that I was opening up Jonas to possible motive, but I also knew he was innocent of killing our father. Call it putting on blinders, but if Jonas hadn't killed my father after finding my mother hanging in the basement, he never would. He did not have it in him.

I first drove past the police station at the edge of the downtown. It was a squat red brick building set back a little from the street by a circular driveway. It was also locked up tight with a notice on the door that listed numbers to call in case of an emergency. My information about Becky and my father didn't seem like an emergency, but I wasn't prepared to go home yet.

I cruised towards Tobias's apartment building, not really expecting him to be home. I wasn't disappointed. His car was not in its parking spot, and the lights were out in his windows.

He was probably out looking for Becky, if she hadn't been found. I sat in the back parking lot for a full minute, deciding where to look next. It struck me that the best place to find out if Becky had been found would be from Kevin, and I put the car into gear. Hopefully, Tobias had been in touch with Kevin or would be again soon.

Kevin and Becky's house was lit up, a light on in every room, as if Kevin were using the house as a beacon to draw Becky home. His tow truck was in the driveway with a police car parked behind it. I gave silent thanks as I pulled my car over as far as I could on the other side of the road. I stepped out of the car and into a black puddle that wrapped my foot in cold water inside my boot.

"Crap," I said and pushed my other leg over the puddle, managing to keep one foot dry. I shook one leg like a dog in the middle of the road before limping to the Wilders' front door.

Kevin answered my ring almost immediately. His face was haggard, his jowls drooping and his eyes lined with red. I knew immediately that Becky was still missing. I reached partway around his shoulder in an awkward hug.

"No word then?"

"No. Nothing. Come in, Maja. I'm just talking to Tobias."

Kevin stepped back, and I had a clear view of Tobias sitting on the couch in the living room drinking from a mug. He lifted a hand in greeting, his face relaxed and his eyes watchful. From the back of the house, I could hear the television and the murmur of girls' voices, likely the fourteen-year-old twins.

"I just made coffee," Kevin said. "I'll get you a cup."

"Thanks, Kevin. I don't mean to intrude." I pulled off my boots, and the right one came off with a sucking sound that made Tobias smile. I tried to let the carpet soak up the worst of the wetness from my sock as I limped over to sit on the couch next to him.

"I was looking for *you*, actually," I whispered as I sat down. "I have something...private...to tell you."

Tobias's eyebrows went up. "You've come to your senses and know we're made for each other?" He grinned, but it was a tired attempt at levity.

"What makes me think you've used that line before? No, I

need to speak with you alone, in private."

"Alone, in private. I've been waiting for years to hear those words come out of your mouth, Maja."

"This isn't the time to joke. I have information that could be important."

"You're right." His eyes went toward the doorway as Kevin walked into the room. He was holding another mug of coffee as he lumbered toward me. The cup splashed hot coffee onto my hand as he handed it to me, but he didn't notice.

"No sign of Becky," he said as he plopped down onto a wingback chair. The legs bounced under his weight. "It looks like she's left Duved Cove and run out on me and the kids."

I turned to Tobias. "Is that what you've concluded after only a few hours of looking?"

"She's an adult, Maja, capable of walking out and never being found if she doesn't want to be. Of course, we're going to keep looking, but it's a real possibility that she left under her own steam." Tobias's eyes signalled a warning.

I glanced over at Kevin, who looked uncomfortable. He nodded.

"She left one other time, about a year back. Went to her sister's in Wisconsin. I'm hoping that's where she went this time too. I've put in a call, and we'll know as soon as she arrives."

I sipped my coffee. She should already be there, if she'd left the night before. I didn't give voice to my doubt. "I spoke with her last night at the hospital," I offered, and both Kevin and Tobias sat up straighter to look at me. "I went to see Jonas. Becky and I chatted for a minute at the front desk."

"That must have been before I saw you outside around eight thirty. You never mentioned talking with Becky," Tobias said. The lightness had left his voice.

179

"Her shift was over at eight. You might have been the last one to see her besides her replacement," Kevin said. "She never came home."

"Yes, it would have been close to eight. She was reading a magazine."

"Was she upset by anything?" Tobias was now watching me very closely.

"No. Nothing I can think of."

I smiled reassuringly in Kevin's direction, but the truth made my cheeks hot. I thought guiltily of the confession I'd pulled out of her. It had upset both of us, and I wondered if it was the reason she had disappeared from Duved Cove—if she really had left on her own. There was no way I was going to tell Kevin that Becky had slept with my father in high school.

Kevin might have bought my story, but Tobias didn't look satisfied. He gulped down the last of his coffee and pushed himself out of the chair. "I'll see you to your car, if you're ready to leave," he said to me. His offer had an edge to it.

I took a first taste of hot coffee and set the cup on the end table. "It's getting late, and I'm sure you're tired," I said to Kevin. "I'll call again tomorrow to find if you've heard anything."

"Sure thing," Kevin said. "See yourselves out. I have to go check on Timmy. He's having trouble sleeping since his world was turned upside down by this. Becky always tucked him in. He asks for her over and over again, and I have no idea what to tell him."

I hugged Kevin before he left the living room. Tobias shook his hand.

I saved my wet boot for last and grimaced as I pushed my foot into its cold depths. I straightened and Tobias opened the front door, letting in the cold air. We stepped outside onto the porch. Tobias looked down at my face illuminated by the overhead light. A gust of wind collected snow from the roof and swirled into our faces.

"Why don't we go to your house to talk? I know you'd like to change into something more comfortable." He paused. "Or dry anyhow. I'll follow you over."

"Thanks. It's going to be a pleasure to get out of these boots, but that's all I'll be taking off, just so you know." I pulled the hood of my parka over my head for emphasis.

Tobias smiled. "A man can dream. No harm in that." Then he lifted a hand to brush snow from my cheek before he led the way down the steps.

I sat Tobias at the kitchen table and went about making coffee. I hadn't had a chance to drink much of mine at Kevin's and craved a steaming cup to warm me up. Tobias said that he could manage one more mug. I poured a splash of Scotch into mine, but Tobias waved it off.

"Still on duty," he said, but he sounded regretful.

I slid the cups onto the table and sat across from him. Claire and Jonas were upstairs, and we had the kitchen to ourselves.

"What did you hold back in your Becky story?" Tobias asked. "It's obvious you have more to tell."

I took a sip and shuddered at the bite of the liquor. I'd poured a heftier swig than I'd intended. I took a cleansing breath. "I wouldn't normally talk about this to you, but her disappearance changes things." I hesitated, weighing options in my mind. I couldn't come up with a good reason not to tell Tobias something that might explain Becky's disappearance. "I'm really not sure how many people know, probably everyone in town except you." I eyed him like he should have known since he was a town cop. "But it seems Becky was having an affair with my father the last year of his life."

"Are you sure?"

I nodded. "She told me herself a few days ago, and she admitted it again last night."

"She was risking a lot, a husband and three kids." Tobias pondered what I'd said. "Still, it does fit the fact that she left Kevin last year, indicating she wasn't happy with her marriage."

I concentrated on swirling the Scotch and coffee in my cup and brought the mug closer to my face to inhale the comforting fumes. It would be easy to stop here and not reveal anything further about my father. I didn't enjoy sharing our family secrets, especially with Tobias. When I looked across at him, he was waiting for me to continue. It was his non-judgmental approach to the information that I'd already given that decided me. I set my cup on the table and spoke in a rush, getting the words out before I changed my mind.

"Becky told me last night that she'd had sex with my father when she was in twelfth grade—just once, but it made it easier to turn to him when she and Kevin were having trouble this year."

"That must have been painful for you to hear."

"Oh, yeah. It's not sitting well, but I don't doubt my father did it. He was a man who didn't think through how his actions might hurt somebody. They got together just after she and Jonas broke up."

"That's right. Your brother left Becky for Claire. It's a tangled web, Maja."

"Not one I'm proud to tell you about. There's slightly more."

"Another skeleton?"

"This I'm not sure of, and you have to promise to have an open mind."

"I always do."

I studied his face, badly in need of a shave, and his eyes, tired but observant, and decided to trust him. I didn't know how much longer I'd have in Duved Cove and needed to see an end to the suspicions—not for my father now, but for my mother and for Jonas.

"I think, and it's just a half-substantiated rumour, that my dad may have been seeing Claire too. I have absolutely no details or proof, just a gut feeling."

The green in Tobias's eyes darkened. "Why would your father have chosen your brother's ex-girlfriend and his wife to sleep with? Is there something you aren't telling me?"

I had trouble getting the words out and couldn't look at Tobias as I spoke. I'd never talked about these things with anybody but Jonas and Billy. "My father was sort of...abusive, you might say. Verbally, mentally, not so much physically, but sometimes. He was the master, and we were there to serve." I tried to speak lightly but didn't succeed. "If he chose Jonas's women, it would be to prove he was a better man than my brother."

"And your mother...?"

"I don't think she knew about the time in high school with Becky. Becky never told a soul, and my father never would have. He liked to show off, but there was a line he wouldn't have crossed with my mother."

Tobias's eyes were flat and hard to read. He spread both hands on the table and pushed himself to his feet. "What you're telling me explains a lot and could be linked to your father's death. It gives a different direction to the investigation, that's for sure."

He leaned towards me and for one crazy second, I thought he was going to kiss me. I could smell his spicy cologne, and his green eyes were staring into mine. Before I could react, he straightened and ran a hand through his grey hair. He sighed and took a step backward. "Well, I have to go. I'll be doing more digging. Thank you for this information. I'll have to think about where it all fits in and reassess who might have killed your father and what Becky's disappearance means in all of this. There is still an outside chance she just got fed up and split."

"For her sake, I hope so." I wasn't convinced, but I wanted to be.

"For everyone's sake. Get some sleep, Maja. How much longer are you staying?"

"I'll work on cleaning out Dad's house for a few more days. I want to make sure Jonas is okay too. If nothing breaks in the case soon, I'll be leaving by the weekend." I thought of Sam and his ultimatum. I could make the trip if I left Duved Cove in a few days. It would be easiest if I gave in to the trip, and my life could go back to the way it was before Dad's murder.

"Good enough. Hopefully, we'll have some answers by then. Thanks again, Maja. I'll only use this information if I have to." His eyes softened into green pools of concern that reverted quickly into brilliant hardness.

If I hadn't known Tobias better, I'd have believed my revelations had affected him. Still, I was glad he hadn't collapsed into a show of pity or sympathy. I didn't want any when I was a kid, and I couldn't bear any now.

After Tobias left, I tiptoed upstairs and soaked in Claire's claw-footed bathtub for nearly an hour with a tumbler of Scotch on the rocks and a book that I borrowed from their downstairs bookcase. The bathroom had been recently redecorated and papered in vertical mauve stripes with pine wainscoting. It was a restful room, steamy from the heat in my bath and lavender-scented from the generous dollop of bath oil I'd added to the water. The book was a history of Duved Cove written by someone I'd gone to school with. It took my mind off the day's events and relaxed me enough that I fell asleep almost immediately upon climbing into bed.

My sleep was filled with dreams so vivid that I remembered them in detail when I finally woke up. I began by chasing my mother through the darkened hallways of our house only to find her dead at the bottom of the basement stairs. Without knowing how I got there, I was beside her, kneeling on the concrete floor and cradling her head in my lap, her blonde hair spread around her like corn silk, her blue eyes open and staring. I looked back up the stairwell to see my father and Jonas laughing together in the kitchen. Jonas lifted his head and looked at me, and I realized that he had been crying, not laughing as I'd first thought. Tears streamed down his face, and his eyes were the haunted eyes of our childhood. Then, a quick shift, and Katherine Lingstrom and I were walking along the beachfront searching for cigarettes. She was laughing at me and running in the direction of the lake. I ran after her, calling her name, but she disappeared into the frigid waters of Lake Superior. I sank onto the sand, and suddenly I was in Billy's arms with him saying that he'd wait forever.

The dream sequences wove into each other like a whirlygig, no clear ending or beginning. I awoke with the taste of salty tears on my lips and a feeling of unease so strong, I felt sick to my stomach. Some revelation about my father was circling just out of my consciousness, and I struggled to make out the message through the fog of my dreams. It was futile. I drifted back into a deep sleep and didn't waken again until sunlight was pouring thick and bright through the bedroom window.

TWENTY-TWO

Jonas came with me to Dad's early the next morning. We made decent progress packing up the living room and clearing out his bedroom. It was sweaty work, but it felt good to be doing something physical. It took our minds off the horror of our father's murder, for time was making the enormity of it sink in, not fade around the edges like one of the black and white photographs in my mother's albums. Around one o'clock, Jonas went to town to pick up some sandwiches and coffee. We figured a few more hours work in the afternoon, and we'd head to Hadrian's for something to take the dust out of our throats.

After he'd gone, I climbed the stairs and found myself outside the door of my old bedroom. I'd forgotten about the boxes of books. One box had been upended by whoever had ransacked Dad's house, and books lay scattered on the floor. The flaps of the other boxes were opened and the boxes were half-empty. I counted ten boxes in all, ten boxes of books for a man I'd never known to crack a book in his life. I crossed the floor and found a bare space to kneel. I picked up several of the paperbacks and examined their covers, then shook them from their spines so the pages fanned out, hoping something would fall to the floor. Nothing did.

"What were you up to, Dad?" I asked and began stacking the books back into the empty box. Inspecting each one seemed futile. "Why the books?"

When they were all put away, I drifted through the upstairs and down into the kitchen. I was packing pots into a box when Jonas returned. He stomped up the back steps and entered the kitchen with a small box that held two large coffees in Styrofoam cups, submarine sandwiches and bags of potato chips. A skein of frost coated his beard. His forehead and the skin around his eyes were purplish red from the cold wind.

"Temperature's dropping again," he said as he set the food on the table and shrugged out of his parka. "Must be way below freezing."

I stood and stretched. "I'm starving"

"Me too. It's the first time in a long time."

We set to work eating, and for a little while, the only sound was our chewing and swallowing. Jonas looked tired but not as frantic as he'd been before he'd gone into the hospital. His eyes were clear and his hands had stopped trembling. I smiled at him between bites.

"You remembered I like lots of onions."

"But no tomatoes."

"Yes, this is perfect." I wiped my mouth with a paper napkin. "What do you know about the books in my old bedroom?"

"What books?"

"There's ten boxes—paperbacks, hardcovers and bibles. I never knew Dad liked to read, or pray for that matter."

"He didn't."

"Then why does he have ten big boxes of books upstairs?"

"He was storing them for somebody. Chief Anders, I think."

"That makes absolutely no sense, Jonas."

"I guess. Never thought much about it before."

"How long has Dad had the books?"

"I'm not sure. I saw them in the fall when I was putting on

187

storm windows. There were more than ten boxes though."

Jonas's eyebrows rose, and his forehead crinkled as he pondered the implications. "The room was half full as I recall. I asked Dad what was going on, and he said he was just storing them for Anders. Yeah, it was Anders. Do you think it could mean anything?"

"Seems odd to me. I know Dad and Anders stayed friends, but why store books for him? Anders has a big enough house."

"It's coming back to me now. Dad said that Anders' wife was renovating, and they needed storage space."

"Well, that might explain it." I reached over and touched Jonas on the arm. "You know I'm going to share the money from this place with you, Jonas. You deserve it more than me."

Jonas lowered his sandwich to the table and seemed to fold in on himself. He tucked in his chin so that his beard was touching his chest and kept his eyes focused on something straight ahead. He spoke dispassionately. "If Dad wanted you to have it, that's cool with me. I don't care about the money."

"Well, you should care. It was cruel of him to cut you out of the will, and it makes me mad. I'm not letting him get away with this." I was surprised at the anger that rose from deep in my chest. "Somebody should have stood up to him a long time ago."

Jonas turned his head so that he was looking at me. "Honestly, it doesn't matter. The money doesn't matter. You don't need to do this for me, Maja."

"Maybe not, but I need to do it for myself."

I stood and swept up our sandwich wrappers into a tight ball in my fist. I banged my hand down on the table. "I've spent my life pretending that what he did to us, to our family, didn't matter, but you know something, Jonas? It left its mark under my skin, where it will never heal. I won't be the victim any longer. Our

188

father is not here sleeping with a loaded gun under the bed. He doesn't have that hold on us any longer. We owe it to our mother to rail against this...this acceptance of what we've become. You can't give in. I won't let you give in."

Jonas lifted his head and looked at me. His eyes reflected the light, the opaque eyes of a stranger. His voice was flat."This emptiness sometimes, it makes me question...sometimes it's like I'm not sure I can keep it going. I'm not sure anything really matters in the end."

"You can't give in to it, Jonas. Promise me you'll never give in." I knelt beside him and rested my head on his arm. "I don't want you to leave me, Jonas," I whispered. "You can't check out on Gunnar and Claire. Not that way."

"Sometimes I think they'd be better off without me."

I closed my eyes. The tears seeped out from under my eyelids.

Jonas stood then, and I felt the sudden strength of his arms wrap around me and pull me to my feet. "It's okay, Maja. I'm not going anywhere. I promise." His voice was penitent, the one he'd always used to keep the peace. I didn't trust it.

"You have to really promise." I was crying now in big gulping sobs.

"I really promise."

"You have to mean it."

I could hear the smile in his voice."It's like we're kids again, Maj. You tell me I have to mean it, and I say it's the meanest mean-it you've ever seen."

I laughed through my hiccups. "A mean mean-it is binding."

"Till the end of time."

I stepped back. "I love you, little brother," I said.

This time, Jonas looked me in the eyes. "And I love you back."

We were middle-aged and we were young, forever joined by

blood and the years we'd shared as children. His pain was my pain, and it was impossible to tell where his began and mine left off. This blood connection meant I would never be free of Jonas's torment nor he of mine. What joined us was as simple and as uncomplicated as the coupling of our parents' flesh, the randomness of birth. Yet, it was so much more. I could no sooner walk away from Jonas than I could walk away from myself, and God knew, I'd tried for over twenty years. My flight had led me back to where it all began—back to Duved Cove and this house where my mother had hanged herself and my father had lain dying in the snow—back to my brother who had been slowly dying inside from the moment he tried to breathe life into my mother's lifeless body.

Jonas wanted to skip Hadrian's and go home to rest. By the progressive paleness of his skin as the afternoon wore on, I didn't argue. He hadn't been out of the hospital long, and the packing had zapped his energy reserves. He sat at the kitchen table while I wrapped the last of Dad's coffee mugs in newspaper before placing them into a box on the counter.

"Does Dad still have that wine stored in the basement?" I asked. He'd had a wine rack built into the coolest part of the basement and had kept it well stocked when we were kids. If he had anything half-decent stored there, it would be a pleasant addition to my evening. It might help Claire relax and start talking to me.

"I think so. He was always going on about how much he paid for a bottle. He took wine courses a few years ago, so of course he became the expert." Jonas snorted. "From alcoholic to sommelier. It's all in the way you market yourself, I guess."

"It's the yuppie idea of class." I thought of Sam and his

pretentious palate. He wouldn't touch a glass of wine from a bottle worth less than some arbitrary price he'd set. Trouble was, if you only drank the expensive wine, you grew to tell the difference. Luckily, a wine's pedigree hadn't mattered all that much to me. I'd grown up on cheap wine and Minnesota beach parties.

Even from the time I was a little girl, I hadn't liked going into the basement by myself. It was nothing I could explain, except that it was the feeling of being below ground and trapped. I opened the basement door, clicked on the light and looked down the steep concrete steps. I realized I'd avoided going down there since I'd been in the house. The light bulb at the bottom of the stairs had burned out, and it crossed my mind to forget about the wine. I turned back to look at Jonas, who was putting on his parka.

"I'll just go start the car while you get the wine," he said. "Where are your keys?"

"In my jacket on the back of the chair. God, Jonas. It smells like something is rotting in the basement. Was Dad keeping meat down there?"

"More mess to clean up," Jonas sighed. "His freezer must be on the blink. I guess whatever has gone bad can wait one more day."

I looked back into the shadowy depths of the basement then closed my eyes and pictured the layout. My father had panelled half of it as a rec room in knotty pine years ago and framed off the unfinished half, which held the furnace, freezer, washing machine and clothes dryer with two clothes lines strung across the ceiling. The wine rack was in a small, cooler pantry at the far end of the unfinished section. I decided quickly. I'd hold my breath, make a dash for the wine rack and be back upstairs in seconds flat. Hopefully there wouldn't be too many cobwebs along the way. I had a real problem with the feel of them on my face. It was an irrational phobia that I should have outgrown but hadn't.

I took tentative steps down the dark stairwell, picking up speed as my eyes adjusted to the gloom. The smell got worse as I got closer to the bottom, and I put a hand over my mouth. By the time I reached the bottom step, dread had begun stealing up my legs and into my arms. It was all I could do to keep moving forward. I felt along the wall until my hand landed on the wall switch. The room jumped into light, and I looked left toward the finished section. The seating area looked much as I remembered it, two couches and a few recliners arranged around a flat screen television, which had to be new, and beige carpeting that I was certain was new, marking off the space. I turned my head right toward the doorway to the laundry room, and the smell got stronger and more putrid. I wanted to race back up the stairs, as far away from the disgusting air as I could get. Instead, I forced myself to cross the threshold into the laundry area, swallowing the bile that rose hot in my throat.

I saw her body almost immediately, shoved between the freezer and washing machine like a pile of dirty laundry. Becky Wilders lying on her stomach, arms stiff at her sides, head turned to one side with a trickle of blood dried on her chin, her eyes wide open and staring into death. Her hair was matted and stained through with dark dried blood. I was a doctor, but this was the first time I had stumbled upon a murdered friend, and the shock of it was too much to take in. I crossed the short distance as if in a dream and kneeled beside her, reaching out a hand to feel for a pulse. The smell of rotting flesh was overwhelming, and I knew it was a futile gesture, but part of my mind could not accept that she was so brutally gone.

She was wearing her winter coat, a navy knee-length parka with a hood lined in fake fur, and black knee-high boots that looked oddly childlike on her tiny feet and slender legs, a red skirt visible where the coat twisted around her waist. I could imagine Becky picking out these clothes and trying them on, turning to study herself in front of a full-length mirror, liking what she saw. The sadness of what had happened to her struck me like a blow to my heart, and I struggled to keep from sobbing. Becky would never be trying on clothes again or feeding Timmy Cheerios or breathing another breath. My stomach rolled then, and I stood to heave into the laundry sink, retching up my lunch until nothing more was left. I raised my head, swallowing the burning in my throat. I could hear Jonas walking across the kitchen floor overhead. He stopped at the head of the stairs and called down to me.

"Maja! You coming?"

I couldn't let him see her this way. I swiped at my face with the back of my hand. "I'll be right there!" I called and turned on the tap to rinse out my mouth and clean out the sink. I stumbled out of the laundry room, but I wasn't quick enough. Jonas met me halfway down the stairs.

"You look like you've seen a rat," he said. "Phew! It does smell pretty bad down here. Did you find anything?"

That's when I should have lied. Instead, I remained silent, not trusting myself to speak. Jonas stared at me, and his face turned whiter than it was already. He tried to push past me, but I held my ground.

"We have to call the police," I said at last. "We shouldn't go back down there. It's not good, Jonas."

"What's happened? Somebody's dead, aren't they?" His voice dropped to little more than a rasp. "Not Claire. . .?"

"Becky," I said, and the word was enough. Jonas loosened his grasp on my arm.

"I should go see her," he said, but I could tell he didn't want to go any further into the cellar.

"I don't think we should disturb the scene. There's nothing to be done for her. She's been there...for quite some time."

Jonas nodded. He turned and climbed like an old man back up the stairs. I followed him, unable to erase the image of Becky's lifeless eyes from my mind, wondering why my brother thought his wife was the one lying dead in our basement.

Tobias was the first to arrive, quickly followed by David Keating and Chief Anders, paramedics from the hospital and lastly, the coroner, each greeting us quickly before descending into the basement. All the while, Jonas and I sat close to each other in the kitchen without talking. Jonas's hands trembled whenever he ran them through his hair. Devastation lined his pale face. I made tea and forced a cup into his hand. He took a few sips before setting the cup down and letting the tea go cold.

David emerged from the basement. He sat down across from Jonas next to me and pulled out a notebook. "Who found her?" he asked.

I raised my head. "I did. Jonas was waiting for me outside while I went to get wine from the basement. I felt for a pulse, but that was all. I knew she was gone."

David's eyes fixed on mine. "Blunt trauma to the head was likely the cause of death."

"Just like Dad," Jonas said.

"Looks much the same," David agreed. He shifted his gaze to Jonas. "I know this must be hard for both of you, but if there's anything you can tell us that would help..."

"She must have been killed that night she never made it home. Did she die in our basement?" I asked. The thought that she'd been lying in the basement the whole time I was working upstairs was an awful thought.

"I can't say, Maja. It's too early."

"Whoever broke in didn't do any damage in the basement. If they had, we might have gone into the laundry room and found her when we were cleaning up." I shuddered.

"Don't think about that now."

We gave the rest of our statements, which didn't amount to much. David snapped his notebook shut and told us we could go home.

"Who will tell Kevin?" I asked as I stood to put on my coat.

Chief Anders entered the kitchen from the basement steps. He walked heavily towards us, his eyes rimmed in red as if he'd been crying. "Tobias will be heading over there now to break the news. This is an awful thing. An awful thing." His head shook from side to side.

I heard someone else climbing the stairs. If it was Tobias, I didn't want to talk to him. I stood and grabbed my coat. "Coming, Jonas?" I asked. I nodded at Tobias, who'd made it into the kitchen as I opened the back door and stepped outside into the fading afternoon light. He'd looked as devastated as Jonas. I could hear my brother saying goodbye as I fled down the steps toward the car.

When Jonas slid in next to me, the car's heater was blasting cold air, and I was shaking. He looked across at me and huddled deeper into his parka. "Let's go to Hadrian's. We could both do with a drink," he said.

"Are you sure you're up for it?"

"I won't be able to rest now.

"Okay. I could do with something stronger than tea."

I navigated my car past the police cars and an ambulance with two paramedics in the act of lifting out a gurney as we put space between us and my father's house. It would take some time before I could put the same space between us and the deaths that had happened there—three deaths counting my mother—three violent deaths in my parents' house that could not be explained.

TWENTY-THREE

Entering Hadrian's was like stepping into another world, one of music and laughter, colour and warmth. It seemed a lot of others had come in out of the cold to search out pre-dinner drinks, because there wasn't a spare table to be found. Jonas and I snagged the last two stools at the bar. Hadrian had enlisted the help of a girl who looked too young to be serving alcohol. She had a cascade of black curls and a morose face that looked a lot like Hadrian's.

"Hi, Sarah," Jonas said. "Two double Scotch on the rocks."

Sarah shifted the gum in her mouth to the opposite cheek and nodded as she chewed. Before long, she slid two tumblers in front of us and took Jonas's money without comment. The first swallow hurt my raw throat, but it was a welcome pain. It beat the numbness that had stolen over my other senses. Hadrian was talking to Wayne Okwari at the other end of the bar. They both looked over at us, so I turned my head toward Jonas.

"How long do you think before the town knows?"

"They probably know already."

I nodded. Duved Cove's grapevine had tendrils everywhere. I looked over Jonas's shoulder and pointed. "Look. A table's open."

"Let's go."

Jonas grabbed both our drinks, and we made our way through the crowded room to the table near the gas fireplace, which was not turned on. The table was the same one we'd sat at the night before. We took seats elbow to elbow.

"So how are you doing?" I asked. "You know, mixing alcohol and your medication probably isn't the best idea."

"I'll just have this one and then head home. Claire will be wondering where I am."

"Is everything all right between you and Claire?"

"Is everything all right between you and Sam?"

We looked at each other and smiled.

"Okay. I see where this is heading," I said. "Mutual confession time."

"Only if forced."

"Sam and I have seen better days. He's been having an affair with someone at work. He doesn't know that I know, and I've never let on."

"Are you sure?"

"I saw them together, and there've been other signs. I've chosen not to confront him for reasons that seem unimportant now."

"Will you be able to work it through?"

"I'm not sure. Since I've been back here, I've started questioning if I even want to. It's been good in a way, having people see me as Maja Larson and not Maja Cleary."

"What was wrong with Maja Cleary?"

"She got lost in the shuffle. I'm not even sure how or when it happened." Misery filled me, and I took a drink from my glass. I didn't want to think about it any more deeply. I cleared my throat. "And you?" I asked.

Jonas sighed. "Claire's tired of living in Duved Cove. Has been for a long time. My bouts of depression haven't helped."

"Do you think it's affecting Gunnar?"

"I'm sure it has. If you haven't noticed, Claire is overly protective and not adjusting to the fact that he's becoming a teenager. I've given up trying to intercede."

"That isn't good, Jonas."

"I know, but in some things with Claire I have no say. That's just the way it is."

I wanted to ask about Claire's relationship with our father, but now was not the time. There might never be a right time, and perhaps there was no need to even discuss it. Jonas was the one to bring up Becky, the subject we'd been avoiding since we sat down.

"Becky never forgave me for picking Claire over her. We were on friendlier terms the last few years, but Becky sleeping with Dad wasn't easy to digest. I never let on to Becky that I knew."

"Who told you? Dad?"

"No, although he hinted enough. It was actually Claire who made the big announcement in one of our fights. She wanted to hurt me because she thought I still cared for Becky."

"And did you?"

"Not the way Claire thought. I made my choice in high school, and I never regretted it."

"Did you ever bring up the subject of Becky to Dad?"

Jonas grunted. "I wouldn't give the old bastard the satisfaction."

"We should probably go," I said.

Jonas shook his head. "No need. Claire will figure out where we are, and I don't think going home will make either one of us feel any better."

We ordered two more drinks—another double Scotch for me and a ginger ale for Jonas. I felt the effects of the first drink. It was nice to feel the sharp edges of grief slipping away. Still, I had to keep some of my wits about me, so I ordered a plate of cheese and salsa-covered nachos. I considered what it could mean that Claire still hated Becky.

People came and went. We overheard people talking about the murdered woman found in our father's house. They looked at us as they talked, but nobody came over to our table. It was as if we had a "do not approach" sign flashing over our heads. Hadrian put on a tape of Scottish ballads and turned up the volume. Another round of drinks arrived, compliments of Hadrian. He waved at us from across the bar.

"I'm thinking you might need to drive us home, Jonas," I said.

"No problem. We got all night."

The phone rang at the bar, and Hadrian stood speaking into the receiver with one hand over his other ear. He dropped the receiver and came over to our table. His eyes were question marks, but he kept his voice neutral.

"Claire wants you to come home," he said to Jonas. "Sounded kind of upset."

"Sure thing," Jonas said. After Hadrian was out of earshot, he added, "She must have heard about Becky. You stay and finish your drink."

Jonas had just pushed himself to his feet when the front door of the bar opened. I looked over my shoulder and saw Tobias standing in the entranceway. He surveyed the room until he met my eyes. Then he started walking in our direction.

"Hey, Tobias," I said as he sat across from me. "Jonas is just heading home to see Claire." I fished in my pocket and handed Jonas my keys.

"I'll bring Maja home if she wants to finish her drink," Tobias said to Jonas.

I looked at my empty glass and the full one next to it on the table in front of me. No wonder I wasn't as upset as normal at Tobias's presence. Jonas was looking tired again, and I nodded.

"I'll get a lift with Tobias. You go home and rest."

"See you back at the house then," Jonas said. He patted my shoulder before he weaved his way through the tables to the door.

Tobias went to the bar to order a drink while I sat and contemplated life. He was back before I noticed, carrying a cup of coffee and a big bag of chips.

"Still on duty?"

"Yeah, still on duty."

"You told Kevin. . .?"

"Yup. It went about as you'd expect."

"He obviously had no idea what had happened to her."

"Obviously. The man's in shock, as near as I can tell."

"Do you have any leads?"

"Now, you know I can't talk about that, Maja." We were silent for a bit. Then, Tobias said, "Are there any leads you'd care to give me?"

"None that I can think of."

"Damn. I can't say any of this is adding up."

We sat nursing our drinks and munching on chips. I noticed the other patrons stealing looks our way but trying to be subtle about their interest.

"Was the door locked when you and Jonas arrived today?"

"I think so, but maybe not. We never used to lock it but have been now that it's vacant most of the time."

Jonas tilted his head. "The thing is, somebody killed her at a different location and placed her body in your laundry room. We found her car in the back of the hospital parking lot behind the dumpster."

"So she was either abducted or she trusted her killer enough to take a ride with them."

Tobias's eyes were fixed on mine. "I also have to wonder if the method of death for Becky and your father was a coincidence."

"Was Becky hit with a shovel?"

"Not sure. We're sending her body to the forensic lab in Duluth for testing, and we'll know more in a day or so."

Another few days. It was going to be impossible to make Sam's trip. The distance between us felt like a fresh sprain that I didn't want to put much pressure on just yet.

Tobias looked past me to the bar and nodded. I turned in time to see Wayne Okwari motion with his head toward the washrooms. I turned back around, and Tobias appeared to be studying his coffee cup with curious interest. After he'd eaten the last of his chips, he said, "If you'll excuse me for a minute, I'm hearing the call of nature."

"A call you should always answer," I said. I watched him thread a path quickly between the tables toward the washroom. It couldn't be a coincidence that Wayne Okwari had disappeared in the same direction moments before.

When Tobias returned a few minutes later, I already had my coat on and was waiting by the door. He grabbed his parka and followed me out into the parking lot.

"The temperature has dropped again," I said, blowing a plume of white frost in front of me as I talked.

"My car'll heat up fast."

Tobias opened my door first and shut it behind me. I shivered as the cold from the seat penetrated my pants and coat. Tobias let in another blast of winter air when he slid into the driver's side. He started the engine and turned on the headlights, then he rubbed his gloves together. "Damn, but it's one cold night. I think there are icicles on the icicles. You and Stan have it warmer up there in Ott-ee-wa?"

"Sam. His name is Sam, and yes, Ottawa has its cold snaps

too." I leaned closer so I could watch his face in the dashboard light, "What was that all about anyhow?" I asked.

"What do you mean?"

"You and Wayne Okwari. In the men's room."

"You are one curious woman, Maja Larson. I never met Wayne in the washroom."

Tobias looked at me then over his shoulder as he backed out of the parking spot. He glanced at me again as he straightened the wheel, but he didn't say anything more about Wayne. After a while, he made small talk about changes to the town. I half-listened. I was mulling over why Tobias suddenly seemed to be hiding something and why a feeling of unease made me wary of confiding in him. Perhaps it had to do with the look in his eyes when I'd asked him about Wayne. His words had been light, but his face had been guarded. After all, what did I really know about Tobias except from when we were kids? People changed. If my father had been up to no good, who better to help him than Tobias, who'd told me the first time we talked that he was planning to head south, just like my father and Chief Anders?

The connections in my brain started to become disturbing. Wayne Okwari was always hanging around the bar, and I'd seen him the day I'd gone to visit Billy and Fortune Bay Casino, the same casino my father frequented—my father, who worked at the border. Now, Tobias and Wayne were giving each other signals across a crowded bar and holding a secret meeting in the public washroom. Small town police forces got into things they shouldn't all the time. They could be as corrupt as big city forces. They had better ways of covering up than the average citizen. The law was on their side and a good front for illegal activity.

Once the ideas started falling into place, it was like a set of dominos tumbling across the floor. There were hidden relationships in Duved Cove, and I needed to get away from Tobias to think them through. I needed to come up with a plan to bring the truth out into the open.

"You seem lost in thought," Tobias said as we pulled into Jonas's driveway. "A penny for them." He flashed me a smile. His face was open but his eyes were holding back secrets. I was wary.

I swung my door open and set one foot on the ground before I turned to give him a shaky smile. "I'm just tired and maybe had one more Scotch than I should have. Thanks for the lift, Tobias. I owe you one."

I darted out of the car and slammed the door without giving him time to respond. My feet slipped dangerously as I made my way up the icy driveway to the back steps. I kept my head down and concentrated on keeping my feet under me. There was no way I intended to fall with Tobias watching.

TWENTY-FOUR

Billy Okwari visited me that night—not in person, but in my dreams. This time, his visit filled me with sadness. We sat in the shadows of the spruce trees in my front yard, nestled against the roots of a giant cedar. Billy needed to tell me something, and his words kept slipping in and out of my consciousness. His eyes were inky pools burning into mine. I tried putting together the pieces of the dream as I drifted back to sleep, but by morning, the threads had nearly disappeared from my memory. All that remained was a bittersweet heaviness, like honey on my tongue, that would stay with me throughout the day.

A long time after the sunlight had begun to weakly filter through the bedroom window, I lay on my side, focusing on the play on shadows on the wall and trying to piece together all I'd witnessed over the past week, trying to reconcile this new reality with images from the past. Somebody had dumped Becky's body in our house, and the choice of location had to mean something. Following the trail of relationships, her killer was logically someone who knew of her affair, with my father and who harboured hatred in their heart. Becky's husband Kevin Wilders, Claire and Jonas had all been hurt by the affair and each had opportunity. I refused to believe that it was Jonas. That left Claire and Kevin, but I didn't like either option. Was somebody else part of the equation of whom I wasn't aware? Could that person be Tobias? It was a small town, and he was a single, attractive man who had flirting down to an art form. His path would have crossed Becky's often, not to mention that she was needy, or *had* been needy. I still couldn't believe she was dead.

I climbed out of bed and changed quickly into jeans, a white turtleneck and emerald green fleece. It was Saturday, and nobody was up. I went through the morning coffee ritual and drank the first cup while eating a bowl of cereal. Sam would be leaving in two days for Bermuda. I had no doubt Lana would be going with him. I wouldn't think about it yet. I felt restless and knew I needed some exercise. I was used to going to the gym at least four mornings a week in Ottawa and keeping a full work schedule. While packing up my father's house was work, it wasn't the workout my body was used to.

I put on my parka and boots and went outside, intending at first to go for a walk along the highway. A second look at the tree line made me suddenly long for a view of the lake, and I went back inside for my car keys.

I parked my car in the barely plowed parking area and started down the path towards the beach. It was slow going, because the puddles of melting snow had frozen over, but I took my time and stepped carefully. Another set of footsteps was visible, leading the way toward the lake. Perhaps, I should have been cautious, but there was no other vehicle in the parking lot, and the prints had to have been made the day before. If I hadn't been so preoccupied, I might have noticed that the footprints were leading to the beach with none returning. That would occur to me later.

I kept my head down, watching where I was going. A strengthening in the wind was the first signal that I'd exited the woods, and I lifted my face in the direction of the lake. When I looked past the huge chunks of ice along the shoreline, I could make out the blue-grey water that bled into the horizon. The sun was a watery ball hovering in the sky, obscured by ribbons of cloud. The snowmobile trails that crisscrossed the snowy beach were icier than on my first visit but still manageable. I started walking, glancing around me as I went, inhaling the fresh air in deep drafts and enjoying the gusts of wind that buffeted me at steady intervals. I wasn't a quarter of the way into my journey before I stopped to survey the wide expanse of beach, and it was then that I spotted the dark mass ahead of me, closer to the frozen shoreline. It looked like a black blanket, lying in a sea of white, billowing when the wind caught under its folds.

I moved cautiously closer, visions of Becky's body flooding back to me. I was a few hundred yards from the dark form when she lifted her head to look back at me. The relief I felt that this was not another dead body was equaled by trepidation. I moved closer, not taking my eyes off the round, pale face and grey strands of hair whipping across her forehead and plump cheeks. The eyes, when I got close enough, were older and faded, but they were the eyes of my childhood friend.

"Katherine," I called across the distance that separated us. "Katherine Lingstrom! It's me, Maja Larson."

I continued to step cautiously closer even as she turned her hooded head back towards her study of the lake. I was sure she'd heard me. I came alongside her and squatted on the ground, not certain how to approach her, matching my silence to hers. Katherine was sitting squarely on the snow, her long black parka protecting her from its coldness. Even still, she must be feeling the chill of the ground and the wind off the lake. I was close enough to smell her acrid sweat and unwashed hair. At last she stirred.

"I knew you'd find me," she said, her eyes still on the horizon.

It was Katherine's voice, but it was not. The youth and strength had gone.

"It's good to see you, Katherine." I wanted to hug her but could see no indication that she would welcome my touch. Instead, I waited and kept my eyes also focused on the horizon. I felt her body shift as she turned to look at me.

"You came to visit Mother."

"Yes. She said you were away on holiday."

"That's what Mother would like to believe. Katherine's on a holiday somewhere warm and safe. It's easier than believing her daughter has gone mad."

"Surely not, Katherine. We all struggle now and then. It's no sin."

"The sin is what's behind the pain."

I looked in her eyes and saw a raw emptiness that spoke of torment to which she'd surrendered. I said gently, "If I can help in any way, Katherine, I would do anything."

She looked back toward the lake and was silent for a long time. When I'd almost given up hope that she would speak again, she began to talk. It was a toneless monologue that needed an audience and so I sat quietly next to her on the snowy beach and listened.

"Brent and I were never good from the beginning. I tried to act like a good wife, as if I liked being married, but I was no good at it. We have two kids, two girls, and I never wanted them. I did everything I could to give them a good beginning, to act like I loved them, but I'm so damaged, Maja." Her voice broke and she stopped talking. When she started again, her voice was dreamy. "I come here every day. Every day, I sit here and wait. I saw you that day you walked along the beach. I wanted to talk to you, but I was afraid then. It was too soon after...I had to figure out what to do. Mother wanted me to go away. I come here every day and

I wait...." Her voice trailed away.

"What do you wait for, Katherine?"

"I didn't mean to kill your father."

A shock travelled up my spine like an adrenaline rush. I closed my eyes and tried to will away the black dots blocking my vision. I was close to passing out and breathed deeply to still my heart. "What did you just say?" I whispered.

"I went to see him. To confront him. All those years ago, he ruined me. All through my teen years, when I should have been so innocent. He ruined my chance to be a wife to Brent."

I bowed my head. "Oh my god, Katherine. I am so sorry."

"I wanted to tell you, Maja. I felt so dirty every time it happened. But then, I'd see your father again and I...it would happen again. I wanted him. I hated him."

The monster in our house was real. I needed to get up and run. Run as far away from Katherine Lingstrom and what she was telling me as I could get. But I couldn't move.

"You did leave him though...eventually. You can be strong, Katherine."

"I only left him because the guilt I felt for your mother was more than I could face."

"But my mother wouldn't have known. He always made sure she didn't know."

Katherine turned to look at me again. "She knew. We were in her bed when she came home early. The next day...she was dead."

"Oh my god. Oh my god." I wrapped my arms around my middle and rocked backwards and forwards.

"The afternoon she found us together, your father left with me. He didn't go back that night because he took me to a motel. I told my mother I was spending the night with a girlfriend. When your dad went back home the next morning, your mother had killed herself. Jonas found her hanging in the basement. I never slept with him again. I just left town and went to work in Duluth, where I met Brent. He was my chance to save myself, but I can't do it any more."

"It wasn't your fault. You were too young to know, and my father was so manipulative."

"I knew enough. I was thirteen the first time, but I could have stopped it. That night last week when I told him he'd destroyed me, you know what he did? He laughed. He laughed and said I was being ridiculous. Can you believe it, Maja? After all the years I'd lived hating myself? He couldn't have cared less."

"I believe it, Katherine. I forgive you. You have to let this go."

"I begged him not to sell his land for the new highway. They wouldn't pay for Mother's property, and it wouldn't be worth anything once word of the highway got out. She only wanted to spend her last years in quiet. That wasn't too much to ask, was it? Your father should never have laughed at me. He owed me that."

"No, he should never have laughed at you, Katherine, but he wasn't a giving man. It wasn't in him to show compassion."

"I told Mother that hiding what I did wouldn't work. I needed to tell you the truth. I can't do this any more." Katherine had begun wringing her hands, red knuckles chafed from the cold. I covered them with my own.

"Katherine, I'll come with you to tell Tobias Olsen. He'll understand and make this easy. It was an accident." I could understand why she would kill Becky too. She'd have known that they were sleeping together, and Becky would have been as tainted as my father. She might even have seen them together. Katherine was mentally ill, and that would certainly be a defense. I didn't dare leave her alone.

"I don't care any more, Maja. I'll talk to Tobias. Mother is going to be very angry that I told you, but it doesn't matter."

"Let me help you, Katherine. I'll stay with you. I'll explain."

I stood and tried to get the circulation back in my legs. The cold had seeped into my bones, and my knees creaked in pain. I bent down, took Katherine's arm and helped her to her feet. We huddled together and walked like two damaged women as we made our slow way through the icy snow and down the forest path to the road. We reached my car at last, and I kept one hand firmly clasped on her arm as I searched for the keys in my pocket with my other. Katherine stood motionless facing the deeper woods, her eyes fixed on a point somewhere over the car roof.

"You never told me what you were waiting for, sitting on the cold beach day after day," I said, the wind snatching away my words so that I wasn't sure she'd heard me. I didn't expect an answer. Her behaviour had lost rational moorings long ago. *It probably doesn't matter,* I said to myself.

I unlocked her door and swung it open. I used both hands to guide Katherine toward the door. Before she sank into the cold interior, she leaned against me. She spoke into my ear, and strands of her hair whipped against my cheek. Her words were a breath of frost against my cold skin. She turned her vacant eyes toward me, and her desperate words held no emotion. "I was waiting for the ice to melt so I could walk into the lake and never come back."

I drove Katherine to the police station, and the woman at the desk radioed a call to Tobias. He arrived with David Keating following in a separate car soon afterwards. I explained what had happened on the beach while Katherine sat zombie-like in the waiting area, still huddled in her black coat with the hood up.

211

Tobias and David listened without comment until I finished all I had to say.

Tobias glanced over at Katherine and back to me. "Okay, Maja. David will take your statement and then we'll try to get Katherine's."

"Please...she's not well, Tobias. I don't want her to suffer any more."

"We'll go easy." Tobias walked across the space toward Katherine. He knelt in front of her and took one of her hands in his.

David lingered in front of me. "You okay?" His eyes were concerned.

I nodded. "I'm glad to know the truth, but it's difficult."

"Let's go into the back, and I'll get your statement. Shouldn't take long."

"Okay."

He took my arm and called to the officer at the desk, "Could you make some tea for Maja and Katherine? Milk and lots of sugar. They both need something to warm them up."

Within an hour, David had typed up my statement, and I signed the two sheets of paper. He helped me into my parka.

"Will you be heading back to Ottawa soon?" he asked.

"I think tomorrow. I was going to stay for Becky's funeral, but I need to get home, and it looks like I have the answers I came for." I was suddenly very tired.

"Don't worry about Katherine. We'll see that she gets medical help. Off the record, she may never go to trial for the murders. She's obviously off-balance."

"Has she confessed to both?"

David shrugged. "We have to go carefully. She's very confused.

I'll be helping Tobias to sort it through."

"This is all so sad. At least we have some answers though. Thanks for everything, David." I reached out and shook his hand.

"No problem. You take care, Maja. My condolences again for your dad."

I walked to the front door, meeting Chief Anders on my way. He was standing at the desk talking into the phone. He hung up and held out his hands to me. I extended mine. His eyes were sad and the lines on his face had deepened.

"I'm so sorry about all this, Maja. I had no idea."

"It's okay," I said quickly. "Nobody could have known." I didn't want him to spell out what my father had done, the lives he had ruined. I felt a rush of guilt for ever thinking badly of Chief Anders and Tobias. It looked like the casino angle had been nothing but a red herring. I was glad I hadn't made any accusations that would come back to haunt me, and yet, greed might have been easier to deal with than my father's black soul.

"What will happen to Katherine now?"

"Well, we can't let her go free. I've asked her psychiatrist to admit her into the hospital in Duluth. She's spent some time there over the last few years, sad to say. I just spoke with her mother, and I'm sending someone to bring her here to stay with Katherine. The two have a strong connection, and Katherine needs all the support we can offer. I also want to find out what the mother knew. I suppose we'll let her go with Katherine to Duluth."

"Good. I don't want Katherine to be alone through this."

"No. I'll make sure she gets the best treatment. You take care too, Maja. Put this behind you and Jonas. It's all you can do."

"Easier said than done, but thanks, Chief Anders. We'll try."

"I know you'll both make it through okay. We're here if there is anything we can do to help."

TWENTY-FIVE

We ate a late dinner of herb and cheese omelettes that Jonas prepared while Claire and I sat at the kitchen table drinking the red wine that I'd picked up on the way home from the police station. We were all in a state of shock and had spent the last hours together in the kitchen, while the fingers of sunlight deepened into dusk, trying to sort out the enigma that was our father and the broken people left in his wake. Claire, at first, had railed against what she'd called the slandering of our father, but she hadn't been able to hang onto her version of the truth for long. By the time we started into the second bottle of pinot noir, her disbelief had been replaced by anger at my father for all he had done: the lies, the betrayal and the seduction, for I had no doubt that he had seduced Claire too. I could see it in her eyes and in the depths of her revulsion once she accepted the truth. My sorrow for her wasn't as strong as it was for Katherine, Becky and my mother, but I still grieved for her, because she'd been a victim too.

Gunnar emerged from his bedroom to eat with us, grumbling about the lateness of the dinner hour. With his arrival, we all stopped talking about Katherine and my father and the sad events of the last few days. Claire was particularly quiet, studying Jonas when he wasn't looking. By the expression in her eyes, I realized that she was beginning to understand the broken part of him. The anger she'd held onto since I'd arrived had eased. Even the way she held herself had softened, and the lines in her forehead were less pronounced.

For once, Gunnar ate with enthusiasm. Earlier in the day, we'd told him of Katherine's arrest and the two people she had killed, and he'd shrugged without comment. Still, I thought I'd seen relief on his face, and his appetite reinforced my suspicion. Had he *believed* one of his parents capable of murder?

Meal over, Gunnar disappeared into his room again. I cleared the table and made tea while Claire sat and smoked. Jonas was restless.

"I'm going to the workshop for a bit," he said at last after circling the kitchen for the tenth time.

"Sounds good," Claire said. "Maybe I'll come see what you're working on after my tea."

Jonas raised his head and looked at her.

She met his eyes and a smile played around her lips. "But only if you want me to," she said.

He looked at her a moment more. "Okay." He moved across the kitchen with his shoulders straighter to pull his jacket off the hook by the door. He stepped into his boots and opened the back door. "See you in a bit then," he said before clumping outside into the early darkness.

I set two mugs of tea on the table and sat across from Claire.

"I'll be leaving tomorrow," I said. "The only flight that suited was early Monday morning, so I'll spend Sunday night in Duluth at a motel near the airport."

"You'll miss Becky's funeral."

"I need to get back to work." I could have added that I needed to get back to the normalcy of my life and away from the pain that was Duved Cove.

"We could have an early lunch before you leave."

"I'd like that."

Claire stubbed out her cigarette in the ashtray with more force than was necessary. Her voice became ragged with anger. "Your father hid a lot. I had no idea. No idea at all. All these years, and you and Jonas never said a word about what went on in your house."

"We couldn't talk about it."

"Why not? How fair was that to the rest of us who fell under your father's charm, his manipulation? Who had no idea? All the young girls..."

I hung my head. "I didn't know about Becky and Katherine," I said. I could have added Claire's name, but I didn't. "Do you think I wouldn't have done something if I'd known? The rest of the things that my father did, well, we just learned to live with it. We took the cue from my mother and never talked about his drinking or...what was going on in our house. We all felt such shame. He controlled us in a way I can't explain, even now. It wasn't all bad, you know. When he was happy and feeling in control, life was good for all of us. It was something we clung on to during the bad times. You don't know how hard we tried to keep him happy, to please him."

"Could that be hereditary? That controlling, narcissistic personality, I mean?"

"Jonas isn't like my father, if that's what you're asking. We both take after my mother, for good or bad." *I had to believe.*

Claire swallowed some tea and stood. She still looked worried. "You are so lucky that you can just leave all this behind and return to your wonderful life with Sam. We will have constant reminders of your father for the rest of our lives."

I watched Claire put on her coat and boots to go join Jonas in the workshop. Her movements were jerky and her face distressed. As she bent to tie her hiking boot, I found my voice. "Is Gunnar my father's child, Claire?" I asked.

Claire's hands went still, her boot laces left hanging. She straightened and turned her back on me, reaching for the door latch. "I know you think badly of me," she said, her shoulders hunched. She pushed the door open. "We've all been guilty of keeping secrets. They always come back to hurt."

Then she was gone, a cold blast of air momentarily replacing the warmth from the wood stove. I could only sit and stare at Claire's empty chair, my limbs too heavy to move. The other shoe had dropped. If Gunnar was my father's son, that would make him Jonas's and my half-brother. It explained the tension in the house...and Gunnar's fear.

I tried calling Sam. I suddenly longed to hear his voice. My husband was an opinionated man who didn't allow for uncertainties or self-doubt. At one time, I'd found strength in his strength, and I needed to believe in that now. I was close to breaking and wanted to hear him tell me life would continue as it had before. If I hurried, I would be home in time to go to the tropical island with him. I would be able to run away from the horror of this past week.

The operator recording told me that Sam's cell phone was off and to try again later. I didn't have the option of leaving a message. I pressed the off button and dialed another number. Fiona answered her phone on the third ring. I could hear music and people talking in the background.

"Maja! It's so good to hear from you. When will you be back?"

"Monday afternoon. Are you having a party?"

Fiona laughed. It was good to hear her familiar joy across the wire. "Yes. We're celebrating my father's seventieth. Can we meet for lunch on Tuesday?"

"I'd like that, but I might be away with Sam. I'll call you when I arrive in Ottawa from Duluth to let you know what I'm up to. You should get back to your guests."

"I'll hear from you in two days. Everything going okay?"

"I'll tell you all about it when I get home."

"Good. I'll be waiting. Safe trip, Maja."

"Two days," I repeated and dropped the phone back into its cradle. Nobody to talk to about what was going on. I might as well go pack for the trip home. I'd bring the remaining half-bottle of wine for company, and with any luck, the pain I was feeling would float away after a few more glasses.

The next morning, I rose early, a headache hovering behind my eyelids. The rest of the family was still sleeping, so after I'd showered and dried my hair, I drove to Frida's for a final breakfast. It would give me a chance to drink in the beauty of the lake one last time.

The girl who poured me a hot mug of coffee before taking my order resembled a shorter, plumper version of Hadrian, dark brown curls tumbling down her back, her eyes sharp and brilliant blue. Obviously, Hadrian had done his part to keep the population of Duved Cove from decreasing. His progeny was keeping the workforce well stocked. I'd intended to order the healthy yoghurt and poached eggs on brown toast, but at the last moment switched to French toast and maple sausages, the house specialty, if I believed the menu. Somehow, today, watching my diet didn't seem so important.

While I waited for my meal, I mindlessly watched the wind

blowing snow across the frozen bay and bending the boughs of the pine trees outside the restaurant window. Chickadees played around a bird feeder that hung on a swaying branch, birdseed scattering on the snow. The sky was flushed pink above the waterline in a thin band, but grey clouds hovered, promising more snow. It was peaceful here, and a calm haven in the emotional storm that had swirled around us all week.

The front door opened and closed. A woman's voice made me look toward the entrance. Patricia Reynolds was talking to the dark-haired waitress near the counter. She was dressed head to toe in a leopard-skin coat with brown leather boots that angled down to pointed toes from six-inch heels. Her platinum hair was braided into two pigtails, and large rectangular sunglasses dominated her small features. She looked like a cross between Heidi and a porn star, not a lawyer in a conservative town. She spotted me and removed her sunglasses. She said something to the waitress before crossing the room to sit at my table. The fragrance she was wearing settled around us like a heavy floral bouquet.

"I'm so glad I caught you. I was sure you'd gone and was actually on my way to the office to get some documents ready to courier to you tomorrow." While she spoke, she was shrugging out of her coat. She draped it across the empty chair between us. Under the coat she wore a tight, wrap-around red top and a black skirt. "I just came from the seven a.m. church service. I like to start the days off early even on the weekends."

My meal arrived, and Patricia ordered the poached eggs I should have had. The French toast was thick, crusty slices of bread fluffed up with egg batter and capped with strawberries and whipped cream. It was the only good thing that had happened in two days. I didn't regret my choice, even with Patricia looking at me like I was on the way to joining the seriously obese. I glanced at her as I chewed my first mouthful. I wouldn't have taken her for the church-going type. I swallowed and said, "I thought we'd completed all the paperwork."

"No, that is, some of the tax forms weren't ready yet and need your signature. Can you drop by the office with me after breakfast?"

I shrugged. "Sure."

She leaned closer. "My god, the news of Becky Wilders' murder is all over town. We all knew Katherine Lingstrom had gone odd, but this is beyond the pale. Such a relief to know the murderer has been caught, but I'm sorry it was Katherine. I remember what good friends you both were back in grade school."

I looked into Patricia's inquisitive eyes. She was waiting for me to elaborate on the arrest, to give some glimpse into what had really taken place in our lives.

"It is all very sad," I said. "I'm glad it's over with. I'm heading to Duluth tonight to catch a flight home."

Patricia straightened and picked up her fork as the girl slid a plate of eggs and toast in front of her. She waited until we were alone again.

"I can understand you not wanting to elaborate. I suspected all along that there was more to Peter...your father than he ever let on."

"Oh, what makes you say that?" I wasn't sure why I was playing along, but Patricia had made me curious.

"It was just the way he had of looking at people. Like they amused him. Yes, amused is the word I would use."

She'd gotten it about right. My father had toyed with people. It seemed he'd slept with all of the young girls in Jonas's and my circle for his own entertainment. He got them at a vulnerable time in their lives and used his considerable charm to get them to trust him. Patricia hadn't been part of our group, but now she packaged a sexuality that would attract any man with an ounce of testosterone. A sick feeling filled me.

"And did you amuse my father?"

Patricia laughed. "I probably would have, except I'm otherwise taken." She leaned forward again, showing off her deep cleavage. "You know, all those years in high school when I was a nobody, I so much wanted to be you. All the boys were falling all over themselves to catch your eye, and you could have cared less."

"I never saw it that way."

"And that was the beauty of it. You weren't even trying to lead them on, and that drove them wild. I had such a crush on Tobias Olsen, and he never even looked my way. All he could think about was you."

I shifted uncomfortably in my seat. I hadn't noticed, because I'd only had eyes for Billy.

"I'm sure Tobias would be interested in you now, Patricia. You're beautiful and intelligent..."

"Don't patronize me, Maja. I know what I am."

We both lifted our coffee cups at the same time. Patricia set hers down and looked out the window. A skein of frost had crept up the glass, making gossamer patterns.

"I went away to university and got all this work done on my body and came back with every intention of winning over Tobias Olsen, but he was engaged to Lindsey Schnerring. That didn't stop me from trying, though. I drank enough one night to get up my courage to track him down. I let him know that I was the one he should be with, not Lindsey. He wasn't interested. Oh, he was kind enough about turning me down, but you can't fake that kind of disinterest."

"I'm sorry, Patricia."

She waved a hand in front of her face. "It's nothing. I'm over it."

"You said that you've met somebody?"

"Yes. Life always works out one way or the other. You just have to give it time."

"I'm glad we ran into each other this morning too," I said. "I was going to phone you before I left, but now I won't have to. I want you to draw up papers to give half of everything my father left me to Jonas. You can courier the papers to me in Ottawa, and I'll sign and return them. I'd like you to take care of this as soon as possible."

Patricia lowered her piece of toast. "Are you sure about this, Maja? We're talking a large amount of money. Your father was quite clear that he wanted the house and land to go to you."

"I've never been more sure of anything."

She studied me as if she were seeing me for the first time. Finally, she nodded. "All right then."

We ate in silence for a few minutes. She drank from her coffee cup and wiped her mouth on her napkin. I felt her watching me and raised my eyes.

"Your father said one odd thing to me the last time I saw him. He asked that I tell you, but it slipped my mind until now."

"Oh, what was that?" *Probably one last piece of nastiness.* I immediately regretted asking.

"Let's see. He said to tell you that if he died to remember the last place you'd ever look. He was adamant that I remember to tell you. Sorry that I forgot." She shrugged. "Does that mean anything to you? Because it means absolutely nothing to me."

I shook my head. "Not really." I looked down and made a pretense of straightening my plate and cutlery. My hand was shaking. I lifted my fingers from the fork and slid my hand under the table. "My father and I lost our connection many years ago. I have no idea what would make him say anything to me at this point, let alone why he would have thought that I'd understand some cryptic message."

I reached for my parka. We both stood to leave.

"This is on me," Patricia insisted. "I'll meet you at the office, and you can sign those documents. It won't take but a minute. I'll draw up the other papers and get them to you by end of week."

"Okay," I agreed, "and thanks for breakfast. You've been a bright light in this dreary town."

Patricia's smile flashed. "You're welcome. I'm glad you've made the trip home, even though I wish it had been under happier circumstances. Next time, maybe we'll have a chance to visit longer."

I sat in my car waiting for the heater to rattle out something besides cold air. I'd go sign the papers before making one last trip to my father's house, a place I'd intended never to step foot in again. That had all changed with one sentence.

Patricia had no way of knowing the importance of what she'd forgotten to tell me. Somebody had torn the house apart looking for something my father had concealed in Jonas's and my childhood hiding place. It was now up to me to find it. My father had been frightened of someone before his death, in all likelihood because of what he'd been hiding in the secret spot. I needed to find whatever it was and lay the last of the mysteries to rest.

TWENTY-SIX

I knew Jonas and Claire would wonder what had happened to me if I was away too long, so after I left Patricia's law office, I drove directly to their house. I'd eat the lunch Claire had promised, load up my suitcase in the rental car and then stop at my father's on the way out of town.

The smoke rising from the chimney led me to Jonas and Gunnar in the back workshop. Their blond heads were bent over a canoe paddle that was taking shape from a planed piece of cedar. Both looked up at me as I entered. For the first time since I'd arrived at their house, Gunnar smiled at me and said, "Hello, Aunt Maja."

"Hello, Gunnar. What are you up to?"

"Dad and I are making a paddle for my school project," he explained. He rubbed his hand lovingly over its smooth reddish surface with something close to reverence.

"It's a beauty," I said, moving closer to inspect their handiwork.

Jonas put an arm around my shoulder. "So how are you today? Did you have one last tour of the town?"

"Something like that. I'm good, Jonas. How are you doing?"

"Getting there. Gunnar and I are just planning a spring canoe trip." He ruffled Gunnar's hair. "We're thinking we'll make more trips this year and start doing some wilderness camping."

"You make me want to move back. I miss Minnesota in the summer."

"Well, why don't we plan a trip in August? Could you get a week off?"

"I'll see. I guess we should make time for what we want to do."

"Not good to keep putting things off," Jonas agreed. "Claire's up at the house fussing over a couple of ham and cheese quiches. She said she wanted to see you when you got back."

"I'll head up then."

"Tell her we won't be far behind."

I found Claire bent over the stove, putting the pies into the oven. She straightened when she heard me come in. Today, her black hair was held back with a paisley scarf, and she'd applied makeup liberally to bring colour to her pale cheeks.

"There you are," she said. "I got up early this morning to talk to you, but you'd already gone. I need to explain. . ." Greyish shadows circled like half-moons underneath her eyes.

"There's nothing to explain, Claire. I'm not your conscience, and I'm certainly not one to judge you."

"You asked about Gunnar. The thing is, I'm not sure who Gunnar's father is. He was conceived during a period in our lives when Jonas was away during the week renovating a house in Lutsen. I was angry with Jonas over something—I can't even remember what now—and your father just started coming around. Gunnar could be your father's or Jonas's. God, I can't believe how awful that sounds."

"Why would you think he's my father's?"

Claire moaned. "Gunnar resembles your father so much, and he acted like Gunnar was his. I fell into believing him, because Jonas and I had trouble conceiving when we tried before."

"Does Jonas know?"

Claire bit her lip and thought over my question. "Sometimes, I think he does, but I can't be sure. Your father used to threaten to tell Jonas if I didn't let him spend time with Gunnar. He made it sound like he wanted a relationship with his grandson—or his son—but now, I'm not so sure. That also sounds horrible when I say it out loud."

"Jonas loves you, Claire. He loves Gunnar too."

"I know. I just need some time before I tell him. I'm beginning to realize what it is I have with Jonas. I don't want him to leave me."

"I'm not saying anything to him, Claire. This is your life, your family. I'm not even so sure bringing this out into the open would accomplish anything now that my father is dead."

"Thank you, Maja," Claire whispered and her eyes filled with tears. "Actually, talking about this with someone is such a relief. You don't know how angry I've been at myself and at Jonas. I believed if he'd paid more attention to me, not gotten sick all the time, I wouldn't have turned to your father. I know that sounds weak, but that's how I felt. It seems so selfish now."

"Perhaps your anger would have been better aimed at my father."

"I see that now. I...what we did was a pattern with him."

I nodded and looked away. There was nothing more I could say to make it better. I raised my eyes and smiled at her, pointing to the lettuce and carrots on the counter. "Can I make the salad?"

Claire dabbed at her eyes with a tea towel and laughed self-consciously. "Yes and while you do that, I'll throw together the apple crisp. I want us to have a nice meal before you head back home to Sam."

I nodded again, but this time I couldn't get any words out without giving away my own sadness.

We said our goodbyes at two o'clock. It was later than I would have liked, and I would be driving into Duluth after dark. The sky had turned a sullen grey over the lunch hour, and a light snow had begun falling by the time I turned onto the road that led to my father's house. The windshield wipers beat in time to my own heart, which had started pounding faster as soon as I'd started on this journey to unearth the secret of my father's last years.

If Sam had been with me, he'd have questioned why I cared enough to do my father's bidding in this, his last request, before he died. Sam would stare at me with his piercing stare as if he could see inside my head to see the machinations of my brain. I would raise my palms and tell him that he had not lived with a parent who'd never loved him back. I would not tell him that I was always searching for answers for what I did wrong. It didn't matter that there were no reasons, no answers. I would continue to search. I would continue to cling onto the times when my father showed me kindness, even now choosing to believe that it was love, even now when I knew better.

I slowed as I passed by the Lingstrom house. It looked empty, the blinds and curtains drawn and a front porch light on even though it was mid-day. Mrs. Lingstrom had gone with Katherine to Duluth. Once the snow stopped falling, Jonas and Gunnar would come to shovel her driveway as they had all winter. The swing set in the yard looked to be tilted at a more alarming angle. It would fall over in a good wind. I longed to run across the yard to straighten it out.

I continued on and turned off the highway into our long driveway, rutted and layered in thick ice and snow. It would take spring melt to wash away the bulk of it. As the car jostled up the drive, I could still make out the indentations of a crisscross of tire tracks from the police vehicles and ambulance that had come to take away Becky's body only a few days before. The house stood forlorn and brooding, all lights extinguished, as if it knew its days were numbered. Bulldozing the house and pushing a highway through our property seemed a fitting end to a place that had brought my family so much pain. I would miss the pine and spruce trees but nothing more. The good memories, and there had been very good memories, were with me always and could not be plowed into the earth like so much timber.

I left the car and circled around to the back steps. Footprints were frozen into the packed snow and up the stairs. I checked that the door was locked before turning the key to pull the door open. Silence greeted my entry. I called hello to be sure nobody was inside and felt foolish immediately afterwards. Still, I made sure the door was securely locked before I undid my coat.

I walked through the kitchen and down the hallway to the front staircase, glancing up at the light streaming through the slatted blind at the landing. It was close to golden in hue, like honey, and it warmed me even though the furnace temperature had been lowered. Then I kneeled and ran my hand across the carpet on the bottom step. This close, I could smell the carpet's factory newness. The green and brown swirling pattern hid the deep slit from one end to the other at the base of the riser. I ran the tips of my fingers along its length, feeling for a place to leverage the carpet up. The fabric held firm to the wooden step beneath. I needed something to pry under the edge of the stair. I ran into the kitchen and pulled open the cutlery drawer. I couldn't find anything strong and thin enough. I thought of my father's tools in the basement. I was scared to go back down there. I pulled open the cupboards, knowing I'd find nothing. I glanced toward the basement door.

"Oh my god," I groaned and closed my eyes to regroup. "Get

yourself down there, Maja, and don't be such a baby. Nothing can hurt you in this house."

I crossed the kitchen and turned on the basement light as I pulled open the door with my other hand. The light at the bottom of the stairs was still out, but the second light in the main room cast enough light so that I could see my way down the steep steps. I took a deep breath and started a careful descent. I began humming, a tuneless buzz that didn't resemble music. It was just a comfort to have a sound that drowned out the rush of blood in my ears.

Somebody had dragged Becky's lifeless body down these same steps. Katherine? I stopped and reached for the banister. Was that a sound on the floor above my head? I cocked my head and held a hand over my heart, trying to still its pounding inside my chest.

Nothing.

I again started down the stairs, this time moving with speed. I reached the bottom and turned on the lights before running across the short distance to the laundry room. Once inside, I glanced at the spot between the washer and dryer. An outline of Becky's body still lay chalked on the concrete. I forced myself to keep moving, past the laundry basin to the shelves at the back wall near the furnace. I knew my mother had hanged herself somewhere in this room, but I'd never asked which beam, and for that, I was thankful. I scanned the shelves, my hand reaching through a cobweb for the crowbar that rested next to the handsaw. This would do nicely. Its heavy feel in my hand gave me sudden strength. I had a weapon. I put my head down and strode for the stairs, taking them two at a time, relieved to set foot in the kitchen and slam the basement door behind me.

I returned to the staircase at the end of the hall. It took me a few tries before I got the crowbar safely anchored under the edge of the bottom step. I cranked hard on its length, putting my full body weight onto the shaft. In time, the board shifted and gave under my weight. I leaned onto the crowbar again and again until the step and the carpet ripped away. I knelt and pulled the stair upwards with both hands. My fingers seeped blood from the sharp ridges in the wood, but I wiped them on my pants and quickly forgot the pain, because I could now see what my father had hidden away.

Packets of white powder nestled in the cavity of the exposed stair. I began to lift them out of their hiding place, one by one. There had to be a small fortune in drugs lying at my feet, for I had no doubt this was heroin or cocaine or something of equal value. My hand settled on a paper that had been lying underneath the stash and I lifted it out, flattening out the page to read the words written in my father's hand. This time, when the stair creaked above my head, I didn't stop reading. It was the sound of a familiar voice echoing down the staircase that made me freeze in fear.

"Maja Larson. I knew you'd figure it out eventually. It sure took you damn long enough."

TWENTY-SEVEN

I kept my head down. For a moment, my brain went into automatic pilot, and my eyes focused on the words in front of me without really seeing them. When I finally lifted my eyes to look up at David Keating, he was halfway down the stairwell, his service revolver in his hand, swinging lazily at his side. He was dressed in a black duffel coat and black skull cap. Bottle green aviator sunglasses hid his eyes, and he'd shaved off his moustache, leaving a white area under his nose and around his mouth. I felt so exposed—like I had a foot caught in a trap, and I couldn't get away. My heart beat erratically inside my chest.

"David, why?" was all I could manage.

He stood two steps above me and removed the sunglasses, tucking them into his coat pocket. His face, half in shadow, was a curious mixture of guilt, resignation and determination. "Money, of course. Olive has expensive tastes, and I would have done anything to keep her happy."

"Four kids cost a lot on a police salary." I tried to sound sympathetic. I was afraid I sounded condescending, but David didn't seem to notice.

He shrugged. "You have no idea. Olive spends money on our kids like it grows on trees, and I have to keep pumping it out. A guy can only do so much overtime. Our second oldest has juvenile diabetes, and it costs me a fortune in medical bills. Now Olive wants a fifth kid, and I've barely started paying for the fourth."

"I'm sorry, David." I had to keep him talking while I thought of how to get out of this mess. My mind began its clinical assessment of his vital signs. Eyes dilated. Colour elevated. Sweat on his forehead. He was in control but definitely agitated. "You were the one who searched the house?"

"Yeah. I knew your dad had hidden the crack somewhere. He got scared there at the end when Rainy Wynona disappeared. The Motego brothers were cutting into our business, making threats."

"What happened to Rainy?"

David shrugged again. "He's probably being eaten by the fishes at the bottom of Lake Superior. Who knows? No big loss. Anyhow, your dad and I figured one last run, and we'd call it a day. Thing is, your father started getting paranoid. He began thinking everyone was out to get him, including me. That's why he hid the drugs and told me he'd left insurance if something happened to him. Probably the letter you're reading now."

David reached out his hand to take it from me.

"But Katherine Lingstrom killed my father."

David laughed. "Yeah, ironic, huh? He should have been more scared of the women he'd screwed than me or the Motego brothers."

I handed the paper over. I'd only managed to read the first two paragraphs, where my father pointed the finger at David and Rainy. My father's outrage at their betrayal was evident. Dad took the credit for the operation, as if it were some kind of accomplishment. The beginning of the letter had been a condemnation of others while he bragged about being the ringleader.

"How many bags are there?" David asked.

"Six. They're all yours. I have no interest in any of this." I desperately wanted him to believe that I was washing my hands of my father and him. I needed him to let me go.

David reached inside his coat and pulled out a folded canvas bag.

"Put them in here, and we'll take the bag out to your car."

"Okay." I took the bag and held it in one hand while I reached into the step and pulled out the packets of cocaine one by one. I stuffed the drugs inside the canvas bag and held it out to David. "You can have my car if you want. I'll walk home and get Jonas to drive me to the airport. I won't tell him anything."

David waved off the bag and laughed. "Actually, you'll be driving me to the border, Maja. You'll be telling Customs that you decided to drive back to Ottawa with your cousin."

"Why don't you just go across yourself? They won't question a police officer."

David wouldn't answer. He pointed the gun toward the back door. "Let's get going."

A storm was moving in. The leaden sky had darkened, and it felt closer to nightfall than mid-afternoon. The wind was whipping up the snow, and it was a struggle for me to carry the bag to the car without stumbling. David stayed close behind me, steadying me under my elbow once when I tripped over an ice chunk. I opened the trunk to put the bag inside.

"You were on your way to Duluth then," he said, nodding at my suitcase and carry-on bag. "Lucky for me."

He slammed the trunk shut and motioned for me to get into the driver's seat. At the same time he made for the passenger door. I didn't dare try to get away. David had the advantage of a gun, and we were in the middle of nowhere with nobody as witness— and he had the eerie calm of a man with nothing to lose.

I got behind the wheel at the same time as he slid in on the other side. I could see my breath, and my cold hands fumbled with the keys before I finally got the car going. It wasn't happy with the call to action and took several tries before the engine agreed to turn over. I coaxed it into gear, and we rattled and jostled down the driveway to the highway. Looking out the front windshield was like trying to see through a piece of gauze. I sprayed washer fluid several times. The wipers barely cleared away the wet streaks and the ice.

"Can't you crank the heat up any higher?" David asked. He huddled into his coat and pulled up the collar. The gun was in his lap, pointed in my direction. I hoped he had the safety on.

"It's up as high as it goes. We should be warm by the time we hit the border." I mumbled the last bit more to myself than to David.

He pointed for me to go left, and I pulled slowly onto the highway. My tires spun on the ice before grabbing. We passed a few homes tucked into the woods, but this stretch of road was desolate. We'd gone a little ways when David squinted out the front windshield.

"Pull over here."

"Here?"

"Yeah, just down this road."

I could make out tire track ruts on a road I knew led to the lake. We followed what was little more than a trail for half a mile or so. The snow banks swooped up beside the road on either side of us like angel wings. At last, we reached a turn-around spot where David's police car was partially hidden by a snow drift.

"Pull alongside," David ordered and I did as he asked. "Leave the car running."

We both got out and went to the back of the police car. David opened the trunk. A suitcase and two boxes filled the space. He had me take the books out of one of the boxes until we came to a row of bibles. I pulled six out, one by one, and opened them to find hollowed out cores, just the size for the bags of cocaine. I looked at David, and he smiled. He'd brought the bag of drugs from my father's house with him when he'd left the car, and he dropped it at my feet. I withdrew each plastic bag of cocaine and inserted it into a gaping Bible. By now, my hands were numb again, and I had trouble inserting the bags. David watched but didn't say anything. There were an additional three hollowed-out Bibles that I left in the trunk.

"Do you want the drugs divided between the two boxes?" I yelled over the howling wind.

"No. The other box is a decoy."

I finished repacking the box and transferred both to my trunk. As David instructed, I placed the decoy box in front. I managed to get his bag into the trunk after I removed my carry-on bag, which I threw onto the back seat before sliding back behind the wheel. My hands and face were now beyond cold, and I shivered uncontrollably, partly from the cold and partly from fear.

"Good work, Maja," David said. "Let's get back on the highway."

I looked at him and took a breath. I placed both hands on the steering wheel, my eyes straight ahead as I tried to control my voice. Even so, it came out small and afraid. "What do you intend to do with me after we get across the border?"

"Don't worry, Maja. I'm not going to hurt you, if that's what you're thinking. People are waiting for me, and I'll be long gone before anybody figures out I've split."

"What about Olive and the kids? You have a new baby."

"Olive's better off without me."

"But you've been together such a long time. It's not too late to go back."

"Drop it. It *is* too late. Just drive and don't talk any more."

I'd hit a nerve. David tapped the gun on his leg, his agitation palpable. I stayed quiet for several miles. I concentrated on keeping the car on the road and out of the drifts of snow that were sloped across the highway. The storm was intensifying, if anything. Traffic on the highway was almost non-existent. We passed a snow plow going in the other direction. David shifted in his seat and looked over at me.

"I'm sorry about this, Maja."

"I know, David."

"Sometimes things just happen. You know, you take a step in the wrong direction, and before you know it, you're sucked into something you can't get out of."

"Did my father...did he pull you into this?"

"Not exactly. We were approached by Rainy Wynona. It seemed easy enough. I'd go into Canada and pick the drugs up at a secondhand bookstore on my way to buy cheaper prescription insulin and supplies for my son. I had a valid reason for going into Canada so often, and your father made sure I was waved through this side without a search. I timed my trips to coincide with his shifts."

"But my father had the drugs in his house."

"Yeah. I'd transfer the drugs to your father's trunk, and he'd bring them to his house for the pickup. His was the logical place, in the middle of nowhere."

"Where did you deal the drugs?"

"Rainy had a trucker from down the road bring them points south. I never bothered too much with that end of it."

I thought of the day I'd stopped at Verl's restaurant on my way to Fortune Bay Casino. Wayne Okwari had enquired about the grandson who drove a transport south. Perhaps he was the link.

"How did you know I'd be back to my father's house today?"

"I didn't. I was upstairs searching when I heard you pull up."

"But your car was hidden away in the woods a few miles away."

"I didn't want anyone to know I was at your house again. I had to hide the car and run back. It didn't take too long, since I've been training for the marathon. I was going to leave town one way or the other today, with or without the drugs."

"But why now? Nobody could link you to the drugs."

David chewed on his bottom lip. He began tapping the gun on his leg again, and I stopped talking. The car swerved on a bit of ice, but I managed to straighten the wheel. The wipers were trying their best to clear the crusty snow from the windshield. Gusts of wind buffeted the car whenever we came to a flat stretch of road. For the most part, we were protected by the dark miles of forest on either side of us. Tree boughs swayed back and forth in the wind, and snow drove sideways across the road. The car's heater had begun to pump out warm air, and the numbness in my fingers had given way to sharp tingling. I kept telling myself that this was David Keating beside me, a boy I'd known since grade school. He wasn't going to hurt me.

I slowed going up a hill. I could see headlights behind me, but the vehicle was keeping its distance. Even if it caught up to us, there was no way I could signal what was going on. I'd have to hope I had a chance to get away at the border crossing. We'd been on the road almost an hour, and I knew it wasn't far ahead. If not for David, I would have been pulling into my motel in Duluth about now. I wondered if anybody would notice my absence. Probably not. I hadn't made plans with anybody for the evening and hadn't phoned Sam to say when I'd be home. He was likely getting ready for the trip. I had intended to surprise him.

David started to look out of the windows, now more nervous than he'd been before.

"How long has that car been behind us?" he asked.

"It just turned on the highway a mile or so back," I lied.

David swung back around in his seat. "We're almost at the border. You'll tell them you're heading home after your father's funeral. Say you're a doctor and I'm your cousin, Ben Larson."

"You have a passport to that effect, I gather?"

"Yes. And Maja, anything goes wrong, I won't hesitate to shoot someone. Canada Customs won't be bothering with us in this storm unless the officer gets suspicious. I'm counting on you to make sure that doesn't happen."

"Okay," I nodded. "I'll get us across the border, but then what, David?"

"Then, I meet my friends, and you'll be detained for a bit while we get away."

"You'll make sure they don't hurt me."

"You have my word."

We reached the crest of the hill and rounded the corner. The road carved through a rock cut that towered above us on both sides. I let out a scream and began pumping the brakes. Across our lane was a Ford truck, spun out on some black ice and facing into the rock cliff. I saw it and my brain registered it, but I reacted on instinct, nothing more. I felt outside my body, watching somebody else getting ready to die. My mind recorded facts. There were no other vehicles on the road. The truck was black. Its front bumper was smashed into the rock cut. We were going to hit it. Snow was falling in slanting lines. *Please don't let me die this way.*

My tires began sliding, and I frantically pumped the brake pedal while steering into the skid. David thunked hard against the side door and cursed. "What the hell? Shit!" He grabbed onto the dashboard,

I steered into the skid as I'd been taught so many years ago in driver's ed, back in high school. Back when life had been simple. Back when I was whole. The brakes caught. The car righted itself. I let my breath out in a whoosh.

We came to a stop a few feet from the truck. My heart was pounding like my chest would explode, and I was breathing heavily. I rested my arms on the steering wheel and my head on my arms. I was tired. I wanted nothing more than to lie down in the snow beside the highway in a fetal position.

Someone knocked on my window, and my head jerked upwards. A hooded figure stood next to the car in the pelting snow.

"David?" I asked. I needed his permission to talk to this stranger. I didn't know what he would do.

David looked all around and back at the person huddled in a black parka standing beside our car. He tucked the gun behind him so that it was out of sight. "Okay, ask if he needs help and tell him we'll send somebody when we get to the next town. Nothing else, Maja, or he'll regret ever stopping us."

The intensity in David's voice was palpable. He was as scared as I was.

I nodded. Now I was responsible for this stranger's life as well as my own. I lowered my window halfway and turned my head to look at the person, not knowing how I was going to get rid of him. I opened my mouth to say something and found myself staring into the glittering black eyes of Wayne Okwari.

TWENTY-EIGHT

"D o you need help?" I managed to say, then things began to happen very fast.

Wayne reached in and pulled up the lock in one swift motion before he opened my car door, unhooked my seatbelt and yanked me out. I hadn't noticed that another man had come up on David's side of the car, and he opened the passenger door at the same time as I flew out my side. I landed on the ground, and Wayne covered my body with his own. The car that had been following us was suddenly flashing red lights and had pulled up behind us. I heard a gunshot. When I was finally pulled to my feet, David was spreadeagled against the car being searched by two men. Wayne kept one hand under my elbow.

"You okay, ma'am?"

He sounded so like Billy, I wanted to cry. "What's going on?" I asked instead as I wiped snow from my face. I'd scraped my cheek and forehead on the ice, and they'd begun to sting.

"I'm an undercover cop. We were watching your father's house." Wayne started walking me toward the truck.

"Then you know about the cocaine in my trunk?"

"We figured it was in the car somewhere." He grinned wryly in my direction.

I stopped walking and held out my arms, palms up. "Why didn't you stop us before we got this far?" The shock was starting to settle in, and the anger. We could have been killed with the

240

truck-across-the-road stunt.

Wayne turned and took a step back towards me. "The agent saw you leaving the house with Officer Keating, but we needed time to mount the takedown. We thought we'd lost you along the highway, and it took a while to track you again."

"We made a detour to pick up David's car. He had it parked on a side road down the way from my father's house." I caught up to Wayne, and we started walking again.

"You had us worried. We were scared he'd done something to you. We had to move faster than we'd have liked, so we improvised. The truck idea was mine. I knew Keating wouldn't let you stop if he suspected the accident was staged. It had to look real."

"David wouldn't have hurt me. He was going to let me go after we got into Canada."

We reached the truck, and Wayne opened the door for me to get in. His eyes were black and fathomless, like Billy's. He said softly, "We had every reason to believe he would hurt you, Maja. We're certain he killed Becky Wilders to keep her from talking. We believe she must have known he and your father were smuggling drugs across the border, and she made the mistake of confronting him, whether about your father's death or the drugs, we'll never know unless David decides to tell us. Anyhow, I got a call from Tobias about the time David was taking you from the house."

I began to protest, but I remembered David's grim resolve. I turned my face away. Through the side window, I watched an officer leading David toward the back of the cruiser. David seemed to hesitate and turned just enough to look in my direction. Then he was being ushered into the backseat, his hands cuffed behind him. Even knowing what David had done, it was painful to watch a police officer and childhood friend brought to this and to know what lay ahead for him.

Oh, David, why ever did you get involved in something that could only end so badly?

I spent the next few hours at the police station giving my statement. Tobias met us there after a difficult drive to Duved Cove from Duluth, where he'd been questioning Katherine Lingstrom in the hospital. It was during that questioning that he'd learned that she hadn't killed Becky. We'd all leapt to the wrong conclusion because we couldn't get our heads around the fact that there were two murderers at work in our town. When Tobias knew for certain that Becky was only responsible for my father's death, David had again become his main suspect.

Tobias had been working for some months with Wayne Okwari, an undercover narcotics agent, to pin the drug trafficking on my father and David Keating. They'd set up surveillance on my father's house after he'd died, but not before David had torn the place apart looking for the bags of cocaine. Tobias knew David hadn't recovered the drugs, so they'd kept a watch on the house. They'd almost given up on the surveillance until David showed up today...followed soon after by me. It was about the same time that Tobias phoned in to Wayne Okwari and Chief Anders that Katherine had not killed Becky. News that David had likely killed Becky made everyone edgier when they realized I was being taken against my will. I liked to think that David wouldn't have killed me once we crossed the border, but the more I dwelled on that, the more naïve that seemed. He couldn't let me go before he was safely out of the country, and I wasn't sure how he'd intended to keep me quiet.

Tobias walked with me from the room where I'd been interviewed to the main desk. He was exhausted and obviously not pleased about arresting a colleague and friend he'd known forever.

"Can I take you to Duluth? The storm's let up, and it's the least I can do now that we've confiscated your rental."

I thought about taking him up on his offer. I'd grown to like Tobias and felt like I owed him for ever having believed him to be involved in the murders. His green eyes watched me with an interest I might have returned if things had been different. I pulled my eyes away from his and looked past him, through the main door to the street. The snow had stopped falling, and I had a clear view to the truck idling out front.

"Thanks, Tobias, but I have a ride." I reached out my hand and shook his. "Thanks for your help, and I know we'll meet again."

"You'll be back this way?"

"I promised Jonas I'd be back in August for a fishing trip."

"Well, I'll see you then. Looks like I'm going to have to postpone Florida for a while."

"I'll see you then."

"You can count on it, Maja Larson."

I retrieved my bags from the floor and pushed the door open. It was cold but I hardly noticed. I walked toward the truck and Billy, who was leaning on the side, watching me come toward him. He pushed himself off the fender and stepped towards me to take my bags.

"Hey, Maja," he said, his hand touching mine in passing.

"Hey, Billy. You taking me to Duluth?"

"If that's where you're headed."

"I can't think of anywhere else I need to be tonight." Billy smiled at me, and his eyes were blacker than I'd ever seen them.

"Sounds good," I said. I climbed into the passenger seat, and Billy got in his side. I watched his profile as he eased the stick shift into drive, and we started down the street, the tires crunching on the icy snow. I tried to imprint every part of him into my memory, from his straight black hair that lay below his collar to his high cheekbones and the slightly crooked line of his mouth.

"You all right?" he asked without taking his eyes off the road.

"You never told me your nephew was undercover."

"I knew he was involved in something, but I wasn't sure. He told me to trust him when I asked."

Billy reached over to turn down the radio, and he glanced at me before looking back at the road. "I never thought it involved you or your father, or I would have tried to do something. I don't know what, but I wouldn't have left you to face all this alone."

"How did your fishing trip go?"

"The clients were from Texas, with more money than brains. The three-day trip ended up being four days. They paid well. I hated being away thinking you were still in Duved Cove."

Then I knew how our story should end. In that second, I made up my mind. Maybe I'd made it up when David had pulled the gun on me, and I wasn't sure how it was all going to turn out. "Can you stay with me tonight?" I asked softly. "I know we have people counting on us, but maybe we owe each other something for all these years." I was suddenly shy and couldn't look at him.

"I'll stay with you," Billy said. "We still have a connection, Maja. I was going to suggest you shouldn't be alone tonight."

I looked over at him then and felt a fluttering begin under my rib cage. This was the man I should have spent my life with.

"It will just be tonight," I said. "You don't need to promise me anything more."

Billy nodded. "I loved you all those years ago when we were kids, Maja, and that will never change. You are the other part of my soul, no matter where you go or who you are with. That is just the way of it. I can't promise you my life, but you have the rest."

I reached over and took his hand in mine. "Knowing will be enough," I said, and I looked out the window to stop him from seeing the tears sliding down my face.

EPILOGUE

I was late, and the restaurant was busy. I scanned the window seats and spotted Fiona sitting in the far corner. She wore a white suit with an indigo scarf at her neck. She looked stunning, not like someone who'd just spent her day with troubled adolescents. When she saw me crossing the floor, she stood and wrapped her arms around me in a hug.

"My god, you're looking good," she said as we sat down.

"I could say the same of you." I smiled and handed her a photo of the two of us that I'd placed in a frame. It had been taken after I'd returned from Minnesota, when I looked like I'd been to hell and back. "So you don't forget me and all that you mean to me." I dropped the manila envelope I'd also been holding onto the bench next to me.

Fiona studied the picture, then looked at me. "How could I forget you, Maja? I'll miss you, that's for certain."

"And I'll miss you."

A waiter appeared at Fiona's elbow with a bottle of champagne. He popped the cork and poured us each a glass in crystal flutes. A plate of prosciutto and melon appeared between us.

"This is lovely, Fiona."

"To new beginnings." Fiona raised her glass to mine.

"To new beginnings," I echoed. I took a sip and set my glass down.

"What time does your flight leave tomorrow?"

"Early. Five a.m., and I have the international check-in, so I should be at the airport two hours ahead at least."

"I'm so proud of you, Maja."

"It's a big step, but I know this is what I want to do."

"Do you plan to go back every summer?"

"If they'll let me go. I start my new job in Thunder Bay in late September, but I've asked for next summer off."

We both reached for the same piece of melon and laughed.

"Maybe, I'll join you in Africa next year. Doctors Without Borders might be able to make use of a child psychologist."

"I'm sure there's lots of work for you. That would be wonderful if you came."

"And Sam...?"

"He wasn't happy about my leaving, as you know, but when I told him I didn't want half his business, he came around." I smiled. "He really had no choice."

"So you'll be doing plastic surgery on some pretty ravaged people in Africa."

"Yes, there's a great need, and I can't wait to get started. Oh my, the faces of those children in Darfur. The world must not forget..."

I could feel Fiona watching me, and I grinned self-consciously. I turned my palms upwards on the table. "I still want to make a difference, and I guess that sounds trite."

"Oh no, my friend. It's just so good to see you passionate about your life, your work. I'll bet you know what you want to order from the menu tonight."

I laughed. "I may not always know what I'm going to order, but I'm getting there. No more waffling."

Fiona raised her glass again. I clinked my glass against hers and drank.

"So, what have you decided about Billy?"

I took my time answering. I'd confided everything to Fiona when I'd returned from Minnesota, when I'd bottomed out, but already, I didn't want to share this part of my life. It wasn't that I regretted telling Fiona; it was just that I'd stopped needing to talk about it.

"Billy has a wife and child. It would be too complicated. I'm letting him go." I said the words and took strength from them. "Not that I ever had him to let go. Just knowing he cares for me is enough to help me carry through with this life. I feel like I've resolved that part of my life—that he's forgiven me for having the abortion and running away from Duved Cove."

"Will he let you go so easily?"

"He has a wife." I shrugged. "When I move to Thunder Bay, near the border, I'll be able to spend time with Jonas, and that's why I accepted the position. I want to be close to what is left of my family."

"Not to be closer to Billy?"

I studied Fiona across the table. She'd asked the words lightly, but we both knew my answer would determine the direction my life would take.

"I'm moving forward, Fiona. I am not moving to Northern Ontario to be closer to Billy." *And if I said the words often enough, someday I would believe them.*

The waiter chose that moment to appear for our orders. Fiona smiled at me above the top of her menu before looking up at the young man standing between us.

"All set to order, ladies?" he asked.

"Yes," I said, and this time I knew what I wanted.

Fiona ordered her meal after me and then went to find the washroom. I studied the people walking past the window on

Richmond Road. The buds on the trees had begun opening, and the sky was creamy blue. It was going to be a good summer. I picked up the brown envelope I'd dropped next to me just as Fiona returned.

"What's that?" she asked as she slid into her seat and replaced the napkin in her lap.

"Another fresh start." I smiled. "It's for my sister-in-law Claire. This is a report I was able to get on my father's medical history."

"Oh? And why is that important?"

I smiled again. "My father lied about many things in his life, Fiona, and I knew he would lie about anything that kept people in his power. I had to find out about Gunnar."

"Your nephew?"

I nodded. "My father had a vasectomy after Jonas was born."

"So your father could *not* have been Gunnar's father."

"Exactly," I said. "The control he holds over Jonas and Claire is about to end."

Fiona leaned across the table. "You're going to make it, you know, Maja," she said, her eyes bright with tears.

"I know," I smiled. "There are no happily ever afters in life, but there are happy beginnings if you can just trust yourself enough to let go and give life another shot."

"Hear, hear!" said Fiona.

We raised our glasses and drank again, long and deep, to all the possibilities that were spread out before us like so much sunshine on a field of Minnesota snow.

Brenda Chapman grew up in Terrace Bay, Ontario, near the border with Minnesota. She began her fiction career with children's novels. *Running Scared* (Napoleon Publishing, 2004) was her first YA novel featuring Jennifer Bannon. She went on to pen three more in the series. *Hiding in Hawk's Creek* was shortlisted for the 2007 Canadian Library Association Book of the Year for Children. *Where Trouble Leads* and *Trail of Secrets* concluded the series. *In Winter's Grip* is her first mystery for adults.

More information on her work can be found at www.brendachapman.ca

Acknowledgements

I would like to thank Sylvia McConnell and Allister Thompson of RendezVous Crime for their dedication and support. Thank you also to Emma Dolan and Frank Bowick for the stunning cover images and design for *In Winter's Grip*. Thanks to Rachel Sentes, whose expertise has been invaluable.

I am grateful to Katherine Hobbs, Darlene Cole, Mike Levin, Lisa Weagle and Alex Brett, who critique my manuscripts and keep the stories from straying. Thank you also to Louise Penny, Gail Bowen and Mary Jane Maffini for critiquing early drafts of this manuscript. The mystery writing community is strong and growing—I would like to acknowledge the continuing support of Capital Crime Writers and Crime Writers of Canada.

The unwavering support from my family and friends, fellow authors, book store owners, librarians and fans is a constant source of strength—thank you to each of you for taking this writing journey with me and for sharing my belief in the power of stories and the magic of language.